Praise for Wendy Delaney's

THERE'S SOMETHING ABOUT MARTY

"Packed with small town innuendo and gossip, this engaging cozy mystery delivers rich, eccentric characters and a cleverly crafted plot."

~ Chanticleer Book Reviews

"A well-written, wonderful mystery!"

~ Lisa K's Book Reviews

"Delaney writes with an equal amount of finesse and humor to keep the reader hanging on every page while laughing out loud."

~ Kimmy's Korner

"A fun murder mystery that is well-written and well-executed."

~ Anna Smith for Readers' Favorite

"Char's third escapade as a human lie detector in the Working Stiffs Mystery series kept me turning the pages and tickled my funny bone, too."

~ Jacquie Rogers, author of the
Honey Beaulieu–Man Hunter series

Also by Wendy Delaney

THERE'S SOMETHING ABOUT MARTY

A WORKING STIFFS MYSTERY
BOOK 3

WENDY DELANEY

THERE'S SOMETHING ABOUT MARTY

Cover by Lewellen Designs
Editing by Mimi (The Grammar Chick)

Printed in the United States of America

First Edition
First Printing, 2016

ISBN-13: 978-0-9969800-5-0
ISBN-10: 0996980059

SUGARBAKER
PRESS

To Estelle Landry, my favorite cat lady.
Thanks for letting me borrow your name.

Acknowledgments

Writing a book might appear to be a solitary endeavor, but this book wouldn't have happened without some special people in my corner.

First of all, I must thank my husband, Jeff, for being my "guy stuff" advisor. I can't imagine a better guy to have with me on my life's journey.

Thank you, Ann Charles, for being with me on the first few legs of my writer's journey.

Marianne Strnad, you saved my bacon. Bless you for sharing your technical expertise.

Diane Garland, Jody Sherin, and Jacquie Rogers, I owe you a big debt of gratitude for talking me down from the ledge on this one. If ever I need my head screwed on straight (or whacked!), I know where to go.

Lastly, my heartfelt thanks go out to my dream team of beta-readers and supporters: Diane Garland, Jody Sherin, Denise Keef, Bob Dickerson, Lori Dubiel, Amber Jacobsma, Susan Cambra, Toni Mortensen, Denise Fluhr, Heather Chargualaf, Deb Tysick-Hawrylyshyn, Lisa Hintz, Brandy Lanfair, Wayne Roberts, Cindy Nelson, Barb Harlan, Beth Rosin, Vicki Huskey, Laurie Burbach, Corie Carson, Brenda Randolph, Marnia Davis, Christie Marks, Kimber Hungerman, Laurie Anderson, Elaina Boudreaux, Jan Dobbins, Debbie Rhoades, DeAnna Shaikoski, Lisa Norvell, Mattie Piela, Amber Lassig, Claudia Stephan, Hope Goodlaxson, Kim Braumann, Ashlee Weeks, Liz Schwab, Linda Roberts, Dixie Daniel, Deidre Herzog, and Karen Haverkate. You all rock!

Chapter One

THE LAST THING I'd expected to hear this morning was Patsy Faraday chirping a greeting like a songbird.

The plus-sized, self-appointed hall monitor sitting outside the Chimacam County Prosecutor's office hadn't once offered me a snark-free morning pleasantry in my seven weeks of sharing a boss with her.

As the low man on the office totem pole, I'd become the designated delivery girl of the department's Friday morning doughnut order. Since those doughnuts came from my great-uncle's cafe and I couldn't just pick up and run without a bit of conversation, I was more than my usual five minutes late to work. But Patsy hadn't spared a glance at the clock ticking next to her computer monitor to serve me her usual version of a tardy slip.

I stopped in my tracks. Something felt very off, as in *Invasion of the Body Snatchers* off. I looked around to make sure she was talking to me and saw two assistants down the hall clicking on their keyboards, but there was no one else within earshot. "Good morning."

Not that I'm any more suspicious than the next person, but when something stinks I'm not one to pretend that it passes my sniff test, so I held the bakery box filled with assorted doughnuts in front of me like a peace offering. "Want one of the apple fritters before they all disappear?"

Much like the finger-licking good pastry I'd devoured on my way to the courthouse, it was no mystery why they disappeared. My great-uncle Duke made the best apple fritters in Port Merritt, maybe even in the entire state of Washington. I should know. He'd been satisfying my sweet tooth ever since my grandmother first took me to breakfast at Duke's Cafe. My thirty-year love affair with his danged apple fritters was one of the many reasons I had yet to lose the eighteen pounds I'd packed on since my divorce earlier in the year.

With fritter love as one of the few things Patsy and I had in common, I'd hoped to tempt her with one as a sugar-glazed conversation starter.

She sharpened her gaze on the pink cardboard box in my hands. "I'm on a low-carb diet. Lost ten pounds in two weeks, so no."

Ten pounds! I'd probably gained a pound in the last hour thanks to that apple fritter and the two slices of bacon I'd sneaked while I got caught up on the local gossip. And sadly, the scoop du jour featured the sudden death of Marty McCutcheon, a Duke's regular and the owner of a flooring shop three blocks down on Main Street.

"Good for you," I said, making an effort to keep the envy out of my voice.

With a smile tugging at her lips like she had a secret, Patsy pushed out of her chair, a note of Chanel rising with her. Patsy's plaited hair, tawny without its usual telltale gray roots, swept over her shoulder as she snatched the bakery box out of my hands. "I'll take this to the breakroom for you. Frankie wants to see you."

Ten pounds, expensive perfume, a new dye job, *and* Patsy was being nice to me? She had a secret all right. If I was reading the clues correctly, it was a new man in her life. Either that or this bird was chirping because I was about to be fired for being late one time too many.

Since I was still paying off my divorce lawyer and needed to keep my job, I wanted to believe in the transformative power of new love. But I also had a sinking feeling that trouble waited for me inside Frankie's office.

Swallowing the lump in my throat, I knocked on the door to my right, and my boss waved me in.

Sixty-year-old Francine "Frankie" Rickard had recently been reelected to a third term as the Chimacam County Prosecutor. Because the uninhabited acres of timber-rich forest in the county outnumbered her constituency, she also served as County Coroner.

Based on the color of the file folder open in front of her—blue, the color used in the office to distinguish coroner's cases from criminal cases—I hoped that I'd been summoned to her office not as an administrative assistant in need of a reprimand but as one of her deputy coroners.

Frankie leaned back in her chair. "Good morning, Charmaine," she said with a quick smile. Since it seemed to be forced and the coffee mug next to her was empty, I guessed that her work day had started hours earlier than mine. And because of the presence of that blue folder, not by choice.

"Morning. You wanted to see me?"

She pointed at one of the two gold-patterned brocade high back chairs facing her, and I took a seat. "I received a call from Darlene McCutcheon early this morning."

Since Frankie wanted to talk coroner business, I breathed a sigh of relief. But that didn't reduce the palpable tension in the room. Probably because that call from Marty's ex-wife couldn't have been a pleasant one.

"I heard about Marty," I said, thinking that it was strange that Darlene would be the one calling Frankie when there was a new Mrs. McCutcheon in the family.

Frankie pursed her peony pink mouth, creating tiny puckers out of the fine lines surrounding it. "News travels fast around here."

Especially when hospital staffers stopped in for an after-shift breakfast at Duke's, where the waitresses were always eager to exchange some daily dish.

I glanced down at the blue folder with Marty McCutcheon's name on the tab. "I thought he'd died from a heart attack."

"Actually, cardiac arrest. Given Marty's history, most likely from cardiovascular disease according to Dr. Cardinale."

I knew Kyle Cardinale. Hunky ER doctor. Great hair. He might be an impossible flirt, but I trusted his judgment. "You think there may be more to it?"

She leveled a gaze at me over her wireframe bifocals. "I highly doubt it, but Marty's ex seems to think that his new wife is responsible for his death. She was quite insistent that something happened at Marty's birthday dinner last night." Frankie pushed the folder toward me. "So, if you can make some time this morning, get her statement."

Of all the deputy coroners on Frankie's staff—and because of budget constraints that included almost everyone with a desk on the third floor of the courthouse—I was typically the one who went into the field to interview witnesses and gather statements. As a deception detection specialist it was next to impossible to pull the wool over my eyes, and since a lot of the locals knew of my reputation as a *human lie detector*, I had an advantage my coworkers didn't: people were often afraid to lie to me.

It certainly made my job easier—something I expected to be the case when I interviewed Darlene McCutcheon, an old friend of my grandmother's.

"No problem. I can make time." Especially since the criminal prosecutor I assisted was at an offsite meeting, and other than keeping his staffers caffeinated with fresh pots of coffee, the only work waiting for me would be the usual end-of-the-week filing.

Frankie nodded. "Talk to everyone who was at that dinner. I'll send his fluids to the crime lab. Then maybe Darlene will settle into some level of acceptance about what happened."

"I'm sure time will help." If the state crime lab was as backed up as it typically was, that amount of time would be a minimum of six weeks.

I scanned Frankie's handwritten notes for a list of who had attended that dinner and cringed when I read Austin Reidy's name.

Crap.

After managing to avoid him for the last eighteen years I was going to have to schedule some face-time with the boy who gave me my first kiss.

Right before I threw up on his shoes.

Chapter Two

JUST AS I remembered from past ventures out to Gram's favorite yarn supplier, once I passed the turnoff for the tiny town of Clatska and crossed the old stone bridge spanning Whisky Creek, a carved wooden sign pointed the way to Mystique Meadows, the alpaca farm owned by Darlene McCutcheon. What I didn't remember was all the kidney-bruising potholes in her dirt driveway, and I immediately regretted driving my Jaguar into farm country instead of Gram's SUV.

I know. What was I doing driving a Jag? A most impractical car for a girl on a budget, but I had needed a set of wheels to move back to my hometown of Port Merritt, so my ex-husband's shiny silver XJ6 had been awarded to me as part of the divorce settlement. It leaked oil like a sieve and half of last week's paycheck went into keeping it purring, but at least the temperamental minx had been getting me where I'd needed to go for the last four months.

Based on the scraping noise I'd heard when the Jag bottomed out in a deep rut, I only hoped I wasn't leaving a trail of auto parts that I was going to need for the thirty-seven mile drive back to the courthouse.

As I pulled in front of the side yard of the rustic red farm house and parked in the shade of two big leaf maples shimmering in autumn coppers and golds, I had the distinct feeling I was being watched. When I climbed out of my car I saw the crowd gathering twenty feet away—a dozen inquisitive alpacas behind the twin Great Pyrenees barking at me through the chain link fence separating us.

"Jake! Elwood! That's enough," said the sixtyish woman as she stepped out of her house, her salt and pepper curls bouncing against her broad shoulders.

A little shorter than my five foot six with rounded hips and a thick roll over the waistband of her blue jeans that her purple University of Washington sweatshirt didn't disguise, Darlene outweighed me by at least thirty pounds.

Shielding her eyes from the midmorning sun, Marty McCutcheon's ex-wife stood next to her Ford Bronco and aimed a frown at me as I approached. "Charmaine? If you're here for your granny's yarn order, now's not a good time."

"I'm not." I fished out a business card from my tote bag and handed it to her. "I work for the County Coroner. I think she told you someone would be coming to get your statement."

Still frowning, Darlene looked down at my card like she didn't want that someone to be me. "Well, Charmaine Digby, Special Assistant to the Prosecutor/Coroner, aren't you coming up in the world. Last I heard you were bussing dishes for Duke."

I didn't like the edge to her voice. I knew I should cut her some slack because her family had suffered a devastating loss, but it seemed like she needed a target for her bitterness, and I was the lucky sap who had just appeared in her crosshairs.

"I helped out at Duke's for a couple of months while one of the waitresses was on maternity leave." I felt like mentioning that her ex-husband had eaten at Duke's fairly regularly, had been a great tipper, and had been much more pleasant to be around than she typically was, but instead I clamped my mouth shut.

She continued to study my card. "I see you went back to using your maiden name."

"I wanted a clean start after the divorce." And absolutely nothing to do with my ex aside from the use of his car.

"I thought about using my maiden name after Marty and I divorced. My two kids were grown by then, but still…. I didn't want to separate myself from the rest of the family." She swiped at a tear trickling down her cheek. "Thought I was done crying, but after forty years with someone in your life…it leaves a hole." She pulled a tissue from her jeans pocket and wiped her eyes. "A big one."

"Maybe we could talk inside." We were getting nowhere in her driveway, and her dogs were staring at me like they saw a couple of meaty bones under my khakis. I took a step toward the house with the hope that she'd follow my lead.

"Sure." Darlene blew out a breath. "Might as well get this over with."

I followed her up a staircase to a long and narrow kitchen that had changed little in the last few decades with the exception of the new refrigerator/freezer hugging a dingy creamsicle wall.

She pointed at the oak claw-footed kitchen table in

front of a large picture window. "Have a seat. I was about to have some coffee. Can I pour you a cup?"

I never turned down free coffee. "Yes, please."

Taking the chair facing the kitchen, I grabbed a pen and a notebook from my bag.

Seconds later, Darlene placed a steaming cup on the coaster in front of me. "I'm lactose intolerant, but I can offer you almond milk if you don't take it black."

"Black's fine." I reached for the dark blue mug and read the bold white lettering inches from my nose: *Thank God It's Friday.* Those four words pretty much represented how I had felt when I woke up this morning, when I was about twelve hours away from a dinner date with Steve, one of my oldest pals and my current...

Actually, I wasn't sure about the current state of our relationship. He was the friend and neighbor I'd been doing a lot more than pal around with for the last month, but we had yet to have a *real* date, so I had been eagerly anticipating this particular Friday.

I didn't need to be able to read Darlene's body language to see that she hadn't been eager to face any of the events of today.

Easing into a seat at the table as if her grief were weighing her down, she looked past me. "Oh, honey, I'm sorry. Did we wake you?"

I turned to see Nicole McCutcheon Reidy emerge from one of the rooms behind me. The last time I'd seen the pretty golden-haired girl who had been a year ahead of me at Port Merritt High, she had been at Duke's, smiling across the table at her dad. This morning there would be no smiles, and her dark eyes were almost swollen shut. No doubt from a long, tearful night. From her icy stare I knew she didn't want me intruding upon her misery.

"I couldn't sleep," she said on her way to the coffee pot.

"I took the last of it, but you can have it." Darlene pushed her cup toward the empty seat between us as Nicole shuffled toward the table. "Honestly, I've probably had enough caffeine to keep me awake for the next week."

Since she looked as dead on her feet as her daughter I didn't believe that for a minute.

I set my cup in front of her. "I know I have, so I think I'll pass on the coffee. Thanks anyway."

Nicole sat to my left and wrapped her hands around the coffee mug like she needed the warmth. "What's going on?"

Fidgeting with the *Thank God It's Friday* mug, her mother cleared her throat. "You remember Charmaine Digby, don't you, honey?"

"Of course I remember her," Nicole said, sitting very still as if every word hurt. "Why is she here?"

Darlene leaned toward her daughter. "I called the Coroner about your dad."

Nicole stared into the inky depths of her coffee mug. "You mean about Victoria."

Frankie's notes had listed the former Victoria Pierce as the second Mrs. McCutcheon and Darlene's primary suspect as the one responsible for her ex-husband's death.

"Charmaine's here to get my statement." Darlene patted her daughter's hand. "Probably just a formality. There will be an investigation into his death, right, Charmaine?"

"Uh…" Not unless the report I submitted after all

these interviews contained something that resembled a smoking gun. "That's a definite possibility."

Nicole narrowed her glassy eyes at me. "A possibility? That woman killed my father."

If I'd learned one thing in my seven weeks on the job, it was that every stakeholder had someone to blame. And based on the venom stirring in Nicole I wasn't surprised to hear her make the accusation against her stepmother.

"Why do you say that?" I asked.

Her gaze tightened. "Are you kidding? Victoria's had three husbands in the last seventeen years. All of them had money and each one died very suddenly."

That didn't mean that she had killed them, but I could see how this looked from Nicole's point of view. I captured her words in my notebook.

Darlene nodded. "I knew from the first moment I met Victoria that she'd be trouble."

I didn't doubt for a minute that Darlene believed what she was saying, but it sounded to me like the anguish over her ex-husband's death was what was bolstering the conviction in her statement.

"But I never expected her to be a black widow," she added.

Seriously?

Considering that I'd served Marty McCutcheon some of the double beef cheeseburgers and chocolate shakes that probably contributed to his heart ailments, I thought calling her successor a *black widow* bordered on the melodramatic. But since Darlene and her daughter were dragging me down this improbable path I had no choice but to keep up. "Uh-huh, and when did Mr. McCutcheon marry Victoria?"

"Last September. Right before Dad's sixty-third birth-day." A flicker of a smile passed over Nicole's lips. "He didn't want the announcement in the *Gazette* to say that he was twenty years older than Victoria." She dabbed a napkin at the tears pooling in her eyes. "Like an age difference of nineteen years sounded so much better."

Darlene pursed her mouth. "The damned fool. Never thinking with the right head."

Nicole cringed. "Mom!"

"Sorry, but you don't know your father the way I knew him. He was a man with needs, and I bet Victoria didn't mind filling them—for a price."

Nicole hung her head. "I don't want to hear this right now."

I did. "What price?"

"The house, the store, all the stocks and bonds, plus everything he inherited from his father earlier in the year." Darlene turned to her daughter. "You told me yourself that your dad changed his will to leave her almost everything."

"You're overstating it. It's half the store. Jeremy and I split the other half."

Darlene's unpainted lips tightened into a sneer. "Whatever. The fact remains the same—she's getting quite the windfall for her twelve months of service."

I could practically taste her sour grapes. Not that Nicole would be any less biased, but I wanted to hear what she had to say on this subject. "Do you agree with your mom that Victoria was after your father's wealth?"

Shoulders slumped, she shook her head. "Maybe. All I know is that he used to joke that he was more worried about her poisoning him than having another heart attack.

That she was trying to slowly kill him."

I leaned forward so that I could get a better angle on her face. "How?"

"She created a special tea blend that was supposed to help with his joint pain. He'd been drinking it for the last few months. Said it tasted nasty."

"Cutting back on the cheeseburgers and losing fifty pounds would have helped more," Darlene muttered as if reading my mind. "He might even still be alive."

Nicole swiped at a tear running down her cheek. "It never occurred to me that there might be something in that tea that could actually hurt my dad. But after hearing him retching in the bathroom..." Her breath hitched. "He was so sick."

Nothing in her expression made me doubt she was telling the truth. Quite the opposite in fact, my eyes burning with unshed tears as I observed Nicole.

"Did he have some of that special tea last night?" I asked, trying to rein in my emotions.

She nodded. "At least I think it was tea. One of the guys had bought him a bottle of scotch for his birthday, so he might have been having a drink to celebrate."

I made a note about the drinks. If there were anything in them to make Marty McCutcheon sick it should show up in the crime lab's toxicology report. "Did your dad eat anything special that you noticed? Anything that you didn't eat?"

"Victoria made his favorite cheese enchilada casserole. I don't do cheese and didn't touch it."

"I don't imagine Jeremy did either," Darlene said. "My kids take after me—no dairy."

"Dad spread some sort of extra hot green chili sauce

on it—something that someone in the office gave him for his birthday. I didn't have any of that either."

"Who gave him the hot sauce?" I asked in case I needed to speak with the person.

Nicole's puffy eyes welled up with more tears. "Phyllis. She and my dad were *close*."

Darlene snorted. "That's one way to put it. She was an old girlfriend of Marty's. Compared to Victoria put some emphasis on *old*."

It sounded like good ol' Marty got around a little bit more than I would have imagined, but I found it difficult to believe that a former girlfriend would intentionally try to hurt him. Assuming, of course, that there had been no recent attempts to rekindle that relationship.

I locked gazes with Nicole. "Anything else that your father ate or drank last night that you didn't?"

"Maybe something from the taco salad bar that Victoria set up." She wiped her eyes. "Honestly, at the time I wasn't paying that much attention."

Ordinarily, any sentence beginning with *honestly* would set off my *liedar*, but since the emotion behind her words was real, I believed her.

I looked across the table at Darlene. "Anything you want to add?"

A crease between her dark brows deepened. "That woman did this. I have no doubt. Marty might have had his faults, but he was a kind and loving father, and deserved a lot better than what he got last night."

Or it was just his very bad luck to have a massive coronary on his birthday.

I pushed back my chair. "I think I have everything I need for now. If you think of anything else you'd like to add to your statement, don't hesitate to give me a call."

Darlene frowned up at me, her arms folded across her ample chest. "What happens next?"

I planned to interview the other witnesses, type up a report for Frankie, and then wait up to two months for the crime lab's toxicology results to come back. Since I figured both these women wouldn't be happy with any response that didn't include a mention of Victoria McCutcheon's imminent arrest, I decided that it was in my best interest to end this conversation on a vague note.

"I'll get the statement of everyone who was at dinner last night and then…" *Don't make it sound like this is an official investigation.* "…I'll turn over that information to the Coroner."

Perfect. Short and sweet with no promise of anything I couldn't deliver.

Still frowning, Darlene blinked. "Will she keep us informed of any developments during the investigation?"

I couldn't leave letting her think she'd be hearing from Frankie sometime next week. "These things can take some time."

"When do you think we'll hear something?"

In six to eight weeks. "I can't speak for the Coroner, so I really don't know."

Darlene heaved a sigh.

In the silence that followed I stepped toward the door. "Thank you again for your time." I met Nicole's gaze. "I'm very sorry for your loss."

I was three feet from making my getaway when Darlene called out my name.

Turning, I planted a pleasant smile on my face.

"I have your grandmother's yarn order ready so we

might as well save her a trip," she said as she led me down the stairs. "It's in the yurt."

"The what?"

"My fiber store."

I followed Darlene to the round tent looming like a giant marshmallow on the north side of the house. Opening the flap she disappeared. "Where the heck did I put it? Sorry, give me a minute."

Catching a whiff of something floral, I followed my nose to the back of the yurt and saw purple clematis and iris dwarfing a plant that had only a couple of purplish-blue blooms. At least it fit into the purple theme Darlene had going.

"Where'd you go?" she asked, coming into view with two small plastic sacks.

"I was just admiring your flowers."

"They seem to do well back here. Must be all the light that the yurt reflects." She patted it like a proud mother. "Marty made fun of me when I first bought it, but it comes in very handy."

Whatever.

Darlene handed me one of the sacks. "Five skeins along with the invoice. Tell your granny she can write me a check or pay me in a couple of weeks, when I get my next shipment from the mill." She dangled the other plastic bag in front of me. "And if you wouldn't mind dropping this one off, this is for Estelle Makepeace. The woman has to be at least eighty-five—one of my best customers, but the last time she was out here she backed into my fence. I don't need the aggravation, especially this week, and I doubt I'm going to be getting to town anytime soon."

I didn't need to add yarn delivery girl to my job description, but since Mrs. Makepeace, one of Gram's mahjong buddies, lived a couple blocks from the courthouse, I couldn't say no without coming off like an insensitive bitch.

"I'd be happy to." I took a step toward my car, the bags swinging from my hand. "Again, if you think of anything else you'd like to add to your statement, be sure to let me know."

"I do have one thing, but it's more of a question."

Based on the intensity of her stare I had the distinct feeling that I wasn't going to like hearing it. "Okay."

"You haven't said anything about Marty having an autopsy."

No, and I didn't intend to. "I believe the Coroner has all the physical evidence she needs to proceed with…" *Don't refer to this as an investigation.*

Darlene stepped closer. "The investigation?"

Crap! "I wouldn't call this—"

"That's what it is, right?" she asked, her eyes narrowing as they searched mine.

"In a very preliminary way." I swallowed the curse I wanted to utter because no matter how I guarded my words, I was still making it sound like Marty McCutcheon had been murdered instead of being a casualty of the heart ailment that would eventually be recorded as his cause of death.

Darlene blew out a deep breath. "Well, at least she's launched an investigation. You'll keep me posted?"

I nodded.

Crap. Crap. Crap!

Chapter Three

AFTER A BUMPY thirteen-minute drive on the county road to Clatska, I headed north on Gibson Lake Drive and bordered by fir trees, I came to a clearing where Marty McCutcheon and his wife, Victoria, had been living in a well-maintained two-story home in the center of a wooded acre.

Lace curtains fluttered at the bay window as I climbed the steps to the front porch. The door swung open before I had the opportunity to knock.

I smiled at one of the most beautiful faces I'd ever seen. With her creamy complexion, delicate nose, high cheekbones, and gleaming, shoulder-length raven hair, Victoria McCutcheon reminded me of the porcelain Chinese doll my mother had brought back with her after filming a movie in Hong Kong. Only the dark almond eyes of the woman in front of me detracted from her physical attributes. Not just because they were smudged with what I guessed was yesterday's mascara, but because they looked like that doll's eyes—lifeless.

Since this long-legged, exotic beauty looked even younger than the woman I had expected to see, I thought

I'd better make sure I was speaking with the right person. "Mrs. McCutcheon?"

She nodded. "Yes?"

"I'm Charmaine Digby from the County Coroner's office. I'm sorry to intrude at a difficult time, but I'd like to ask you a few questions about what happened last night."

"Of course." She stepped back to let me in. "I just made some tea. Would you like some?"

I wasn't much of a tea drinker, but since I'd given away my coffee at Darlene's house, my caffeine addiction was in no mood to be denied. "That would be great."

I followed her into a spacious kitchen with walls painted in a warm winter wheat, stainless steel appliances, and a terracotta floor, all bathed in sunlight streaming in from an arched window that stretched the length of the room.

Victoria waved a slender hand at the round white table in front of a set of French doors that afforded an excellent view of the manicured back yard. "Please, have a seat."

A minute later she joined me with two steaming mugs. "Do you take anything in your tea?"

Thinking about what Nicole and Darlene had told me about Victoria's *special* blend, I knew what I didn't want in my tea.

I held the mug she'd offered under my nose and sniffed it. Nothing registered. "What kind of tea is it?"

"A green tea. Sorry, I don't remember which one. I know I bought it at the Chinese herbal store in Port Townsend."

Good enough for me. I took a sip. "It's fine just as it

is. Thank you."

She sat ramrod straight, staring across the table at me. "You said you had questions."

I pulled out my notebook. "Yes, I understand you had a small birthday party here for your husband last night."

She didn't blink, didn't flinch at what should have been a painful memory. "Yes."

From what little I'd gleaned in mystery novels, black widows typically poisoned their victims, and a dinner party with some spicy food might provide the perfect opportunity to eliminate a rich husband.

"Who prepared the food?" If she really were the black widow type that Darlene and Nicole tried to make her out to be, Victoria would probably want to cast some suspicion on as many people as possible.

"I did."

So much for casting a wide net of suspicion. "All of it?"

The corner of Victoria's mouth tugged into a hint of a smile. "Every bit of it."

I didn't know what to make of the smile. It seemed incongruous with her otherwise solemn demeanor, but I didn't get the sense that she was telling me anything that wasn't true. "Can you describe everything that you think your husband ingested?"

She listed the casserole and green chili salsa that Nicole had mentioned along with chips and dip, and jalapeno poppers. She also confirmed that Marty had poured himself a scotch.

"Any other liquid? Coffee? Tea?" I asked, watching carefully for a reaction.

I saw no emotional response.

"He only drank tea in the morning," she calmly stated.

"What kind of tea? Green tea like this?"

"No. A special therapeutic tea to ease his joint pain."

"Was this also from the Chinese herbal store?"

"Actually, my father practices herbal medicine in Santa Barbara and prescribed this treatment for Marty's arthritis."

"Anything in it that might be considered dangerous?" Or lethal?

Her brow crinkled, but her gaze was unwavering. "I think I understand what you're asking. I wasn't trying to slowly kill him contrary to what he used to say. He just didn't like the taste of it."

That statement led me to believe that either Victoria McCutcheon was one of the most skillful liars I'd ever met or Nicole's suspicions about this tea were totally without merit.

"Did your husband consume anything that you didn't see anyone else eat or drink?"

"Other than the scotch that someone might have helped themselves to while I was in the kitchen, maybe the salsa. Marty poured that over the enchilada casserole. Don't know what that said about my cooking other than the fact that my husband liked a lot of spice in his life."

I assumed that included her since she was twenty years his junior.

She reached for her tea. "He was in the middle of eating it when he said he didn't feel well."

"Then what happened?"

"He rushed to the bathroom and became violently ill."

"Did anyone suggest calling for an ambulance?"

"No, because I told Marty I was going to take him to the hospital, but he refused to get into the car. Said it would pass." She shook her head. "It was his stubborn male pride talking, and I was a fool to listen for as long as I did. When I saw how much worse he was getting I called nine-one-one, but it took almost an hour to get him to the hospital. Minutes later his heart stopped, and he was gone."

She didn't seem too broken up about it, but everything she'd said rang true. "That must have been a tremendous shock."

She blinked as if she were processing my words. "It still is."

"Had your husband mentioned anything about not feeling well prior to sitting down for dinner?"

"No, he seemed fine. I think he ate something that made him sick. Possibly the salsa."

"Do you still have the bottle?" Not that I knew exactly what Frankie might do with it, but on the offhand chance that some toxin actually showed up in Marty McCutcheon's blood and urine, I'd be stupid not to take it as evidence.

"Of course."

"What about the enchilada casserole?"

Victoria McCutcheon set down her mug with a steady hand. "I have everything just as it was when we left for the hospital last night."

Because she couldn't bear to deal with it just yet? Doubtful. So far she'd impressed me as someone who had no difficulty compartmentalizing her emotions. "Could I take a look?"

With a nod she rose from her chair. Grabbing my cell phone, I followed her into the dining room where, if I hadn't known better, it appeared that a dinner for six had just been interrupted.

She placed her hand on the back of the chair facing the window. "Marty sat here."

From the unappetizing greenish-yellow mound on his plate, it looked like he had been working on the salsa-covered casserole when he started feeling discomfort, supporting what both Nicole and Victoria had told me.

Using my cell phone camera I took a close-up of Marty's plate and then stepped toward the doorway behind me to get a longer view of the entire table. "Where did you sit?"

"In front of you, to Marty's right. Across from me, Marty's daughter, Nicole, and her husband. At the end of the table, Marty's son, Jeremy. Then Cameron sat next to me."

All I knew about Cameron was what I had read in Frankie's notes—that he worked at Marty's store. Seemed a little unusual that he'd been invited to the birthday party since everyone else was family.

"Who's Cameron?" I asked.

"Marty's son from a relationship he had when he was still married to Darlene."

Another son? I met Victoria's gaze. "I spoke with Nicole earlier. She gave me the impression that she only had the one brother."

"She doesn't know. Marty only found out two weeks ago and had been waiting for the right time to tell her about her half-brother." Victoria took in a shaky breath, the first chink I had seen in the emotional armor she'd been wearing since I'd arrived. "Jeremy, too."

Wow. Keeping that kind of secret from his family had to have been a weighty burden to carry around. It made me wonder if it had added to his stress level last night.

"Did Marty seem nervous, or did he say anything about breaking the news during dinner?"

"No, he wanted to talk to his kids privately— tomorrow or the next day, so last night seemed like any other dinner party we'd had here."

"Even with Cameron here? That didn't seem odd to Nicole or Jeremy?"

Victoria shook her head. "Everyone who worked at the store was invited."

And yet only Cameron—the son Marty hadn't known existed until two weeks ago—had taken his father up on the invitation. Something about this dinner party didn't pass my sniff test.

"It's a tight-knit group of three employees besides Jeremy. Cameron was just the only one who said yes," she explained as if anticipating my next question. "Phyllis wouldn't come to our wedding either, so I'm not surprised she declined the invitation."

Phyllis was the former girlfriend who had given Marty the salsa. I wasn't surprised to hear that she didn't want to sit ringside and bear witness to Marty's wonderful life with Victoria. At least what had appeared to have been a wonderful life.

A tiny frown line etched its way between Victoria's perfectly arched brows a second before she broke eye contact. "And I can't tell you why Bob didn't come," she said with a lip press that suggested that she couldn't tell me because she didn't want to.

"Bob?"

"Bob Hallahan, the assistant manager at the store and one of Marty's best friends."

I knew Bob a little from having waited on him a few

times at Duke's.

"He gave Marty the bottle of scotch when they went out for lunch yesterday. It's…" She hesitated, seemingly censoring herself. "…not typical for Bob to turn down an invitation to dinner."

It would be if something were to happen that he didn't want to see.

Criminy! Darlene and Nicole's claims that Marty McCutcheon was poisoned were rubbing off on me.

I needed to rein in my imagination and focus on doing the task at hand: getting statements from everyone who attended the birthday party, which meant retrieving my notebook to capture the information Victoria had just provided. "I'll be right back," I said on my way to the kitchen table, chiding myself for acting like a rookie.

Death investigations weren't an everyday occurrence in rural Chimacam County. I'd only participated in one, and today was just my third time to venture out of the courthouse on official coroner business. Still, I needed to get it together and not wear my inexperience on my sleeve.

Seconds later, I met Victoria mid-stride in the center of her kitchen.

She offered me a box of plastic wrap. "Would you like to wrap this around Marty's plate so that you can take it with you?"

Clearly she wanted me to. Again, not what I'd expect to hear from Darlene's black widow.

I'd seen and heard nothing to give any credence to the former Mrs. McCutcheon's accusations, but Victoria's action struck me as being a little too helpful—as if she'd known that someone from my office would stop by today and she had mentally prepared herself for that knock on her door.

Tucking my notebook under my arm I took the box of plastic wrap from her. "Yes, thanks. Out of curiosity, did anyone from the coroner's office call you this morning?"

"No. You're the only person I've talked to today. Well, aside from Jeremy. He called to make sure I was okay." She drew in a deep breath. "And to let me know that his mother might make some trouble. I assume you've already talked to her?"

I nodded. "She has some concerns." To put it mildly.

Victoria McCutcheon met my gaze, her dark eyes hard like flint. "So do I. That's why I called the Sheriff the moment I got home last night."

That tidbit of information wasn't in the file Frankie had given me.

"A deputy arrived about an hour later. He took my statement much like you did, snapped a few pictures, and then very politely reminded me that they did everything that they could at the ER, but until the sheriff's department is told otherwise, my husband died because he had a bad heart."

Despite the fact that I was willing to take some bottles and leftovers back to the office with me, I knew that I was accomplishing little more than that sheriff's deputy.

"So please, take whatever you need and find out what killed my husband," Victoria said with an icy intensity that made my skin prickle with gooseflesh.

❋

Returning to the courthouse forty minutes later, I

walked into the bowels of the third floor carrying a paper sack containing the remains of Marty McCutcheon's last meal, a half-empty bottle of green chili salsa, and a nearly-full fifth of scotch whisky.

Karla Tate, Frankie's death investigation coordinator in charge of cataloguing the evidence brought into the department, looked up at me over her computer monitor. "Brown bagging it today?"

"It's evidence. Maybe."

She arched an eyebrow. "Maybe?"

"If Marty McCutcheon ate or drank anything that caused his heart to stop last night, it's evidence."

Leaning over her desk, Karla frowned at the bag. "Is that a bottle of booze in there?"

I nodded and told her the rest of the contents of the bag.

She puckered, accentuating the network of wrinkles that decades of smoking had carved into her upper lip. "You know that if there were any real indication that Marty died from anything other than a bum ticker, the Sheriff would be storing that stuff in his evidence room instead of us cluttering up ours."

"I know it's a big *if* and we'll probably end up throwing all of this into the trash, but if there's even a chance that Frankie wants something analyzed after the labs come back...."

"Fine," Karla muttered on a sigh. After pulling out some evidence tags from a drawer, she led me down the hall to the storage closet that doubled as an evidence room.

It contained a four-tier wire rack unit that shelved boxes of holiday decor and party supplies, coils of

extension cords, a cardboard box piled high with tele-
phones that appeared to be leftovers from the last
century, and a covered plastic storage bin containing a roll
of aluminum foil along with assorted sizes of baggies and
gloves.

To the right of the shelving unit stood a tall, two-door
gray metal cabinet. Filling up the majority of the remaining
space a white refrigerator/freezer softly whirred.

Nothing about this closet screamed *Evidence Room*
except for the fact that both the cabinet and the refrigerator were secured with padlocks.

"Glove up," Karla said, reaching into the plastic bin
and handing me a pair of nitrile gloves. "I assume you
were wearing gloves when you removed this stuff from
the house?"

"Uh, no, but I only handled the plate after wrapping it
in plastic and the other two bottles already had their lids
on them."

Karla heaved another sigh as she snapped on a pair of
gloves. "If this ever goes to court the defense attorney will
rip you to shreds for not following protocol. In the future,
if you think we need to collect some evidence, call me."

My cheeks burned from the criticism of the senior
staffer who had been training me to be her backup. I'd
made another rookie mistake.

She pulled the plastic-wrapped plate from the bag.
"This looks nasty."

I couldn't disagree. "Yeah."

Palming the plate she met my gaze with a look worthy
of a disapproving schoolmarm. "And it isn't cold."

"I know. Mrs. McCutcheon left everything on the
table, just as it was after her husband became ill."

"So it sat out all night, uncovered."

"Yep."

"You know what I said about that defense attorney ripping you to shreds?"

I nodded.

"Ditto. Fortunately for us, Marty didn't fall victim to anything more sinister than the poor diet that's been hardening his arteries the last forty years, and your *evidence* won't be needed."

"Right." Try convincing the McCutcheon women that their loved one had simply eaten his way into an early grave.

After another few puckers and sighs, the remnants from Marty McCutcheon's last meal were bagged, tagged, and stored under lock and key, and I was handed a plate to return to his second wife.

Not today, I thought, washing it in the breakroom. My only order of business today was to speak with everyone who had shared that last meal and then get my report to Frankie.

I made a quick trip to my desk to store the plate in a drawer and check my messages, then I headed for the door to interview the next person on my list: Jeremy McCutcheon.

On my way out I glanced up at the brass clock mounted above the front door that, along with the red brick courthouse, dated back to the late eighteen hundreds. Since it was eleven twenty-two and approaching lunchtime for most of Port Merritt's occupants, I figured I had a fifty-fifty chance of catching Nicole's brother at the shop where he'd worked for Marty. The same could be said for Cameron, the half-brother Nicole and Jeremy didn't know they had, Phyllis, the salsa lady, and Bob, Marty's whisky supplier.

With any luck, I'd be able to get most of their statements, take my own lunch break at Duke's, and then walk back to McCutcheon Floors & More to finish the job.

That would leave only one name on my interview list: Austin Reidy. I just needed to make sure that my lunch had settled before I visited Austin. Not that history would repeat itself and I'd cap off our meeting by upchucking on his shoes. That ugly little slice of mortification pie was served only to sixteen-year-olds foolish enough to chug their first beer on a dare. Wasn't it?

I reached into my tote bag and fingered the roll of antacids I kept in a side pocket. Yep, I was armed and ready for Austin Reidy. At least that's what I told myself.

Chapter Four

AS SOON AS the door to McCutcheon Floors & More swung shut behind me, two things seemed very inappropriate given the reason for my visit: the business as usual atmosphere in Marty McCutcheon's store and the bright smile on his son's face as he greeted me.

"How're you doing? Can I help you find something?" Jeremy McCutcheon asked without waiting for an answer to the first question.

I looked up at the younger, golden-haired version of his father. "I don't know if you remember me. I'm Charmaine Digby and I work for the Coroner."

The wattage of his smile dimmed as his heavy-lidded brown eyes scanned my face. "Yeah, I remember you." His gaze dropped to my hips. "It's been a while."

At least fifteen years since I'd served him a burger at Duke's and double that many pounds. "I'd like to speak with you if you could spare a few minutes."

He shook his head. "You couldn't have picked a worse time."

No doubt his father's death had to have made getting through this work day especially difficult.

"We're kicking off our annual fall sale today."

A sale? Today of all days?

He thumbed in the direction of the two couples walking through the laminate flooring section. "I'm kinda busy."

"I can see that." I also noticed a twenty-something dressed in the same polo shirt/blue jeans combination as Jeremy, who was assisting one of the couples. That's where the similarity between the two men ended. Where Jeremy, a solid-packed former state wrestling champion, looked like he'd enjoy the taste of his own blood, the dark-haired guy with the more angular features looked long and lean like a distance runner who preferred fresh air to the stink of a wrestling mat. At least I'd thought they had nothing in common until his gaze met mine, and I saw that they shared the same heavy-lidded, bedroom eyes—Marty's eyes.

This had to be Cameron, and he appeared to be as curious about me as I was about him.

"I thought about closing things down today," Jeremy said as I looked around. "But I didn't think my dad would want us to do that, especially after he spent some bucks to advertise the sale. Instead, when I told everyone the news this morning, I said they could take the day if they wanted."

"Anyone take you up on your offer?"

"Just Bob Hallahan. He and my dad went way back, so he took it pretty hard."

"Understandable."

"If you could come back Monday, after the sale—"

"Sorry, this can't wait, but I promise I'll be brief. Is there somewhere private where we could talk?"

"Of course." The smile crawling back onto his face, he bowed slightly, all politeness like the officious maître d' at my former in-laws' San Francisco bistro. So very accommodating to the big tippers, such a prick to everyone else. "Right this way."

I followed him past stacks of rolled carpet, halfway down a dimly lit hallway into a back office cluttered with catalogs, books of swatches, and laminate sample boards.

Jeremy sat behind the desk and pointed to the two black vinyl chairs facing him. "Have a seat. Sorry about the mess. Pop was the carpet king in town, not the organization king."

Clearly that was the truth, but again it struck me how unaffected by his father's loss Jeremy appeared to be. It was as if he'd shifted into an emotionally neutral state. Assuming, of course, that he was a man capable of experiencing highs and lows on a sliding scale of emotions.

I sat in the chair closest to the door and pulled my notebook from my tote. "First of all, my condolences. I knew your dad from working at Duke's over the years. He was a very nice man."

"We all thought so," he said, his gaze cool as he tapped a steady beat with his index finger.

I took that as a signal to cut the niceties short and get on with the interview. "I understand that you were at your dad's house for dinner last night."

The tapping continued. "That's right."

"Who else was there?" I already had the answer, but I wanted to hear it from him.

"Victoria, my sister, Nicole, her husband, Austin, Cameron, and me."

"Who's Cameron?" I asked to watch Jeremy describe

Cameron's relationship to his late father.

"New guy. My dad took him under his wing when he hired him a couple months back. Even had him to the house for dinner once before."

Again Jeremy was making like Switzerland. Completely neutral.

"So it didn't seem unusual for him to be there with your family?"

"No, and why are you asking about one of our employees?" He sat up straight like I'd just jammed a stick up his backside. "Are you suggesting—"

"I'm not suggesting anything. The Coroner just wants to be thorough. You know, dot all the i's, cross all the t's."

Jeremy vented a breath.

Righteous indignation? If that's what he had intended to convey I wasn't buying it, not with the lack of heat behind the carefully constructed mask he was wearing.

"Whatever," he muttered. "I need to get back to work so what else do you want to know?"

"Tell me about your dad. You must have spent quite a bit of time with him yesterday. Did he say anything about not feeling well?"

"He seemed fine. It was his birthday so Phyllis got him a cake. We all signed a card for him. What can I tell you? He seemed to be enjoying himself."

"And later on at dinner?"

"The same. Laughing, joking around—normal stuff." He knit his brows. "At least until he broke into a sweat."

"When was that?"

"About ten minutes after we sat down to eat. I didn't notice it at first. Victoria did. Asked him if he was okay. Of course the old goat said he was fine. Too proud to admit he was in pain."

Nicole and Victoria had made it sound like Marty had become violently ill from something he ate or drank, but neither one of them had used the word *pain*. "Did he say something about anything hurting to you?"

With a cavalier shrug of a shoulder Jeremy's lips curled into a humorless smile. "Didn't have to. I was there for his last heart attack. Trust me, seeing him go all sweaty and pale—that's not something you forget."

"Did you tell Victoria that you thought your dad was having another heart attack?"

"I tried, but when he started throwing up she got a little hysterical. Honestly, I don't think she heard me."

Hysterical? The cool and calm Victoria I met earlier this morning? Once again, I wasn't buying what Jeremy was trying to sell me. And him throwing in an *honestly* line only served to make him less convincing.

"But if you recognized the same signs that you saw before," I said, struggling to phrase my question in a non-accusatory way, "did you suggest placing a nine-one-one call?"

"Victoria didn't seem to want to call, but finally... after..."

"After what?"

"Dad passed out on the bathroom floor, and I was yelling at her that we couldn't wait any longer," he stated matter of factly as if we were talking about something as inconsequential as the weather, not his dying father.

His version of last night's events was very similar to Nicole's and Victoria's except for the parts where he suspected that his father was having another heart attack and his portrayal of his stepmother as hesitant to get

Marty the help he needed. The unflattering picture he'd painted made me curious about their relationship, especially since I knew that Jeremy was the one who had called to check up on her this morning.

"But with the time it takes for the paramedics to get out to Clatska, it was already too late." He heaved a sigh as if it had been scripted, but behind that sigh—nothing. No sense of loss, no indicator of grief.

What was with this guy?

The finger tapping resumed. "Anything else that I can tell you?"

I knew there was plenty more he could tell me, but it would have been a waste of his time and mine if we were to continue this game of verbal dodgeball.

"That's all I need for now. Thank you. Would you ask Cameron to come in?"

Coming to his feet, Jeremy narrowed his eyes at me, his gaze hard as granite for a split second before he shifted back into neutral.

You don't like me telling you what to do.

"I'll see if he's available," he stated slowly and clearly as if I needed a reminder that he was the one in charge in this office.

Fine. At least he'd revealed an honest emotion. Not a particularly pleasant one since the guy looked like he wanted to wrap his beefy arm around my neck and put me into a head lock, but still, his emotional response told me a lot. Most notably that my read on him was correct.

That didn't mean that Jeremy McCutcheon had anything to do with his father's death. It also didn't mean that he didn't.

❋

Shaking his head, Cameron Windom stared down at
the floor much like he had most of the last seven minutes
we'd shared in his father's office. With his fingers inter-
locked, his elbows propped against the armrests of the
chair next to me, Cameron gave the appearance of
praying, only his lips weren't moving. Instead, they were
clamped shut, making him look a lot like my ex-
husband—a man afraid of digging himself into an
inescapable hole after I caught him kissing our sous chef
in the walk-in freezer.

After several seconds of stony silence, Cameron blew
out a breath, his feet inching toward the door like he
wanted to bolt. "Really, I don't know what more I can tell
you. Like I said, I ate everything that he did, so I don't
know why he got so sick."

You could tell me the whole truth. Which would be
especially useful since the information he was withholding
was making him too twitchy to get an accurate reading.

I decided to take a different approach. "Okay, then tell
me about when you found out that Marty McCutcheon
was your father."

He searched my gaze. "How did…. Does Jeremy
know? I wasn't supposed to say anything until after—"

"Victoria told me, and I haven't said anything about
this to Jeremy, but it will be included in my report to the
Coroner."

Cameron swallowed, his Adam's apple bobbing as he
nodded. "Maybe it doesn't matter now."

I leaned toward him both to see and hear him more
clearly. "What doesn't matter?"

"Without Marty here…" He shook his head. "There's no reason to make the McCutcheons' lives any more complicated than they already are."

Somehow his line felt rehearsed. Maybe the brothers were more alike than I'd given them credit for.

One corner of his mouth lifted. "Too bad. I kinda liked this job."

"Are you saying you're leaving?"

He stared at the floor with such intensity he could have burned a hole in the carpeting with his corneas. "Jeremy doesn't want me here. He's made that pretty clear."

Oh, yeah? "How?"

Cameron shrugged. "He rides me pretty hard when Marty's not around. And now that he's gone, I don't have to put up with Jeremy's *management style*." Another lopsided smile crossed his lips. "It's not like I'm going to be invited to any more family gatherings. No big deal," he said, his eyes reddening with unshed tears as he lied to the both of us. "I don't need any of this shit."

The last part of his statement might have been true, but as a member of yesterday's gathering he was smack-dab in the middle of it.

He turned to me. "Are we done?"

"In a few minutes." Now that we didn't need to skirt around his relationship to Marty, I wanted to revisit Cameron's account of yesterday's dinner party. "When you said that you ate the same food as Marty, what exactly did you eat last night?"

Cameron angled a glare at me. "You want to know every single thing I ate?"

"Yep."

"Chips, dip, a bunch of jalapeno pepper things wrapped in bacon, some sort of enchilada casserole, taco salad, sour cream, more chips. I guess that's pretty much it. Oh, and a beer."

He had packed away that much food, and he was this skinny? Man, I'd love to trade metabolisms with this guy.

I compared the list to everything Victoria had told me that Marty had eaten and spotted one glaring omission. "Did you have any of the hot sauce?"

He shook his head. "I thought about it when Marty dared me to try it, but when Victoria pointed out the flames on the label I decided not to tempt fate."

"Fate?"

"Hot and spicy food can give me some pretty bad heartburn. In fact, that's what I thought was happening with Marty at first."

"When he started getting sick?"

"Right. He grabbed his water glass like his throat was on fire. After he finished his water he drank Victoria's."

It seemed odd to me that she hadn't mentioned this.

"Then he started to sweat," Cameron said.

She hadn't mentioned that either.

He wrinkled his nose. "A few minutes later I could hear him throwing up in the bathroom."

"Cameron, did you or anyone else suggest calling nine-one-one?"

He stared down at his scuffed sneakers. "Sure, but Marty kept saying that he'd be okay—to give him a few minutes." Cameron shook his head. "I think waiting all that time was a big mistake."

Based on everything I'd heard, I couldn't have agreed with him more.

*

Back in the sixth grade Heather Beckett called me a psycho-bitch-freak in front of the entire class. Okay, I freely admit that my competitive nature had gotten the best of me during a game of *Truth or Dare*, and I shouldn't have outed Heather as a liar at her own slumber party. It never occurred to eleven-year-old me that there would be retribution, that my classmates would tell their parents about what had happened, and I would never again be invited inside their homes.

Being the bastard of a B-list actress infamous for her nude photo spread in a men's magazine had branded me as something of a local curiosity. But once the psycho-bitch-freak label was added it were as if Heather had doused me with kerosene and struck a match. The next morning, did I rise from the ashes a new creation? Not by choice, but I had a metamorphosis just the same. Suddenly, it seemed that I was no longer just my mother's bastard.

I had become one scary bastard.

And I knew I was scaring the crap out of Phyllis Bozeman, who was squirming in the seat that Cameron had vacated five minutes earlier.

At least she had stopped crying, which was a good news/bad news thing since she was sitting wide-eyed, staring at me like I was some sort of voodoo princess capable of bending her to my will.

I wished. It would certainly make my job easier, especially today.

"How's Aubrey doing?" I asked, painting an easy smile on my face.

Aubrey Bozeman had been tight with Heather's cheerleader crowd and had treated me like a social pariah all through high school. I had no interest in the latest Aubrey news, but if some polite chitchat helped her mother breathe a little easier, I could fake it.

Unblinking, Phyllis swallowed. "Fine."

"Good to hear." *Relax. Blink!* "I heard she had another baby. Boy or girl?"

"Another boy," she said after several seconds of hesitation, as if too much information about her grandchildren might put them in danger.

"Good for her." I leaned a little closer. "And how is Grandma doing?"

She finally blinked. "What do you mean?"

"I'm sure this has been a difficult day."

Averting her gaze, Phyllis's pale lips thinned, her puffy eyes starting to pool with a fresh round of tears.

I passed her the mini-packet of tissues I kept in my tote for tearful interview subjects. "I'm sorry. I know you lost someone you were close to."

She eyed the packet as if I'd asked her to hold the snake we'd be sacrificing after the interview.

"I'm fine," she stated, handing it back to me.

Sure you are. "Then may I ask you a few questions?"

She pushed back a curl that had escaped her helmet of dyed black hair and nodded.

"Did you happen to see Marty yesterday afternoon?"

"We had a little birthday celebration around one. You know, we all gathered around to wish him a happy birthday and have some cake."

"How'd he seem?"

"Fine." A sad smile pulled at the network of crinkles

around her dark eyes. "Happy."

"No indication of any health issues?"

She shook her head. "Absolutely none."

"Nothing that seemed out of the ordinary?"

"No."

I wrote *seemed fine* in my notebook. "How would you characterize your relationship with Marty?"

"My relationship?" She blinked, sending a tear down her cheek. "We're friends."

"I understand that you and Marty used to be more than friends."

Sniffing, she looked like she wanted to sic that snake on me. "That was a long time ago."

Not that long ago. "And Marty broke it off shortly after he met Victoria."

"It was a mutual decision," she said, taking a swipe at another tear.

I didn't believe her for a minute, but nothing she'd told me had waved any red flags. At least not yet.

I passed her the tissues. "And that probably led to another decision to avoid spending much time with Marty after work."

With no resistance Phyllis reached into the mini-pack and dabbed her eyes. "I may be getting old, but I'm no fool."

"Tell me, considering that your relationship with Marty had cooled, I'm curious why you bought him a birthday present."

That same sad smile blanketed her face. "It seemed petty not to. Just because we're not.... It doesn't mean we can't do something nice for one another."

"What did you get him?"

"Salsa from a little shop we discovered on a trip to Arizona a few years back. We both loved the stuff, so I set it up to get a delivery every year—one for him for his birthday and one for me."

"So this gift wasn't a surprise."

Phyllis narrowed her eyes at me as if she had just realized that I wasn't so scary. I was just frighteningly slow on the uptake. "Hardly, not after three years."

"Did you have the salsa shipped to your house?" I asked.

"No, I've had a problem with things disappearing from my front porch, so I had it shipped here. Arrived late last week."

Where someone could have had easy access to it—someone who knew that a bottle of Marty's favorite salsa would be arriving in time for his birthday, just like it had last year and the year before that.

Chapter Five

TWENTY MINUTES LATER, I was sitting on a bench at the marina munching on Duke's takeout, when Detective Steve Sixkiller pulled up in his unmarked Port Merritt Police cruiser.

"What is this—a late lunch?" he asked, shading his eyes from the sun as he closed the distance between us. "You said in your text that it was an emergency."

"It is." Since I could eat my way through any emergency this guy obviously didn't know me as well as I'd thought he did.

When the object of my first schoolgirl crush sat down next to me, I passed him the grease-stained takeout bag. "Want some fries?"

Crossing his long legs, he reached into the bag and pulled out a couple of lukewarm french fries. "I have a meeting in a few minutes so what I want is for you to give me the short version of this *emergency*."

"Fine. If you've been anywhere near Duke's today I'm sure you heard about Marty McCutcheon."

"Yeah, that he had a heart attack," Steve said, chewing.

"Technically, it was cardiac arrest, but based on what his family members have told me I wouldn't be so cavalier about what caused his heart to stop."

He turned to me, a tic above his jawline keeping pace with the seconds of stony silence between us. "Seriously? Frankie asked you to speak with the family?"

"It was to placate his ex because she was making some accusations about Marty being poisoned."

Steve blew out a weary breath. "Poisoned."

"That's starting to look like a possibility."

He wiped his fingers on one of the napkins I'd stuffed into the takeout bag. "In your educated opinion as an experienced death investigator."

"Okay, I know I'm not—"

"Where did he die?"

"At the hospital."

"I assume that someone from your office talked with the attending?"

"Frankie spoke with the doctor who treated Marty in the ER."

"And?"

"He told her that Marty had a bad heart and a history of cardiovascular disease, and that led to his cardiac arrest."

Standing, Steve tossed the remnants of my lunch into a nearby trash can. "I think this conversation is over."

"But I have two witnesses who were there at dinner when Marty got sick, and they both think he was poisoned."

"Dinner at his house out in Clatska?"

I nodded.

"Outside of my jurisdiction, so I can't help you, Chow

Mein," Steve said, using the nickname he'd given me back in the third grade. He glanced at his wristwatch. "And I need to go."

I tried to keep up with his long strides as he headed for the parking lot. "But what if they're right?"

"People around here don't die from being poisoned."

"There's always a first time."

"I repeat—not likely, but if he ate something that killed him it should show up during the autopsy, and then Frankie will hand this case over to the Sheriff."

"There's not going to be an autopsy."

Standing in front of his car, Steve met my gaze. "Because Marty died at the hospital after he went into cardiac arrest. That's what the doctor said, and that's good enough for Frankie, right?"

Especially since my boss didn't want to bust the county's budget by calling in a forensic pathologist for an unnecessary autopsy.

"Pretty much."

"Then I'd say your work should be about done, Deputy." He tweaked my nose like we were siblings instead of lovers who had been sharing a bed most of the last month. "See you later. Wear something sexy," he said with a wink.

Despite the mixed messages, he left me feeling like the gooey s'mores we used to make as kids. But as I watched Steve drive away a cold reality washed over me, dousing the sexual fire he had ignited. One, because other than a pair of four-inch stilettos I had nothing in my closet that qualified as vixen attire—at least nothing that I could squeeze my bloated carcass into. That meant I was going to have to do some emergency shopping. And two, since I was pressed for time with few local options, that shopping would have to take place at the Valu-Mart south of town, where I'd heard that Austin Reidy worked.

I sucked in a breath, girded my loins, and popped an antacid for good measure. "Austin Reidy," I said as I walked toward my car, "ready or not, here I come."

A half hour later, after finding a swingy black wrap dress with a plunging neckline that hugged me in all the right places, I handed my purchase to the cashier. "Do you know if Austin Reidy still works here?"

"Austin? Oh, he's dat guy in sporting goods," she said in a Slavic accent. "Rear of store."

The sporting goods guy. That seemed pretty appropriate for the former jock, I thought as I ran my credit card through the scanner.

What didn't seem appropriate was me showing up where he worked without first letting him know I was coming. Of course, I didn't have any problem with dropping by McCutcheon Floors & More unannounced. Then again, I didn't have a history of throwing up on any of their shoes.

After the cashier handed me my receipt, I walked past the beauty product aisles and several rows of home decor and took a left, where I spotted a guy in a navy blue polo and khaki pants, demonstrating a treadmill to a customer. I looked around for other males outfitted in navy and khaki, but the jogger with his back to me appeared to be the only one working in Sporting Goods. This had to be Austin.

Hopping off the treadmill and onto a nearby elliptical,

Austin looked like he'd kept himself in great shape, like he could still push a basketball up and down a court while barely breaking a sweat. Unlike me. Beads of sweat were popping out on my upper lip in anticipation of having to face Austin Reidy for the first time in almost twenty years.

"Sheesh, cool it," I told myself when I ducked into a row of automotive accessories and fixed my face in the nearest mirror. It wasn't like I was back in high school and wanted a date to the prom. Thank God. I was just going to ask him a few questions, then I was out of here.

"May I help you?" a male voice said behind me.

"No...I..." I didn't recognize the dark, fleshy circles under his gray eyes or the paunchy beer gut hanging over his waistband, but the tiny mole on the salesman's left cheek was unforgettable.

I pasted a happy smile on my face. "Oh, my gosh! Hi, Austin!"

"Hi." His greeting sounded more like a question, like *who the heck are you?*

Okay, he wasn't the only one who had put on a little weight since high school. "It's Charmaine."

After an awkward moment of silence he cracked a smile as he reached out to shake my hand. "Nice to see you again."

I bet it is.

"What good luck," I said. "I needed to talk to you, but I also needed to do a little shopping on my lunch hour, and now, here you are."

The smile slipped from his face. "Talk to me? Why?"

"Sorry, I should have mentioned that I'm with the coroner's office."

He grimaced.

Not the first time I'd received that kind of reaction. No one liked talking about death and dying. "Maybe Nicole told you that I might be stopping by?"

He gave his head a little shake. "I haven't talked to her since last night."

Curious. She'd obviously spent the night at her mother's, but if I had been Nicole and had just lost my father, I would have expected a call from my husband at the very least.

"Then you don't know that the Coroner has asked for a statement from everyone who was at your father-in-law's birthday party. Is there someplace we could talk?"

"Now?"

"If you don't mind."

Austin blew out a breath that reeked of wine. From his bloodshot eyes and the sheen of sweat on his forehead, I guessed a lot of wine. "I do mind. I'm working," he said.

"It will only take a few moments. Could you take a break?"

His gaze tightened as he looked down his nose at me. "I already took my break. We can just talk back here if it's only going to be a few minutes."

"Fine." I followed him to a rack of barbells hung opposite a display of reflective apparel for joggers, an area of the store my flabby thighs could attest I'd never seen before.

Austin glanced up and down the aisle. "Okay, shoot, and make it quick. I don't need any guff from my manager about being too chatty with the customers."

Which sounded to me like this was something that had happened before. That piqued my interest, but wasn't why

I was here, so I cut to the chase. "Since we're pressed for time, let me ask your impression of how things were going last night prior to when your father-in-law became ill."

"My impression?" Austin shrugged a shoulder. "Everything seemed okay. Marty was in a good mood. The food was great. I don't know what to tell you."

"Just tell me what comes to mind. For example, did everyone there seem to be acting pretty normally?"

"I'd just met Cameron, one of the guys from the shop, but yeah." Staring down at the scuffed linoleum under his feet, Austin pressed his lips together as if he were replaying an unpleasant memory. "Pretty damn normal."

"Everyone getting along okay?"

He smirked. "Sure."

I didn't need to be able to read his body language to see he was lying.

"So, no family drama."

He folded his arms, resting them on his belly. "No more than usual."

"Like what?"

He exhaled, blasting me with his stale breath. "Nic getting pissy about me helping myself to her dad's scotch. It wasn't like he didn't offer it to me."

I didn't care what she thought about her husband's drinking as much as I did about what he had actually consumed. "So you drank some of the scotch your father-in-law received as a present?"

"Yeah."

"How was it?"

A corner of his mouth lifted. "Smooth."

And obviously poison-free since Austin had suffered no ill-effects aside from a possible hangover.

"Excuse me, honey," an older woman said as she reached for a pair of the wrist weights I was standing in front of.

I stepped aside. "Sorry." At least she'd given me a legitimate excuse to escape Austin's wine breath blast zone.

Wrinkling her nose, she sniffed the air and shot me an accusatory glance.

It's not me. You're in the zone.

I motioned to Austin to join me in front of a pink bicycle with training wheels at the end of an adjacent aisle. "I heard your father-in-law also received a bottle of salsa for his birthday. Did you try any of that?"

Austin shook his head as he straightened the display. "Not a fan of green stuff."

Since he was packing around an extra fifty pounds I assumed "green stuff" included lettuce.

"Hey, if a list of what I ate and drank is all you need from me—"

"It isn't." I smiled politely. "Austin, a minute ago you gave me the impression that there may have been some underlying tension at the dinner table."

Staring at the bike, he shrugged while I waited with my pen poised over my notepad.

He knew something; he just wasn't biting.

"That's the one," a little blonde girl said, running down the aisle with her mother trailing behind her, a toddler in tow. "That's the one I want!"

The girl hit the brakes and frowned up at me. "Hey, that's my bike!"

Trust me kid, I don't want your bike. I just needed a couple more minutes in private to wrap up this interview, preferably without becoming asphyxiated.

"Cassidy, don't be rude," the kid's mother said.

Too late. "Not a problem. I was just looking."

"Do you have any questions about the bike?" Austin asked the mother.

Oh, no, you don't. "He'll be back to answer your questions in just a minute." I pulled him into the next aisle, backing him up to a stack of soccer balls. "So, any issues that you were aware of between Nicole and any other family members?"

"Yeah, I suppose you could call it an issue."

Okay, now we were getting somewhere.

"Nic can't stand to watch Victoria wrap her brother and father around her little finger."

Since I had nothing but disdain for one of my former step-fathers, I couldn't blame Nicole for feeling the way she did. "When you say Victoria wraps them around her finger, what does she do exactly?"

He screwed up his face. "Hell, I don't know. She just has a way of getting guys to do things for her. It's like one minute I'm making myself a drink, and the next I'm helping her make a salad, and it feels like it was my idea. It's like a Jedi mind trick kind of thing."

It must have been if Victoria had him in close proximity of vegetables.

"So I stay away from her," Austin said, blasting me with his stinky breath. "I get in less trouble that way."

"I take it then that you two didn't spend a lot of time at her father's house?"

"No more than absolutely necessary." Austin's feet inched toward the kid and the bike he wanted to sell her. "Now, if there isn't anything else—"

"One last thing. When your father-in-law became violently ill last night, why did it take so long for someone to call nine-one-one?"

"Hey, I suggested it," Austin said defensively. "I know something about puke." He met my gaze with a derisive smirk on his lips. "This wasn't normal puke, so I told Nicole we should call for an ambulance. But Victoria thought it would be better to drive Marty to the hospital."

"But that never happened."

"Stubborn bastard refused to leave the house. Said he'd be fine once he got everything out of his system."

Which was pretty much what Victoria had told me. Jeremy and Cameron, too.

"That didn't happen either," I said, thinking aloud.

Austin shook his head.

"What do you think caused Marty to become so sick?"

"My guess—food poisoning. But I never heard of that killing anybody before."

That made two of us.

Chapter Six

"WELL, SHOOT," I said, finding another typo in the report I'd been working on for most of the afternoon. If I was going to inform Frankie that three of my interviewees thought Marty McCutcheon had suffered from some sort of food poisoning, I needed to at least spell poison correctly!

As for the notion that it was done by the hand of a black widow, Frankie would have to make that determination herself, because I'd found nothing in the former Victoria Pierce's history to indicate foul play.

Husband number one, an insurance executive—so some money there—had died from a brain aneurysm after taking a bad fall. Her second husband, a restaurateur, died from an apparent heart attack while jogging, which didn't compel me to pull on my running shoes anytime soon, but it also didn't strike me as suspicious.

"Have a nice weekend, Char," Karla called to me as she headed down the hall.

"You, too," I responded automatically, listening to sirens wailing in the distance. It sounded like someone's weekend was off to a bad start.

I glanced down at the time on my computer screen. Five-thirty-seven! The start of my weekend would suffer the same fate if I didn't hightail it home to my grandmother's house, where Steve would be picking me up in less than an hour.

After I emailed Frankie my report I shut down my computer and raced downstairs, making a mental list of everything I needed to do to get ready for my date.

As soon as I opened the door of the Jag I saw the two plastic bags on the passenger seat—the reminder I'd left myself to deliver Estelle Makepeace's yarn order on my way home.

"Too late now," I told myself as I started the engine and glanced at the dashboard clock. She'd be on her way to mahjong, and I now had forty-nine minutes to get home and get my sexy on.

"Sorry, Estelle. I'll stop by tomorrow." When I wasn't in need of a presto change-o kind of minor miracle.

Forty-seven minutes later, I was in my grandmother's upstairs bathroom, applying another layer of Bronze Goddess, a lipstick from the line of cosmetics my mother repped. The stuff didn't look nearly as good on me as it did on her, but....

I gave my flat-ironed hair another shot of hairspray and then took a step back for a longer view of my reflection. Not bad considering the amount of time I had to transform myself from desk jockey to sexy. Well, as sexy as I could get in a cheap black dress two sizes larger than I used to wear.

I loosened the cinch at my waist to deepen the V neckline and expose a bit more of the girls to focus Steve's attention away from everything that jiggled in my southern hemisphere.

"Okay, I'm as ready as I'm going to get," I said, dashing down the stairs with my stilettos in one hand and the beaded black clutch bag I'd borrowed from Gram in the other.

I was done skulking around with Steve, done with hiding our relationship from public view. Tonight was the night we'd stop by Eddie's Place, the watering hole owned by our friends, Roxanne and Eddie Fiske, and tell them that we were a couple.

As my best friend since the age of nine, Rox wouldn't be happy with me for keeping my relationship with Steve a secret for the last five weeks. Heck, she would probably challenge my sanity for crossing the *friendship* line with him, and after twenty years of keeping my stupid school-girl crush to myself, she had every right to. But I couldn't continue hiding the truth from her, couldn't keep coming up with excuses not to go out with the guys that she and our buddy, Donna, kept trying to set me up with.

Tonight was the night.

I slipped on my stilettos and stood at the door to wait for the very punctual Detective Sixkiller's arrival, which according to the clock on my cell phone should happen any second.

My phone started ringing with Steve's name displayed as the caller. *No!* "You'd better be calling to tell me that you're on your way. I swear if you cancel on me again—"

"Sorry, I'm in the middle of an accident investigation. Give me a half hour."

"A half hour. Not a problem."

"See you then."

"You'd better!" I said, but he'd already disconnected.

Twenty-five minutes later, I was back upstairs in the bathroom, trying to create the instant cheekbones my mother had crowed about in her Glorious Organics infomercial, when my phone rang.

I glared at Steve's name on the display as I answered the call. "Why do I have the feeling that I'm not going to see you on my doorstep tonight?"

He sighed. "Sorry. I think the only way that's going to happen is if I'm bringing over a pizza in a few hours."

Pretty much the way all of our *dates* had gone the last few weeks.

"I'll make it up to you," he added.

I'd heard that before, too. "Uh-huh."

"Call you later?"

"Sure."

"I *am* sorry, you know."

"I know. Do what you have to do and I'll see you later." I disconnected and shut the cosmetic sample box since cheekbones were no longer high on tonight's priority list.

"Well?" I asked my reflection in the mirror. "Looks like you're all dressed up with no place to go." And with my grandmother out for an evening of mahjong with the girls, no one at home to have dinner with.

So much for my plan to make tonight the night I came clean with Rox.

Or could this plan be salvaged?

Really, did I need Steve by my side to do this?

Nope. In fact, it could be easier to talk to Rox if I were by myself.

I could even order a pizza for later. Not a bad plan B, assuming that I could get ten minutes alone with her.

No, check that. I wasn't going home until we talked. Tonight was absolutely positively the night!

Entering the renovated red brick warehouse that Eddie and Rox had transformed into the go-to gathering place for the best pizza in town, I heard a loud clatter of pins in the adjoining eight-lane bowling alley. Judging by the whoops and hollers that followed, someone must have thrown a strike. I took a deep breath and hoped that would be the only kind of hollering I heard after I told Rox my news.

"Hey!" she called out, smiling at me from behind the bar. "Look at you! Somebody must have a big date tonight."

I took a seat at the far end of the well-polished oak bar, two unoccupied barstools separating me from four middle-aged men in matching bowling league T-shirts. Not exactly the most private location to have a heart-to-heart, but between the din of the crowd and the seventies rock music blasting through the overhead speakers, it would be next to impossible for anyone to listen in. "Yeah, I had—"

"Is he meeting you here?"

"Not exactly."

Rox's attention shifted to one of the bowling league guys who wanted a refill. "I feel a story coming on. Hold that thought and I'll be right back."

"I have a story for you, all right." I swallowed the growing lump in my throat as I listened to Billy Paul singing about having a secret thing going on with Mrs. Jones. I glared at the speaker perched eight feet from my head. "Not helping."

"Is this seat taken?" Without waiting for an answer, Kyle Cardinale slid onto the barstool next to me.

Criminy. This was so not the way my evening was supposed to go.

I forced a smile. "It is now."

His gaze raked over me. "You look very lovely tonight." His whisky brown eyes widened as if he'd committed a public gaffe, and he pushed away from the bar. "Sorry, I'm intruding. You're obviously on a date."

"Relax. He had to cancel."

Kyle settled back down on his barstool. "Must be something in the air. My date had to cancel, too."

"Bummer," I said, looking past him at the delighted expression on Rox's face as she approached.

She tossed two coasters in front of us. "Good evening, Doctor. What can I get you?"

"That depends on the lady."

I opened my mouth to speak, but the Adonis next to me was short-circuiting my brain with the smoldering look in his eyes and nothing but a squeak came out.

His gaze traveled south, lingering at my cleavage. "I have dinner reservations for seven at the Grotto."

One of the spendier restaurants over thirty miles away on the Port Townsend waterfront. Either he'd wanted to impress his date or Dr. Cardinale had expensive taste.

And since that date wouldn't be arriving, I saw danger signs flashing between us—danger that I needed to diffuse. "I—"

"Then you'd better get going or you're going to be late," Rox interjected, gathering up the coasters.

I tilted my head at her. *Sheesh, way to be subtle, girlfriend.*

She beamed with satisfaction. "Have fun."

Kyle stood, offering me his hand. "Shall we?"

Again, not the way my evening was supposed to go, but I slipped my hand in his, all too aware of his gentle touch. "Why not?" It was just dinner.

Releasing me to hold the door open, he kept his hands to himself as we stepped outside. "I was just about to cancel my reservation and order a pizza to go when I saw you at the bar."

The breeze off Merritt Bay blew wisps of hair into my face, every one of them sticking to my painted lips as if I were wearing flypaper. "You can still do that," I said, shielding myself from the wind and further hair damage with his broad-shouldered body. And after he left with his pizza I'd lay my soul bare to Rox, preferably following a shot or two of liquid courage.

Kyle turned to me. "Why would I want to do that when I could have the pleasure of your company?"

Standing eye to eye in the parking lot thanks to my four-inch stilettos, I had no answer for him, especially since he was looking at me like he might want to play doctor later.

Loose gravel crunched under our feet as we headed toward the rear of the parking lot. "My car's back here."

I had no idea which of the twenty or so cars in the lot was his, but I hoped we'd get to it soon because my shoes weren't made for traversing rocky terrain. "Okay."

"How're you doing in those shoes?"

"Fine." I wasn't about to admit that my feet were killing me.

"I don't see how you girls walk in them."

"Very carefully, especially in gravel parking lots."

Kyle took my hand. "Wouldn't want to have to fit you for a cast later."

He pulled me closer and my traitorous heart quickened.

Gads. What was with me and Italian men? Being unceremoniously dumped by Christopher Scolari after seven years of marriage should have hardened my heart. But no, mine was racing like a schoolgirl's on her first date.

"Here we are," he said.

I screeched to a stop, staring at the vintage cherry red Jaguar parked next to a beater sedan.

"This is your car?"

"Yep."

I'd seen it a couple of times at the marina where Kyle lived, but I'd assumed it belonged to some rich yacht owner, not an attending at the hospital who was starting to remind me way too much of my ex-husband.

"Nice." Was this supposed to be a joke? The chance encounter with Kyle a set up? I looked behind me to see if Rox were watching us from the kitchen door. Nope. Of course, she wasn't. Roxanne Fiske didn't have a cruel bone in her body. This had to be dumb luck, the universe having a chuckle at my expense. And tonight of all nights.

Not funny, universe.

He opened the passenger door for me. "It was my dad's. He gave it to me when I graduated med school."

No way.

I shivered as an eerie sense of déjà vu washed over me. It was almost the same story I heard when I met Chris in culinary school. The *oh shucks, it was a graduation present from my dad* delivery of their lines was even the same.

Jeez Louise, just when I thought I'd gotten my ex out of my system, he was back—just repackaged with a doctor upgrade.

"It's a sweet ride." Kyle smiled as if I needed some encouragement to get in the car.

"I'm sure it is."

"And we should probably leave soon if we want to make our reservation."

"Right." This was only dinner, I reminded myself, sliding onto the mint condition leather upholstered seat. If the conversation became awkward I could ask him about Marty's cardiac arrest. I breathed a little easier, feeling like I was in the driver's seat. Okay, technically, I was in the passenger seat, but I planned to maintain complete control of tonight's freak show.

"Hope you're hungry," Kyle said, fastening his seat-belt. "I hear the seafood at this place is great. They also have some good Italian food. One of the nurses mentioned the manicotti. I think *to die for* were her exact words."

If he thought anything Italian was going to touch my lips tonight he could forget about it!

✳

"What sounds good to you?" Kyle asked, sitting across from me at our white linen-covered table for two. "A bottle of pinot grigio? A nice shiraz?"

Pinot grigio? Chris's favorite? Not a chance.

"Either would be a delightful pairing with the manicotti." Our waiter pointed at the wine list in Kyle's hands. "I might recommend a zinfandel to accompany the lady's salmon. We have several excellent Washington varieties."

Sure. Fine. Whatever. I just wanted my empty glass filled with something alcoholic, stat.

Kyle met my gaze. "The zinfandel then?"

I forced a smile. "Can't wait to try it." Truly.

With a polite nod our waiter left with our order. I estimated that we'd have at least ten minutes to kill before our overpriced salads arrived. Since we'd spent most of our time in the car talking about our jobs, I figured it wouldn't seem too out of context to ask a few more work-related questions of one of the last people to see Marty McCutcheon alive.

I stared into the flickering tealight candle creating dancing shadows on the wall next to me. "It's nice that you have this weekend off, especially considering the long hours you had to work last night."

"Well, I'm certainly enjoying how it's starting," Kyle said.

The low level of light in the restaurant made it difficult for me to read his face, but the easy smile on his chiseled lips told me that he was definitely enjoying the moment.

His gaze dipped to the breasts my wrap dress was doing a miserable job of containing, lingering like he wanted more than the taste I was offering.

I sat up a little straighter to minimize the peep show. "Me, too."

Seriously? Is that the best you can do? You're in the driver's seat, remember? Drive! Ask about Marty.

"I understand you were working last night when—"

I looked up at our waiter, back with a bottle of

zinfandel, and watched him pour a small amount in a long-stemmed wine glass. Kyle tasted it and nodded his approval.

Good. Fill our glasses and go away.

Once our waiter stepped away from our table, I tried to pick up where I'd left off. "About last night, I wanted to ask you about Marty—"

"Charmaine, let's not talk about work anymore. In fact…" Kyle raised his wine glass. "Here's to leaving work behind us for one night."

No, no. Not when I had Marty McCutcheon's ER doctor sitting two feet in front of me.

I took a drink of wine. "Fine. No more shop talk. Just let me ask you one question."

Swallowing, he set down his glass. "Okay, one question."

"Did you find anything at all unusual about Marty McCutcheon's cardiac arrest?"

"Unusual? Not really."

"You don't have any unanswered questions as to what caused his heart to stop beating?"

"With his medical history? No." His dark eyes narrowed. "And you and I can't discuss this further unless you're going to tell me that you're asking on behalf of the Coroner."

I shook my head. "But she did ask me to talk to the family, and there's strong concern that he ate or drank something that made him sick and led to his death."

"Yeah, I heard as much from Frankie when I talked to her this morning."

"The family wants an investigation."

Kyle blew out a breath. "And you want to know if I

think it's warranted."

I nodded.

"Like I told your boss, Mr. McCutcheon was in ventricular fibrillation upon arrival. Despite our best efforts and those of the medics, he went into cardiac arrest. My best guess as to the underlying cause is coronary artery disease."

"Sure came on fast though. One minute he was fine. The next he was in the bathroom, puk...er...retching."

"That's not that unusual in cases like these."

"Hmmm." Seemed pretty unusual to me, but what did I know?

I leaned back as the waiter arrived with our salads.

Kyle pointed at his plate of greens with his fork. "If Mr. McCutcheon had eaten more of this instead of the cheeseburgers at Duke's, we probably wouldn't have had this discussion."

Since he had just echoed what Darlene had told me yesterday, I made a mental note to cut back on the cheeseburgers.

He shot me a lopsided smile. "Hope I didn't ruin your appetite."

"Not at all." But I saw someone waving at me from a table across the crowded dining room who might. Donna Littlefield.

Donna, one of my best friends since grade school, was a drop-dead gorgeous cosmetologist and owner of Donatello's, one of the two beauty parlors in town. If Duke's Cafe was Gossip Central, Donatello's was Gossip South. I loved Donna like a sister, but I knew that I'd have to act fast if I didn't want to eclipse Marty McCutcheon as this weekend's top news story.

Laying my napkin on the table, I grabbed my clutch bag.

"Would you excuse me for a minute? My phone's been buzzing. Probably my grandmother. I just need to make sure she's okay."

"Of course." Kyle set down his fork and smiled politely.

I'd give the most popular ER doctor in town points for good manners. Steve would have challenged me on the lame story about my grandmother with his mouth full.

"Start without me," I said, stepping away from the table. "I'll be right back."

Donna's eyes tracked me as I approached. As I passed her table I pointed in the direction of the ladies' room, where she joined me a minute later.

She slapped my arm the second the door closed behind a little girl and her mother. "Why didn't you tell me you were seeing Kyle Cardinale?"

"I'm not. This isn't a date."

Her full lips curled, her sapphire almond eyes gleaming with satisfaction. "You're certainly dressed for a date."

I couldn't very well tell Donna that I'd dressed for Steve. That would be like striking a match in a fireworks factory. The explosive chain reaction would reach Rox before I swallowed a bite of my salad.

I could outright lie or minimize the damage by fudging the truth. And I was all about damage control tonight. "Kyle and I both had our dates cancel on us, so he invited me to dinner. End of story."

A tiny frown line etched a path between Donna's perfectly arched brows. "Well, that's disappointing." She fluffed my bangs and then stepped back, assessing me.

"Better, but sweetie, you need to come in and let me give you a haircut."

I needed a lot of things and silence on the subject of who I was or wasn't dating was at the top of my list. "I'll make an appointment next week." I gave her a hug. "I'd better get back before he thinks I fell in."

Damage contained, I reached for the door.

"Wait a minute," she said, checking her lipstick in the mirror. "You didn't tell me. Who's the guy?"

Arrgghh! "The guy?"

Donna turned around, her cell phone in hand. "Yes, silly. Who cancelled on you because we should send him a picture to show him what he missed."

Oh, I had every intention of showing Steve what he'd missed. "Just a guy I know through work." Almost true. "It was a first date, so it's not like—"

"Smile!" Donna said, snapping a picture of me. "I'll send this to you in case you change your mind."

I wouldn't because Steve would be seeing the real thing later. "I need to get back. Talk to you soon."

"Okay, but I want news if there are any developments on the Dr. Yummy front."

"Don't hold your breath," I muttered as I stepped out of the ladies' room, arriving back at my table with my clutch bag vibrating.

Sitting behind a mostly empty salad plate, Kyle eyed my bag. "Everything okay with your grandmother?"

"She's fine. Sorry I took so long." I reached for my salad fork and my bag buzzed again.

"You're sure? Because if you need to get that—"

"I don't. She has a new phone and is learning how to text." I rolled my eyes for effect when I heard my phone vibrating for the third time.

Good grief. What was Donna doing?

I pulled my phone out of my bag. "I'll just send her another message to let her know that I can't talk right now. She obviously didn't get the last one."

Pressing a button to view Donna's last three text messages, I saw that she'd sent me two pictures separated by this message: *If you ever want to make that guy jealous, show him this pic of Dr. Yummy.*

I opened the picture attached to her next text—a zoomed-in view of Kyle and me gazing into one another's eyes like star-crossed lovers. "Criminy!" I immediately deleted it.

Kyle reached for the wine bottle to refill his glass. "That doesn't sound good."

"She's playing with her camera now."

He topped off my glass. "Let's see what she sent you."

"Trust me, you don't want to see pictures of her cat." I tucked my phone back into my bag and took a much-needed long drink. "How's the salad?"

"Great. You should try it."

I picked up my fork to give it another go.

"Charmaine?" a deep voice said.

I looked up to see Mitch Grundy, one of my great-uncle Duke's least favorite restaurant equipment suppliers.

Mitch wasn't a bad guy. Duke just hated surprises, and that included cold calls by pushy salesmen.

"Good to see you," he said, extending his hand. "It's been a few years."

Almost eight since the last time I'd seen him was at my wedding reception—something he'd invited himself to after hearing about the open bar.

"Yes, it has." It also felt like years since I'd sat down to eat my salad.

Mitch glanced at Kyle, waiting for an introduction. Probably to see if I was sitting with a potential client. "Excuse me. Mitch Grundy. Dr. Kyle Cardinale," I said, giving Kyle's title a little emphasis so that Mitch would get the clue that there were no business prospects for him at this table.

When Mitch leaned toward Kyle to shake his hand, I noticed a woman standing behind him. *Holy crap!* A very familiar woman.

Mitch put his hand to her back, pressing her closer to the table. "Dr. Cardinale, Charmaine, I'd like you to meet Patsy Faraday."

Pursing her mouth, Patsy looked down her nose at me. "We've met."

Chapter Seven

"MINE'S THE SILVER one over there," I said, pointing to my car parked across from the green dumpster next to Eddie's kitchen door.

"You own that Jag?" Kyle chuckled as he pulled into the adjacent parking spot. "Small world."

More like bizarro world on this freaky Friday. "Yep, very."

He turned off the ignition. "I guess you and I have even more in common than I thought."

Aside from our mutual love of manicotti, a caffeine addiction, and the same shaped car key, I couldn't think of a thing. I also couldn't think of a way to tell him that without sounding ungrateful for the nice dinner he had bought me, so I decided to gloss over pesky details and go straight to the gratitude portion of our evening.

"It was a lovely dinner. I'm sorry your date had to cancel, but—"

"Don't be. I'm not," he said, his gaze dropping to my mouth.

Uh-oh.

He smiled, leaning closer, testing the waters.

I needed to say something, do something to let him know that another ship was already sailing my waters.

"I…" My clutch bag vibrated on my lap. "Sorry, I think I have a call." Pulling out my phone I saw that I had another text from Donna, wanting a progress report on my evening with Dr. Yummy. "Nope, another text. My grandmother's asking when I'll be home, so I should probably get going."

An insincere smile flashed across his lips. "Of course."

He unbuckled his seatbelt and stepped out of the car while the one of us who had needed the dateus interruptus fumbled with her seatbelt.

"Come on!" I muttered under my breath a second before my door opened.

"That belt mechanism can be a little tricky, so allow me." Kyle reached over me, brushing my left breast as his fingers found purchase.

He smelled great, a heady mixture of sandalwood, deodorant soap, and red-blooded American male.

He probably kissed great, too.

What the heck are you thinking? This isn't anything you want to know about. He's Chris 2.0.

"You'd better hold onto me when you get out," he said, extending his hand. "There's a pretty big pothole on this side."

I took his hand, expecting him to let go after we circumvented the pothole but that didn't happen.

I pointed at the kitchen door that one of the pizza cooks kept unlocked for smoke breaks. "I need to go in and see Roxanne for a minute, so thank you again for—"

"I'll walk you."

"I'm fine, really."

"As long as you're in those heels tell that story walking."

I couldn't help but laugh because that sounded like something Steve would say to me. I also couldn't help but like this doctor, even if he was Chris 2.0.

We stepped onto the concrete slab that formed the step to the kitchen door and I turned to him. "Good night, kind sir, and thank you for seeing me safely to my door."

"Good night, Charmaine." Without hesitation he pressed his lips to mine just as I felt a doorknob smack me in the butt.

Standing in the doorway holding a plastic trash bag, Rox's eyes widened. "Sorry!" She grimaced. "*Really* sorry to interrupt you."

Taking a step back, Kyle held the door open for her. "No worries, I was just leaving." He fixed his gaze on me. "Enjoy the rest of your evening."

"'Night," I said to his back as he walked toward his car.

Rox tossed the trash bag into the dumpster. "What are you doing out here anyway? I thought you two would be out making an evening of it."

"I came back…" To talk to you. To order a pizza for Steve. To clear the air so that I could breathe easier every time she saw me with Steve. Instead, I felt like I had just farted into the wind. "…to get my car and I wanted to see you before I left."

She grinned. "To tell me about the great time you had, right?"

"It was more like an okay time."

"Very okay based on the way he was looking at you."

"Don't make too much out of what you just saw, and please don't say anything to anybody." Especially Steve.

"I won't, but…" Placing her hand on my shoulder, Rox softened her gaze. "Honey, is everything okay?"

"Sure. It's just been a long day."

"Then why don't you call it a night. Come over in the morning for coffee if you want to talk."

My phone vibrated again. *Donna! Let it go!* "I do want to talk." I needed to. "I'll see you tomorrow."

After making it safely back to the Jag, I took a look at Donna's latest text. Only it wasn't from Donna. It was Steve, wanting to know if I wanted him to order a pizza before he left the station. Since that meant coming here to Eddie's to pick it up and undoubtedly have a few words with Rox in the process….

I sent him a quick reply. *Nope, already ate.* I tossed my phone onto the passenger seat, started my car, and hit the gas. I had a cop to beat home.

Ten minutes after I'd changed into an old pair of blue jeans and a hooded sweatshirt, I opened the front door to a weary-looking police detective with a bottle of beer in each hand.

"How much trouble am I in?" he asked.

I'd been asking myself that question ever since I left Eddie's. "You're not. I know stuff just happens sometimes." Boy, did I know.

He shook his head, his expression sullen as he stepped past me. "Yeah. The crazies like to come out on the weekend. They just started early today."

I followed him to the living room, where he made a

beeline to the sofa.

"Where's your grandmother?" he asked, holding out a beer as an invitation to sit on the cushion next to him.

That would be cozy, but we needed to talk and I wanted to be able to see his face.

"At Mrs. Doolittle's. It's mahjong night," I said, taking the bottle he offered and planting my butt in the over-stuffed easy chair to his left.

Steve and I locked gazes. After several seconds, a flicker of a smile danced on his lips. "I take it this means you want to talk about tonight."

Want might be too strong a word, but I was prepared to tell him everything that had happened this evening. Well, almost everything.

I nodded, my mouth suddenly dry.

He took a pull from his bottle of beer. "So, how'd it go?"

With what? Dinner? I really didn't want to just dive into the main course of my evening with Kyle. I needed to start with an appetizer, something for him to nibble on. "I went to Eddie's shortly after I hung up with you. You know, to tell Rox about us."

Steve's mouth flat-lined. "I still don't understand why this is such a big deal."

"Of course not. That's because you're a guy."

"Just tell me that you finally told her."

"I tried." I wiped away a drip of condensation trickling down the beer bottle in my hand. "It got busy with a lot of people at the bar." Kyle included. "But I told her I wanted to talk to her and we're meeting for coffee in the morning."

"Good." Steve took another sip of beer. "Are we done

talking?"

I was, at least on that subject. "Unless you want to tell me about your evening."

"Drunk kid versus tree. Tree won. End of discussion."

Bad for the kid, but good for me if that's all Steve had to say.

I pushed out of my chair. "Then I guess we're done talking unless you'd like to tell me you're hungry."

"I'm okay. I had a bag of chips out of the vending machine a couple of hours ago."

"Well, you should just be stuffed then. Gram has some leftover pot roast in the fridge. Want a roast beef sandwich?"

He stifled a yawn. "I never refuse your grandmother's pot roast."

No, he didn't and Gram knew it. Probably why she often featured it for his standing Wednesday dinner invitation.

Steve looked too tired to move, so I handed him the television remote control. "Find us a movie to watch, and I'll come back with room service."

Two minutes later, I was in the kitchen listening to him channel surf when I heard my grandmother open the back door.

"You ladies must have been having quite a game." I glanced at the clock on the stove. "It's almost ten. You're usually home from Mrs. Doolittle's by nine." And since Angela Doolittle lived several miles away on the south shore of Merritt Bay, and my eighty-year-old grandmother didn't like to drive at night, often closer to eight.

Gram set her purse on the kitchen table and dropped into one of the hardback chairs like she was dead on her feet. "We got a late start. Estelle finally called Angela from the hospital to let us know that she couldn't make it."

"Uh-oh." I remembered this morning's commentary about Estelle's driving and wondered if any of those sirens I'd heard were for her. "Is she doing okay?"

Gram blinked her hazel green eyes, slightly magnified behind her trifocals. "Is *she* doing okay? Honey, Estelle's fine. It's her great-grandson who was taken to the hospital. Poor little thing."

Estelle had been a widow for as long as I'd known her and had surrounded herself with such a menagerie of cats, I'd never thought of her as having anything but four-legged children, much less great-grandchildren. "What happened?"

"From what Estelle was able to get out of Phyllis—"

"Wait! Phyllis? Phyllis Bozeman?"

Gram nodded. "The boy's granny on the mother's side."

That meant that this was Aubrey's kid, and we were talking about Marty McCutcheon's former girlfriend, which piqued my interest all the more.

"According to Estelle, Phyllis was babysitting the boys to let the parents have a night out. Then, while she was cooking their supper, the toddler slipped out through the dog door."

I sucked in a breath, a twenty-year-old memory flooding back from when I had babysat Frankie's little kids and the panic I'd felt when one of them pulled a similar disappearing act.

Gram shook her head. "I guess she found him eating some plant in the yard."

"Oh, no!"

"The good news though is that she rushed him to the ER, and it looks like he's going to be fine."

"Thank goodness."

"No kidding. A little kid like that, it wouldn't take more than a couple bites of a poisonous plant to kill him."

I couldn't help but wonder if the same could be said for a man of Marty McCutcheon's size.

"But thanks to Phyllis's quick thinking, she saved him," Gram said, pushing to her feet.

"She also gave him the opportunity to eat the plant, so I wouldn't give her too much credit."

Gram patted my shoulder and headed toward the refrigerator. "I give credit where credit is due. Sounds like the parents did, too. I guess Estelle's grandson went on and on about how grateful he was that Phyllis was a master gardener and recognized that it was a poisonous plant."

A master gardener who knows about poisonous plants and her former boyfriend's penchant for hot sauce?

I shivered, my skin prickling with gooseflesh as my brain churned over the possibility that this was more than a coincidence. "Did Estelle mention the name of the plant?"

"I don't know. Angela talked to her, I didn't." Gram pulled a juice glass out of the cupboard and filled it with milk. "Why do you want to know the name of the plant? It's probably something so common that I have it in my yard."

"Just curious. Stuff like that is good to know."

She narrowed her eyes at me. "Since when do you take an interest in gardening?"

Ever since Phyllis Bozeman's name had come up

twice in the same day.

I shrugged a shoulder as I opened the jar of Dijon mustard that Steve liked. "I'm interested in lots of things."

"Is one of them about to eat a sandwich?"

Gram knew I'd been making a lot of late night trips across the street to be with Steve, so there was no point in denying the obvious.

"He had to work late and missed out on dinner."

She aimed a sympathetic smile at me. "Sorry."

That made three of us.

"And on that not-so-happy note, I'm going to bed," Gram said, rinsing out her glass. "It's been a long day."

It had been a long day. And since I'd barely spent any of it with the guy in the living room, I had a feeling it wasn't close to being over.

I followed my grandmother out of the kitchen with a plate in my hand.

"'Night, Stevie," she said with a wave as she headed up the stairs.

The detective on her sofa didn't respond. For good reason, as I discovered when I set his sandwich on the coffee table in front of him and heard him snoring.

I tapped his foot with mine. "Hey, Sleeping Beauty."

His eyes opened. "Hmmm?"

I took the remote control away from him and turned down the volume. "Dinner's served."

Yawning, he sat up as I joined him on the sofa. "I was watching that."

"You were asleep."

"Well, I'm not now, so—"

"Good." I pointed at the sandwich. "Eat that and let me ask you about something."

"Why do I have the feeling that I'm not going to like this?"

"Shut up and eat."

He shot me a dirty look as he reached for his sandwich.

Since that look was accompanied by another yawn, I figured that I'd better skip the non-essential. "My grandmother just came home and told me a story about a friend's great-grandson who was taken to the hospital after he ate a poisonous plant."

"I was in and out of the ER following up on my guy when they were working on the kid," he said with his mouth full. "He's okay, isn't he?"

"He's going to be. I guess Phyllis Bozeman saved the day by getting him to the hospital as quickly as she did."

"Yeah, I saw her there with Aubrey. They both looked pretty shaken up."

"That's it, just shaken up?"

Steve stared at me. "What else would you expect?"

I'd heard news reports about parents and caregivers who would make children sick on purpose as a cry for attention. "I'm not sure, especially if—"

"If what?"

"If little Johnny's grandma made him eat that plant."

Steve set his sandwich down. "First of all, it's Jordan."

"Whatever."

"Secondly, what you're suggesting is child abuse— something that medical professionals are always on alert for, so if there had been any *real* concern about that I would have been notified."

His implication couldn't have been clearer. My concern was without merit.

"Still, it's quite a coincidence that Jordan Makepeace

had to be rushed to the hospital just hours after you told me that people around here don't die from being poisoned."

"Accidents happen."

"I'm just saying."

"What exactly?" Steve took another bite of his sandwich.

It seemed almost ridiculous to say it aloud, but I had already jumped into this murky water. It was time to start swimming. "Since Phyllis Bozeman seems to know her poisonous plants, what if she decided to get some revenge after being jilted by her old boyfriend?"

Pausing mid-chew, he cast me a sideways glance. "And we're back on the Marty McCutcheon murder train."

"I know it sounds farfetched, but poison is supposed to be the female murderer's weapon of choice, right?"

Steve looked down at the last half of his roast beef sandwich in mock-horror.

"I don't have any interest in killing you." I patted his arm. "I'm not quite done with you yet."

"Very reassuring."

"But vee have vays of making you talk," I said, borrowing the bad Russian accent my mother had used in a Bond movie spoof.

"Sounds like an empty promise to me." He took another bite.

Since some sweet torture with the man had barely registered a blip on my interest meter the last couple of hours, he had me there. "So, tell me straight. Do you think it would be completely crazy to think that Phyllis Bozeman could have slipped something into the bottle of salsa that she bought for Marty McCutcheon's birthday?"

Smirking, Steve slowly shook his head.

I didn't appreciate the smirk. "But if it's at all possible that her grandson accidentally got into whatever she used—"

"The bigger question is whether it's at all possible that you're going to give this a rest anytime soon."

I watched him finish his sandwich. "Like you said, crazy stuff happens on the weekend."

"And I've had enough crazy for one night," he announced, rising to his feet. "Thanks for dinner."

I followed him to the door. "But what if what happened was no coincidence?"

He kissed me on the forehead. "Good night, Chow Mein."

Chapter Eight

AFTER I WOKE up with birds chirping outside my bedroom window I brewed a pot of French roast and then joined Myron, Gram's fat tabby cat lounging in the study, and fired up my grandfather's old computer. The dial-up connection made searching the internet painfully slow, but the price was right and gave me access to a printer.

While I sat at the desk and waited for the ancient PC to yawn to life, I checked my phone for text messages. Nothing but a *CALL ME!* from Donna.

"Forget it."

I had no news for her or anyone else on the Kyle Cardinale front. He was a charming flirt with impeccable manners, and he smelled great. Beyond that, I didn't want to think about last night aside from the confirmation that Kyle had given me that Marty McCutcheon had gone into cardiac arrest almost immediately upon arrival at the hospital. Which led me to my question of the morning: Now that Marty's ex-girlfriend's name was linked to a poisoning incident, could she have had something to do with stopping his heart?

The internet couldn't provide me the answer to that

specific question, but I figured it should be able to tell me if a plant could kill a man twice my size.

After a two-minute wait in which Myron followed me around while I fetched myself another mug of coffee, I had my answer: over a hundred thousand results telling me variations of the same thing. Okay, I clicked on only five of them, but the answer was a resounding yes.

One website featured an article that listed a number of plants under the heading of Cardiovascular Toxicity. I'd heard of almost all of them—foxglove, oleander, lily of the valley, monkshood, rhododendron, azalea. Heck, based on the pictures in the article, Gram had several of these plants growing in her back yard.

Sipping my coffee, I skimmed the article, focusing my attention on the plants in the Cardiac Glycoside group.

In cases of acute toxicity symptoms usually show up within minutes to hours.

My pulse racing, I retrieved my interview notes from my tote bag and reread them. Marty had started to feel ill ten minutes after he had sat down to eat.

I scrolled down to the list of symptoms and compared them to what I'd written in my notebook. *Diarrhea, vomiting, confusion, disorientation, irregular heartbeat, chest pressure, shortness of breath.*

Almost every one of them matched the witness descriptions.

Under the heading of Aconitine group, I held my breath when I read the line: *Late stage symptoms of poisoning include skeletal muscle paralysis, cardiac dysrhythmias, and intense pain. If untreated, death may result from ventricular dysrhythmias or respiratory paralysis within 1 to 6 hours after ingestion.*

"Holy shit!"

"I don't like the sound of that," Gram said, standing in the doorway in her robe and fuzzy slippers.

"Gram! Don't sneak up on me. You about gave me a heart attack." Especially after what I'd just read.

She leaned over to stroke Myron, who had immediately abandoned his least favorite human in the house to demand some attention at her feet. "I wasn't sneaking up on anybody, was I, sweet boy? And what may I ask are you looking at that has you using such language?"

I pressed the *Print* key to show Kyle the article I'd just read. "Nothing."

"You're not the only one who can tell when someone's lying." She was at my side in an instant like she wanted to catch me in the act. "It's not porn, is it?"

I pointed at the plant displayed on the monitor. "Does it look like porn?"

"No, it looks like lily of the valley. I have some planted in a container out back. I can show you if you want to see the real thing."

"No need. I know where it is. I was just…" I couldn't very well tell her that I thought Marty McCutcheon had been murdered. "…researching plant toxins. As a deputy coroner that kind of information might come in handy." Not for the job I was being paid to do, but since Gram had yet to help herself to a cup of wake-up juice, I was banking on the fact that her synapses weren't yet firing on all cylinders.

"Oh. Good thinking." She patted my shoulder and headed for the kitchen.

Yeah, you can tell when someone's lying all right.

I looked over the pages that Gramps's old inkjet printer had spit out. Not the greatest quality but readable.

Tucking them into my tote, I went upstairs to take a shower. I had a coffee date with Rox. After that I needed to see a doctor.

Not even ten hours had passed since Kyle kissed me. Would it give him the wrong idea if I asked to see him?

If Marty McCutcheon's death had been caused by a plant toxin overdose, I shouldn't care how it might look if I called him.

Still, I knew I was playing with fire.

As a pastry chef I'd been trained how to prepare food over an open flame. I'd also been known to singe my fingertips a time or two. When that happened you bucked up; you didn't let anyone see you sweat.

I couldn't guarantee the sweat part, but it was definitely buck up time.

*

I hadn't expected to see so many cars parked outside Merritt Lanes when I pulled in behind Ernie Kozarek's big-assed Buick at eight fifty-five.

"Good morning," the white-haired septuagenarian said as he pulled a leather bowling bag from his back seat.

"Hi, Mr. Kozarek. A bunch of you guys must be starting early today." Typically, Eddie and Rox didn't open until nine-thirty during the weekend.

"Early? Nah." He squinted against the sun's glare reflecting off the cotton candy clouds above us. "The seniors' league meets here every Saturday at this time. 'Fraid we'll be hogging the lanes if you had hopes to get a game in."

I didn't. My only hope this morning was that Eddie

would be keeping Mr. Kozarek and his bowling buddies happy so that I could have twenty minutes alone with Rox—something I was dreading, especially after the kiss with Kyle that she'd witnessed last night.

Heck! I'd meant to call Kyle to see if he could meet with me right after I was done here, and I'd been stressing so much over what I was going to say to Rox that I had forgotten.

Three feet from the door that Mr. Kozarek was holding open for me, I waved him on. "I have to make a call, thanks."

I looked up Kyle's number in my notebook, having collected it when he was a witness on my first assignment. Two seconds after punching it in I heard his voice, inviting me to leave a message.

Dang. That probably meant that he was trying to sleep in on his day off and didn't want to be disturbed.

It also meant that I needed to leave him a message. I hated leaving messages, especially when I needed to choose my words carefully so he wouldn't misinterpret them.

"Hi!" Good grief, I sounded like a breathy teenager. I needed to cool it, sound professional, colleague to colleague. "It's Char. I was hoping to talk to you today about something I'm working on." Not bad. At least I'd made it clear this was a work-related call. "I'm going into a meeting," *so don't call me,* "but I'll try calling you later to see what your schedule for today looks like."

Ending the call, I breathed in a big gulp of fresh air and slowly released it in an attempt to lower my blood pressure, because I knew that the next message I delivered wouldn't be nearly as well-received.

I pushed open the front entrance and took the first door on the right, seeing nothing but empty tables and chairs and no Rox behind the bar. "Hello?" The aroma of coffee wafted from the kitchen, so I followed my nose.

"Hey!" Donna said with a bright smile, stopping me in my tracks as she stepped out of the ladies' room.

"What are you doing here?"

She linked her arm with mine, reversing my course. "A little bird told me you might be coming here for a chat."

A little bird with a big mouth.

Donna led me to a table by the side window. "I knew you wouldn't want me to miss out on your gabfest."

She couldn't have been more wrong. "You don't have any clients this morning?"

"I had a cancellation."

Liar. She'd probably cleared her schedule the moment she got wind that I was coming over.

I looked up at Rox as she placed a coffee carafe in the center of a table that had been set with three cups and spoons. "We were on the phone late last night and…"

Talking about me and Kyle, no doubt.

"…well, I didn't think you'd mind."

I stared at her in disbelief. Inviting Donna was as good as getting all our friends on speed dial for a conference call.

Rox squeezed out an apologetic smile and sat to my left while Donna flanked me on my right.

"She doesn't," Donna said, while Rox filled our coffee cups.

I reached for the creamer. "Says you."

"You don't mean that. Do you know why? Because we're your best friends." Donna scooted closer to me. "So spill it. What's going on?"

I stared into her sapphire eyes. Did I dare answer that question honestly? If I did, anything I said would become public knowledge before the day was out. Was I fully prepared for everyone to know about Steve and me? But wasn't that why I was here, so that I could tell Rox before the news hit the gossip airwaves?

It was now or never. "It's a long story."

"Goody!" Beaming, Donna exchanged a smile with Rox. "I love stories."

I was pretty sure she was going to have mixed feelings about this one.

"A few weeks back," I said, my heart racing, "after Trudy died—"

"Poor Trudy, but that gave you the opportunity to meet Dr. Yummy!" Donna patted my hand encouragingly.

"Right." And not the guy I wanted to talk about. "I…" I heard my phone ring and reached for the tote bag by my feet. "Hold that thought." If it were anyone other than Gram, Steve, or Frankie, they could leave a message.

I recognized the number as the one I'd dialed five minutes earlier. *Seriously?* Hadn't I made it clear that I was going into a meeting? Did being a doctor mean that his time was more valuable than mine?

If I hadn't been so desperate to see Kyle today I would have let it go to voicemail. "I need to get this," I said, getting up from my seat. "I'll be right back."

I answered on the fourth ring. "Hello."

"Hey, sorry I missed your call. I was in the shower."

That's not all he missed. "You must've not got my message."

"I heard enough, but I hate messages, don't you?

Especially when the much more pleasant option is to speak to the real thing."

I should have been flattered, but since Rox and Donna were hanging on my every word, I felt like I was tap dancing around a minefield. I headed for the door to find some privacy. "That's sweet but—"

"I'm glad you called. I had a good time last night."

"Me, too, but about why I called," I said, stepping out into the sunshine. "I wanted to talk to you about something."

"Want to do it over lunch?"

Lunch? I just wanted a quick Q and A session. "I'm in the middle of a meeting and don't know how long I'll be, so—"

"No problem. Come on over when you're done. You know where I live."

Yeah, a nice, cozy sailboat where he had ingratiated himself with my mother when I was working a case a few weeks back.

I cringed, knowing that I needed to pull on my big girl pants and agree to do this before anyone else I knew ended up in his ER.

"Okay, see you later." I disconnected and headed back inside, hoping that I hadn't just made a big mistake.

Both Rox and Donna were sitting exactly where I'd left them, only they now wore big grins on their faces.

How much had they heard? "What?"

Donna fixed her gaze on mine. "How's Dr. Yummy this morning?"

I needed to cool her jets before she went supersonic with the wrong story. "That was about work."

"Sure." She tapped her phone a couple of times and

held it up to Rox. "I ask you, does that look like they were discussing work?"

Rox's eyes misted over as she stared at the picture of Kyle and me at the restaurant. "Awww, look at that expression on his face. I knew the two of you would hit it off if you gave him a chance."

"It was just a dinner," I said. "And that phone call from him was—"

"About work. Right." Rox handed Donna back her phone. "Give us some credit. Plus the acoustics are really good in here."

Donna leaned closer, her smile predatory. "He was calling because he wanted to see you later, right?"

"Yes, sort of, but you two need to shut up and let me tell you something before you jump to some crazy conclusions." Because if I spent one more minute in this pressure cooker I was going to blow my top.

Donna folded her arms across her midsection, show-casing her perky C cups. "Fine, then tell us!"

"I'm seeing Steve," I blurted out before I lost my nerve.

"What?!" they shouted in unison.

"I know." Boy, did I know how unlikely he and I seemed as a couple. "I'm sorry I kept this from you, but now you know that we're…"

…*going out.*

Nope. Technically, he and I had yet to go on a real date.

…*going steady.*

Hardly. And I'd been away from the dating circuit for so long I didn't even know if couples our age did that anymore.

"…together." More or less, and usually at his house in the middle of the night.

"Steve and you," Rox said as if my pairing with one of our best friends left a bad taste in her mouth.

I nodded.

She stared at me. "Together."

I nodded again.

"Holy moly," Donna said on a sigh. "I sure didn't see this coming."

The intensity of Rox's gaze sharpened. "Considering you'd always said that would never happen I don't think anybody did."

Me included. "I realize this is a bit of a shock but…."

"Yeah, understatement of the year." Rox jutted her chin. "Especially since I see you almost every day!"

I didn't know whether to let her vent or try to explain something I barely understood myself. "It just sort of happened."

"When?"

"Around a month ago." Actually closer to five weeks, but I didn't want to make it sound worse than it already did.

Her mouth gaped. "A month?"

Donna swatted my arm. "And you didn't tell us?"

"I couldn't." If it blew up in my face, it would be devastating enough for Steve to walk out of my life. I couldn't risk forcing our mutual friends into a situation in which they had to choose between us, especially Rox and Eddie. "I wasn't ready." Like that day would ever come, but I couldn't keep this a secret forever. Not in this town. And it was killing me to keep it from Rox.

Cocking her head at me, she leaned back in her chair.

"Not ready, but in the meantime you let me and Donna set you up with some dates. Really, don't you think you could have said *something*?"

Donna swatted me again. "Yeah, what's wrong with you?"

"Ow!" I rubbed my arm. "That only happened twice and you practically ambushed me."

"I did not ambush you last night!" Rox protested. "I facilitated."

She and I both knew that was a lie. "Big difference."

"I thought you liked Kyle Cardinale!"

"That was almost two months ago!" I said, matching her volume. "And I was only mildly interested before I found out he was seeing someone else."

Rox's cheeks reddened as if I'd slapped her across the face. "Well, how would I know that when you don't talk to me!"

"So, there's nothing going on between you and Dr. Yummy?" Donna asked, making me wonder if all the years of hairspray had clogged her ears.

"No!" Except one stupid moment when I let my guard down and he kissed me.

Out of the corner of my eye I saw the kitchen door swing open and a frowning Eddie heading our direction. "Everything okay out here?"

Donna answered with a nervous giggle. "Everything's fine. We're just having some girl talk."

"Yeah," Rox said, her eyes aiming daggers at me. "We girls were having a long overdue chat…"

I glared back at her. *Yes, you have a right to be pissed. Now get over it.*

"…and finding out about the new man in Char's life."

Eddie stood behind his wife, his hands on her shoulders. "Yeah? Anyone we know?"

She snorted. "I'd say so because he's your best buddy."

Eddie blinked. "Steve?"

"We've been seeing one another." I braced myself for some teasing.

He gave me a crooked smile. "What do you want from me, my approval?"

"I don't think I need it." But I wanted it just the same.

He winked. "Atta girl."

"So, Steve didn't say anything to you about it?" Rox asked him.

Eddie shrugged. "Why would he?"

"Yeah, why say anything to a trusted friend?" Rox pushed out of her chair and grabbed her cup.

"Rox," I said to her back. "It wasn't about trust." Okay, maybe it was a little.

"I have to get back to work. I'm sure Donna does, too."

The implication was clear. She wanted me out of there. "Okay, I'll talk to you later." Alone and soon, before the damage I'd caused had an opportunity to fester.

Rox waved me off and stalked toward the kitchen. "Sure you will."

Chapter Nine

I COME FROM a long line of women who eat in times of crisis. Not that my last twenty-four hours constituted a full-blown crisis. But with Steve not wanting to talk about the revolving door of poisoning victims at our local ER, and Rox not wanting to talk to me period, it should have come as no surprise when I found myself roaming the Red Apple Market in search of something comforting. It's just that the doctor perusing the deli section wasn't what I had in mind.

I did an about face and zipped into the express check-out line, where I grabbed a candy bar from the rack of sugary treats next to me and tossed it onto the conveyor belt.

Unfortunately, Millie, one of the chattier checkers, was working the register. "I know. I couldn't have been more shocked when I heard about it," she said to the customer in front of me as she took her time scanning a can of dog food. "He was in here with his wife on Tuesday. Pretty thing. Beautiful skin."

I jingled the five quarters in my hand to give Millie the clue that I was in a hurry.

Oblivious, she rested her palm on the second can as if she could divine its price. "I hear she's been through three husbands."

There was no question about the topic of the gossip du jour—Victoria McCutcheon.

The dog food lady glanced back at me and lowered her voice to a whisper. "She either has the worst luck or she knows how to pick 'em."

I felt like telling the woman that I could still hear her.

Millie nodded. "Or both. Still, I feel sorry for her. They were so cute together."

I felt sorry for her, too. Victoria's husband had been taken from her and in one of the most horrific ways that I could have imagined.

"That'll be three twenty-seven, hon."

As the dog food lady rummaged through her wallet I saw a package of brie cheese land on the conveyer belt behind my candy bar. One of the better quality brands, too. Someone knew her cheese.

I looked back to see if the epicurean behind me was anyone I knew.

Correction, *his* cheese along with several large mushrooms, a bunch of chives, and a bag of fresh spinach. All organic, no doubt.

Kyle had a twinkle in his eyes when they shifted to my candy bar. "If you eat that you're going to spoil your lunch."

"It's…" I couldn't think of a believable lie that wouldn't make me look like I was PMSing. "It's a snack for later in case—"

"In case you don't like what I'll be feeding you?" He put my candy bar back on the rack. "Trust me, you're going to like it."

I'd always been wary of men who asked me to trust them, especially the ones who reminded me of my ex.

I smiled politely. "I'm sure I will."

Millie winked at me like we were the second cutest couple she'd seen this week when she rang up his cheese. "Oooh, looks like he's making something special for you."

"Sure looks that way." And way too much like a date, dang it.

I needed to get out of there before anyone else I knew saw us together and came to the same conclusion. "I'll wait for you outside," I said to Kyle.

A minute later, he joined me where I had been staring out at Merritt Bay and wishing I could have a redo of my morning. "So, did your meeting end early?" he asked.

Abruptly was more like it. "Yeah, it didn't last as long as I thought it was going to."

"Want to come over now and make it brunch?"

Not really but I needed to talk to him, and the sooner the better. "Sure, that would be great."

He looked around, squinting against the glare of the sun at my back. "Where'd you park?"

I pointed to the side lot, where I had tucked the Jag away behind a dusty Red Apple panel truck so that I could stuff my face without an audience. "Back there. How about you?" The only red car in the lot was Millie's old Saturn.

"I walked."

Of course he had. The marina was only a block away.

He inched toward my car. "Can I hitch a ride with you? I'd love to check out your interior."

If this had been any other day I would have nailed him

on his double entendre. Instead, I injected enough frost in my glance so he'd know that I hadn't called him to play sexually charged games.

But he had eyes only for the car as we approached. "You don't see the red leather in an XJ6 every day."

"I wouldn't know. It was my ex-husband's." I clicked the remote to unlock the driver's door. "Give me a second and I'll open your door."

"The remote won't unlock it?"

"Nope." That was just one of a long list of things that had gone wrong with the Jag in the four months since Chris handed over his car keys to my divorce attorney.

I got behind the wheel and reached across to open the passenger door.

"Might be the actuator," he said, climbing in.

"Yeah, that's pretty much what my mechanic told me." Actually, my high school buddy, George at Bassett Motor Works, had said that he wouldn't know what was wrong with it until he took it apart. Since that sounded scary expensive I'd been in no hurry to get it fixed.

Looking around, Kyle leaned in my direction to check out the back seat. "Nice."

I breathed in his scent, the same fresh combination of soap and sandalwood that I'd noticed last night, and concurred with him on a sensory level. Then I met his gaze and felt color flooding into my cheeks when I realized that he might not have been referring to the car.

"Okay, then. On to brunch!" I announced a little too loudly as I started the engine.

"Charmaine—"

"Char. Only my mother and strangers call me Charmaine."

I watched the corners of his lips curl in amusement, his brown eyes warm and kind. "Well, I wouldn't want you to think of me as a stranger."

After last night that would be impossible.

I forced a smile and was about to shift into reverse when his hand touched mine.

"And I'd like you to relax. I may have overstepped when I kissed you last night, but I assure you that nothing is going to happen today that you don't want to happen."

He had missed on that promise by at least a half hour, but he was right about the two of us. Nothing was going to happen.

Twenty minutes later, I was on Kyle's sailboat, sipping mineral water at the table he'd set for two. "Are you sure I can't do anything to help?" I asked as I watched him slice the mushrooms he'd bought.

I knew he didn't need me crowding him in his one-person galley, but we had an hour to kill before the egg dish he was preparing would be ready, and I was running out of safe subjects to talk about.

"Nope, I've got this." He transferred the mushrooms into a sauté pan.

"Smells good. What are you making?"

"Spinach brie frittata. My grandmother's recipe."

"Passed down generation to generation?" I asked, imagining Kyle in braces, cooking with his mom.

His face split into a smile as if I'd said something funny. "No, my mother doesn't cook. Everything I know I learned from my nonna."

Sounded like we had that in common, too. Only my

grandmother was English-Irish, not Italian.

"What's your mother do, if you don't mind me asking?"

Focusing on the mushrooms he was sautéing, he shrugged. "Well, she shops and travels, and redecorates the living room every few years."

Jeez, he was describing my mother in the flush years following her TV series.

"And to be fair," he added, "she also volunteers at my dad's hospital and sits on the board of a couple of nonprofits."

"Back up. You said your dad's hospital. He's a doctor?"

"A neurologist back in Boulder. He also teaches there at the university."

"Sounds like someone who has a lot of letters after his name." And some big bucks for each one of those letters. Maybe that explained the sailboat and the expensive dinner last night. Kyle came from money.

His expression darkened as he added several cups of chopped spinach to the pan. "Something like that."

I had the feeling that I'd struck a nerve. Some father-son thing? I didn't want to intrude into Kyle's personal life more than I already had, but this seemed like an opportunity to shift the conversation toward the subject where I needed his expertise.

"Had you always wanted to be a doctor?"

"Heck no, I wanted to be a rock star."

I couldn't help but laugh, but he certainly had the looks to be the front man in a band. "Decided you didn't want to buy a bus and play a different city every night?"

"Hey, when I was thirteen I thought that sounded pretty cool. Twenty years later there are days I still do."

"It must be interesting though, working in the ER." Not the smoothest segue, but it would have to do. "Oh, speaking of the ER, one of my friends from high school was there last night with her two-year-old." I paused, hoping that he'd turn toward me so that I could read his reaction.

When he did I continued. "Jordan Makepeace."

Nothing registered except the same feigned expression of interest I got from Steve whenever I talked about my job.

"His grandmother—Phyllis Bozeman, if you know her—found him outside eating a plant and rushed him to the hospital."

Again, no flickers of recognition. If Phyllis or Jordan had made prior trips to the ER, they hadn't been on Kyle's watch.

"Is he doing okay?" he asked.

"Seems to be. From what I heard it sounds like his grandmother got him there in the nick of time."

"Good for Grandma and Jordan then. Plant toxins can be very dangerous."

Yes, they were, as I had recently learned. "Is that something you see very often?"

He cracked an egg into a bowl. "No, and usually the parents say that they have no idea what the kid ate or drank."

"But you're able to run some labs and find out, right?"

Reaching for another egg, he grinned at me. "Someone's been watching too much TV."

He was sounding like Steve again. "Okay, so it's not that easy, but if Phyllis hadn't known what Jordan ate, there should be a way to tell, right?"

"There'd be traces of the plant in his vomit. But no matter what he ate or didn't eat, he'd present with certain symptoms, and we'd go from there."

I pulled the computer printout from my tote and unfolded the three-page article on the galley counter next to the bowl. "What if you saw these symptoms?"

Kyle removed the pan from the burner, leaning on the counter as he leafed through the pages. Less than a minute later, he handed them back to me, his eyes hooded. "This is what you wanted to talk to me about."

I nodded. "Which I tried to indicate on the phone."

His jaw tightened. "So, you didn't dig up enough information last night about how Marty McCutcheon died?"

"I'm trying to do my job and gather all the pertinent information surrounding his death so that the Coroner—"

"I know what your job is. I can even appreciate that you're willing to do what's necessary to get that job done, but I can't help you. Not this time."

I knew he was referring to a research project he had helped me with when one of his patients died suddenly a few weeks back. "I'm just trying to understand—"

"And I've told you everything you need to know for a cause of death. Mr. McCutcheon was in ventricular fibrillation upon arrival. He arrested about thirty minutes later. That's all I have for you."

"That's all there is to it?" I asked, watching him carefully for a reaction.

"That's all I saw. The medics who brought him in reported he was experiencing paralysis and ventricular dysrhythmias. In other words, his heart was out of rhythm. He had to be shocked, several times."

"But why was this happening?"

"Given his history, like I told you last night, my guess would be advanced coronary artery disease."

He was telling the truth, dang it.

I stared down at the paper in my hands and saw the words, *paralysis* and *irregular heartbeat*. "It seems like one of these poisons would be a great way to kill someone, especially with that kind of history."

"Don't let me give you any ideas, and not that Mr. McCutcheon's death was caused by anything other than a very unhealthy heart, but you're right. It could be an effective way to kill someone."

I stared at him. "Because you can't just run a few labs and find out that someone was poisoned?"

He smirked. "Not around here. Takes some seriously expensive equipment and highly trained toxicologists that county hospitals can't afford."

I sighed. I could only hope that the state crime lab had some of that equipment.

Kyle glanced down at the bowl between us. "If you're done pumping me for information, I'd like to eat sometime today."

"I'd prefer to call it asking a friend for his help with a problem."

He grabbed a whisk. "Yeah, I like that better, too. Still feels like I was pumped for information though."

"Sorry."

"Now let me ask you a question," he said, whisking milk in with the eggs.

"Okay." The flutter in my chest told me to expect that his question wouldn't have anything to do with work.

"Was that the only reason you called me this morning?"

It was a fair question, but there was no way I could give him a completely honest answer without hurting his feelings.

"I was concerned that there might be a connection between why Jordan Makepeace was rushed to the hospital last night and the death of Marty McCutcheon, and I wanted to see what you thought. To see if this seemed like too much of a coincidence." I left the rest unsaid. He was a smart guy. He could read between the lines.

He nodded. "I'm not a big one for coincidences."

"Me either."

"But they happen. You and me, for example. There we were at Eddie's, in the same boat after dressing for an evening out."

"Yeah." Point taken.

"So, the guy who cancelled on you. Is it serious?"

"Maybe." I felt like Steve and I needed more time to figure that out. "I guess I'm not sure yet, but I can tell you that he's important to me."

At the nod of his head I could see he'd gotten the message. "What about you and your date last night?"

He pressed his lips together, deliberating on his answer for a split-second too long. "Just someone I'd gone out with a couple of times."

I seriously doubted that. "Just a couple?"

His mouth stretched into a lopsided smile. "Maybe four. Does that disqualify me from having brunch with you?"

"Nope, especially when I'm hungry."

"Good answer."

While he busied himself in the galley, I studied the

paper in my hands and thought about the one thing that Jordan Makepeace and Marty McCutcheon appeared to have in common: Phyllis Bozeman. Coincidence? Maybe. There was only one person in town who could solve that mystery for me—the lady herself.

✳

"I need a cake," I said to Lucille, one of the two Duke's waitresses working the afternoon shift.

She and I both knew my request was a formality because *the Duke*, Darrell Duquette, was watching us from the cut-out window over the grill to make sure that I didn't treat his bakery profit center like an all-you-can-eat buffet.

Stepping behind the illuminated glass case in her squeaky orthopedic shoes, Lucille pointed at a German chocolate cake missing two slices. "We got this one."

"A whole cake." I leaned closer to check out a platter of cupcakes that might work in a pinch.

Lucille looked at me through the glass, the points of her platinum bob curling into her cheeks. "Where's the party?"

"No party. I just need a cake. Something cheerful looking." I figured the family of a poisoning victim could use all the cheering up they could get.

"We got German chocolate and carrot. If that isn't enough cheer for ya, you need to get your ass back here and bake it yourself."

It wouldn't have been the first time since I graduated from culinary school that I'd availed myself of Duke's kitchen. I'd baked most of the family birthday cakes, even my own wedding cake. But I needed something readily packable into a bakery box if I wanted to catch a grandma at the hospital during visiting hours.

"Lucille, could I get a refill when you have a minute?" called Stanley, one of Duke's more senior regulars from his usual perch at the yellow Formica counter.

She pursed her lips. "The natives are getting restless."

"Go get him his decaf. I'll deal with Duke," I whispered, stepping behind the bakery case like I had countless times over the years while helping stock its shelves.

I pulled out the platter of cupcakes and did a quick count. Ten. Good enough. All I needed to do was dress them up a little, and they would do nicely.

Pushing open the kitchen door with my shoulder, I smiled at my great-uncle. "Howdy! Looks like a pretty good crowd today considering that it's after tourist season."

The curmudgeon wearing the grease-stained white apron glowered at me. "And they might want to take home some cupcakes, so where do you think you're going with those?"

"I'm buying them," I said on my way back to my great-aunt Alice's butcher block worktable.

"You know that's supposed to mean that you *pay* for 'em."

"I was thinking more along the lines of taking it out in trade."

He brightened. "Yeah? A dozen cupcakes to replace those? Okay, you've got a deal—as long as you throw in a chocolate layer cake. We sold the last piece an hour ago."

"Wait a minute," I said, pulling the cake decorating

tray from the storage shelf next to a cooling rack. "Since when is that fair?"

"Since you owe me for the cheeseburger I made you for lunch yesterday, and the apple fritter I saw you sneak on Monday."

"I swear you've got eyes in the back of your head, old man."

He chuckled low in his throat as he flipped the burger sizzling on the grill. "And don't you ever forget it, baby girl."

"Yeah, yeah, yeah." Like he'd let me.

At the worktable I sorted through a box of cake toppers and found three little rainbows, a couple of plastic palm trees, and assorted fondant zoo animals that I could use. "Perfect."

After I placed the cupcakes in a pink bakery box and arranged them like they were having a fun day at the zoo, I fastened the box with a Duke's Cafe sticker and headed for the kitchen door.

Duke pointed at me with his spatula. "You'd better come right back and get to bakin'. I've got an apron here with your name on it."

Unfortunately he wasn't kidding. He'd used that threat on me so many times when I was a teenager, he'd had one embroidered for me.

"I'll be back. First, I need to make a special delivery to the hospital."

Chapter Ten

AFTER A QUICK stop in the hospital gift shop to buy an overpriced balloon, I headed up to the second floor where Jordan Makepeace had been moved after spending the night in Intensive Care.

Standing at the door, I hesitated to intrude on the four generations gathered around the honey-haired little boy's bed. Yes, Phyllis Bozeman was standing at the foot of his bed with her youngest grandchild in her arms, but so was Estelle and I didn't need this courtesy call getting back to my grandmother, especially since it had the potential to go very badly.

"Balloon!" Jordan squealed, pointing at the polka-dotted *Get Well* balloon in my hand.

All eyes turned to me.

I painted a happy smile on my face as I stepped into the room. "Hi, everybody! How's the patient?"

"Better, thank you," his father said with a glance at a frowning Aubrey, as if she could explain why I was visiting their son.

Estelle waved me over to stand next to her. "Oh, boy! I think someone special is getting a balloon!"

As I approached, Phyllis clutched her baby grandson to her bosom like I was going to fly away with him on the broomstick that I'd left in the hallway.

Just keep smiling and think of a way to get Phyllis alone.

"Charmaine?" Aubrey's puffy eyes narrowed as they scanned me from head to toe. "What are you doing here?"

Since I had insinuated myself into the tail end of what had to have been an all-night vigil, I hadn't expected Aubrey to be pleased to see me, especially after twenty-three years of avoiding one another.

"Duke heard about what happened and asked me to bring this brave young man a little get well gift." After handing his father the balloon, I opened up the bakery box and showed Jordan my cupcake zoo.

His eyes widened. "Cupcakes!"

"How cute!" Estelle said. "Which one do you want to try first, Jordy? A monkey or an elephant?"

He reached for the box. "Monkey!"

Aubrey placed her hand on her son's arm. "Granny, don't encourage him. He can't—"

"These will keep in the refrigerator, so when he's ready…" I winked at Jordan. "…that monkey cupcake will still be yummy."

"Hello, hello," a fortyish doctor said as he came alongside Jordan's bed. He smiled apologetically at the two grannies and me. "I hate to break up the party, but we're going to need everyone but Mom and Dad to leave the room for a few minutes."

Aubrey exchanged glances with her mother. "Maybe you should take Joey home. It's past his naptime. Then I'll call so you know what to expect later."

Phyllis nodded and gathered her purse. "Okay, bye,

sweetheart."

Jordan waved goodbye to his grandmother and then looked expectantly at me.

Smart kid. He knew this was my cue as well as I did. "You feel better, Jordan. Enjoy that monkey!"

After setting the bakery box on a table by the door, I followed Phyllis into the disinfectant-scented hallway. "Before you go, I wonder if I could ask you something."

She shifted the baby in her arms. "I need to get him home. Estelle, too," Phyllis said, turning to look behind us. "Estelle, are you ready to go?"

The older woman sighed. "I just need to find a bathroom. Such a nuisance this bladder of mine."

Once Estelle was out of earshot, I pointed at the bench by the elevator. "As long as you have a couple of moments, let's have a seat."

"I can't imagine that we have anything else to talk about if this is about Marty," she said, seating little Joey on her lap.

"I just need you to help me understand something."

"Well, I'll try."

I leaned in to get a clearer view of her face. "I don't know if you realize this, but Marty became violently ill a couple of hours before he died."

She nodded, her eyes downcast as she stroked the fine hair on her grandson's head. "Cameron mentioned that yesterday."

"We are trying to determine if something he ingested led to his heart failure." Okay, *we* was bending the truth into a boomerang that might whack me in the head later, but I needed this to sound official.

Phyllis knit her brows, her dark eyes searching mine.

"Something he ingested? He seemed fine at work, so do you mean something he ate at his birthday dinner?"

"It seems like a possibility."

"Why are you asking me? I wasn't there."

"But you gave him something he ate that no one else appears to have touched Thursday night."

"The salsa?"

I nodded.

"It was the same salsa I always give him."

"Was anything added to it?" I asked, watching her closely for a reaction.

Her nostrils flared, her eyes scarcely more than slits as she stared me down. "Certainly not by me."

Joey started crying as if his grandmother were scaring him.

I know, kid. She can be a little intense. Kind of like my ex-mother-in-law when she was angry. But Phyllis Bozeman was also telling the truth.

I flashed her my best conciliatory smile as she patted the back of the increasingly fussy baby. "I apologize, but I must ask...do you have any reason to think that something might have been added to it?"

"I didn't until now!"

True again. If there had been something poisonous added to the salsa, she didn't know anything about it.

Phyllis labored to stand with Joey in her arms as Estelle walked up behind me.

"Okay, I'm ready," Estelle said, pressing the button for the elevator.

Pushing out of my seat I knew this little interview would be over the second the elevator door opened. "You know, it's just remarkable how well Jordan is doing."

Estelle placed her hand on Phyllis's shoulder. "And this one gets all the credit for that. If it wasn't for her quick thinking, I shudder to think what could have happened to that sweet little boy."

When the elevator door opened, we stepped inside and I pressed the button for the ground floor. "Yes, thank goodness you knew that plant was poisonous, Mrs. Bozeman."

Phyllis sniffed, staring at the elevator door. "I didn't. But I'd never heard of anyone using crocuses in salads or soups, so I just assumed."

Oh.

"Good assumption." On her part, not mine because without the Phyllis Bozeman link between her former boyfriend's death and her grandson's poisoning, I couldn't help but wonder if Kyle was right. Maybe Marty's untimely death could have been avoided if he'd cut back on the cheeseburgers.

After leaving the elevator we headed for the exit while Joey screamed, heading for a baby meltdown.

"Somebody's really tired," Phyllis said, picking up her pace.

Seemingly content to lag behind, Estelle tapped my arm. "Are you going home from here?"

"Back to Duke's actually." To make good on a debt.

"Could you give me a ride?" She pointed at the crying baby. "Plus, since Phyllis is headed over to Clatska, I'm out of her way."

"No problem. In fact, I have some yarn for you from Darlene."

"You do?"

"I was over there yesterday, and she asked me to

deliver it since I'd be coming back this way. I meant to stop by on my way home from work, but…"

"That's strange," Estelle said as we followed Phyllis out into the afternoon sunshine. "I saw Darlene's car parked across the street from my house shortly before I got the call about Jordan. I wonder why she didn't just deliver the yarn then and save you the trouble."

"Me, too."

"I'm on the right here," Estelle said when I turned on E Street, pointing at the house with the oatmeal aluminum siding as if I'd never seen her little rambler before.

Slowing, I looked at the basil green craftsman style house with the cream trim across the way. "That's new." It had been a few years since I'd spent any time in Estelle's neighborhood, but I remembered the house being a lighter color.

She leaned over, looking past me. "Turned out nice, didn't it? Bob's been working on the place ever since he moved in last year."

"Bob?"

"Bob Hallahan."

I pulled into Estelle's driveway and turned to face her. "When you said you saw Darlene's car across the street, did you mean that it was in front of Bob's house?"

"Yep, and right opposite my driveway. I almost hit it when I was backing out to go to the hospital." Estelle rolled her eyes. "She still blames me for taking down that old ramshackle fence of hers. I never would have heard the end of it if I'd hit her car."

Since Darlene had given me the distinct impression

that she wouldn't be making a trip into town yesterday, I couldn't help but be curious about why she visited her ex-husband's best friend. Perhaps she knew about something in Marty's will that concerned Bob. Something that Marty had wanted Bob to have?

But wouldn't that something have remained with Marty at his house, not his ex-wife's?

"Hopefully, the next time she visits she won't park in your way," I said.

"Yes, she should follow the lead of the lady friend Bob's been seeing and park closer to his mailbox."

I hadn't realized that Bob had a *lady friend*. Maybe this was a mutual friend he shared with Darlene and that was what had prompted her visit last night. "Who's he seeing these days?"

"I only caught a glimpse of her last Tuesday evening when I was taking out the garbage. Seemed quite lovely. Chinese, I think."

"Black shoulder-length hair?"

She nodded. "Looked a little young for him if you ask me, but what do I know about these things anymore?"

Since her description fit Victoria McCutcheon, I wondered the same thing.

"Besides, as long as his visitors don't park in my way, who he spends his time with is none of my business." Estelle gathered up her yarn and her purse. "Well, thanks for the ride. For the cupcakes for Jordan, too."

"Those were from Duke."

"Right." She grinned. "That bugger has never given away free food in his life."

Duke had given it to me on sort of a need-to-know basis.

She opened the car door. "You're a nice girl, Charmaine. I'm going to tell your granny so the next time I see her."

I wasn't so nice. I'd used the near-death of a little kid to squeeze information out of his grandmother.

Since Estelle was struggling to get out of the bucket seat, I came around to the passenger side and offered her my hand.

She locked palms with me. "Yep, a nice girl."

Who was feeling guiltier by the second.

"Now, what you need to do," Estelle said as I pulled her to her feet, "is find a nice boy." She winked at me. "Get back on the horse and all that good stuff."

"Yes, ma'am." And I knew exactly which horse I wanted to ride later. Yep, there would be no pillow talk about poison tonight.

After Estelle's door closed behind her I looked at the house across the street, where both Mrs. McCutcheons appeared to have made recent visits.

Strange. Especially since one of them had deceived me about her intention to come into town.

If the subject just happened to come up later, maybe my *nice boy* wouldn't mind offering an opinion about it over a beer.

"He's not *that* nice," I reminded myself. Better make it a home-cooked meal with a big slice of chocolate cake for dessert.

"It's about time," my great-uncle grumbled when I grabbed my apron off a hook in the kitchen. "Did you do rounds while you were at the hospital?"

"No. I was just visiting a friend." Duke wasn't the inquisitive one I needed to worry about in the cafe, so I slipped my apron on knowing that I'd said enough to satisfy his curiosity.

Unfortunately, the same wasn't true for Lucille, Gossip Central's ringleader, who was pushing through the kitchen door. "Would that friend's name be Dr. Cardinale?"

Uh-oh! Someone had blabbed—someone who had seen me with Kyle.

I stared at her, my mind racing for a way to contain the damage without full disclosure. Phyllis Bozeman didn't need the rest of Port Merritt to know that I had thought she could have poisoned her former boyfriend, and neither did I.

"Of course not. Why would I take cupcakes decorated with monkeys and elephants to a doctor?" I headed for the worktable to get this conversation away from the ears of the waitress who was picking up her order at the window.

"Heck, I don't know," Lucille said, hot on my heels. "Maybe the dude's into monkeys."

I cocked my head at her as I pulled a large stainless steel bowl out from under the worktable. "Please. Whoever you've been talking to has it all wrong."

"Funny you should say that because that's exactly what I told Millie when she came here for her lunch break and wanted to know how long the two of you had been going out."

Great.

Her eyes fixed on me, Lucille leaned over the table like a snake poised to strike. "So, the two of you had a lunch date."

"It wasn't a date."

She smiled conspiratorially. "Uh-huh."

"It was more like a business meeting." At least that's what I had intended.

"From what Millie said about the way he was looking at you, it's more like he wanted to get down to business," she said, chortling at her own joke.

"Hardly."

"Oh, you can deny it all you want, but she's not the only one who's noticed how he looks at you."

"Probably because he has a bit of a crush on my mother, and with the right makeup," and bad lighting, "he sees a little of Marietta in me."

Lucille smirked. "Doll, when he's looking at you I really don't think he sees your mother."

Since I was the one with the bad hair and the extra thirty pounds, I didn't take Lucille's opinion as a positive.

"Order up!" Duke barked in our direction.

"Yeah, yeah, hold your donkeys." Lucille pointed an index finger at me. "Don't go anywhere. I want details about this lunch."

"Trust me, the details are going to be very boring."

"Uh-huh. I may not be able to tell that you're lying, but I know you're holding out on me."

"I'm not holding out on you." Much. "And I have nothing else to say on the subject."

Lucille frowned. "You and Steve are hanging around one another too much," she muttered, squeaking away. "He gave me the same *no comment* answer ten minutes ago."

"What?!" I followed her through the kitchen door and locked gazes with the detective sipping a cup of coffee at the counter.

I pasted a smile on my face as I slipped onto the barstool next to him. "Hey."

"Hey, yourself." His tone was cool, his eyes assessing.

"I'm surprised to see you here this late in the afternoon. Did you get a sudden craving for bad coffee?"

"I was looking for you."

"Yeah? Looks like you found me."

He glanced down at my white apron. "What's with the apron? Duke putting you to work?"

"It's payback for a couple of lunches I had earlier this week."

A humorless smile pulled at the corners of his lips. "Payback can be a bitch, can't it? Especially when it comes to lunches."

I had a sinking feeling that it was going to be, and soon. "I know you were chatting with Lucille earlier, so would you like to hear why I had lunch with Kyle Cardinale?"

"Only if you'd like to tell me."

Not especially.

As if on cue Lucille ambled over to refill Steve's cup. "Get you anything else, hon?"

"No thanks," he said, his gaze fixed on me.

I waited for her to leave, but instead she lingered with a sudden compulsion to refill the sugar dispensers at the counter.

"Come with me." I picked up Steve's coffee cup and led him into the kitchen to find some privacy.

Duke frowned as we passed. "This ain't a meeting room, you know."

"We won't be long. I just need to talk to Steve for a

minute in private."

"And I need cake," Duke said, calling after me. "Is that going to happen anytime soon?"

"Yes!" Sheesh, I could only handle one minor crisis at a time.

Setting down Steve's coffee on the worktable, I pulled out a wooden stool for him to sit on. "Okay, I can explain."

He shrugged a shoulder. "You don't have to."

"But I don't want you to have the wrong idea."

"Then what's the right idea?"

"You know how we were talking about Phyllis Bozeman slipping something poisonous into the salsa she bought for Marty McCutcheon?"

"I know how *you* were talking about it."

"I figured Kyle would be a good person to ask about what symptoms he might see in a poisoning victim."

"Uh-huh."

Steve could read micro-expressions almost as well as I could, so I knew I'd best not stray far from the truth. "And when I contacted him he suggested that we talk over lunch."

"Yeah, and?"

"And that's it. He pretty much confirmed what he'd told me before about Marty's cause of death, and then I…" I hesitated telling him anything about going to the hospital since that hadn't been my finest hour.

Steve's eyes narrowed. "What'd you do?"

"I sort of ran into Phyllis."

"I bet you did."

"The good news is that I'm sure that she didn't poison Marty."

Steve exhaled. "Please tell me that you're going to leave the woman alone now."

I nodded.

"Anything else that you'd like to tell me?"

"Just this." I leaned over and kissed him. "Oh, and I told Rox about us."

"About time."

"She's pissed that I didn't say anything sooner."

He shook his head. "Why do you women make everything so complicated?"

"Some things are complicated," I said with more volume than I'd intended. "Relationships for example. They can get complicated fast."

"You've been friends forever. I'm sure you'll smooth it over with her."

I wasn't referring to my relationship with Rox. "Right."

"When are you getting out of here?"

"In a couple of hours. Why?"

"I thought I should make good on that date I owe you."

"Yeah, because if you don't, payback's a bitch."

"So I've heard."

"It so happens that I bought something sexy that you haven't seen yet."

Steve rose to his feet, a glint of carnal interest in his eyes. "Pick you up at seven? We could go into Port Townsend to some place along the waterfront if you want."

Ordinarily, I'd jump at the opportunity, but I had no desire to dine at another Port Townsend waterfront restaurant this weekend. "How about if I come over and make dinner? I can probably finagle some cake out of

Duke for dessert."

"Yum." Steve pressed his lips to mine, gently at first, then he deepened the kiss.

"Mmmm, yum," I said when we came up for air.

"Hey, what do you think you're doing back there? Break it up!" Duke pointed at me with his spatula. "You, get busy baking. And you," he said glaring at Steve. "Out!"

Lucille burst through the kitchen door. "What? What'd I miss?"

"This." I linked my arms around Steve's neck to pull him to me and kissed him long and hard.

"What the heck!" Lucille exclaimed. "I thought..."

I turned to her. "You thought wrong."

Chapter Eleven

FIVE HOURS LATER, I was leaning against Steve's white-tiled kitchen counter and sneaking a peek at my cell phone while he loaded his dishwasher.

My phone displayed the same lack of activity as the last ten times I had checked. No missed calls. No texts. No nothing since I'd outed myself to the two gossip queens of Port Merritt.

Weird.

Totally and unpredictably weird, but maybe Steve had been right all along. Aside from Rox, who had the right to be a little ticked at me for holding out on her, maybe nobody especially cared that Steve and I were officially *friends with benefits.*

Considering how popular a dance partner he had been on Tango Tuesdays at the Senior Center, I found this non-development a little perplexing. But we weren't cheating on any spouses, neither one of us made enough money to make us gold digger-worthy, and no shotgun wedding was on the docket.

Maybe my *big reveal* hadn't been so big after all, and Lucille's cronies wouldn't grill me like a cheese panini the next time I stepped into Duke's.

This was a good thing—a very good thing. But given the bevy of dishy rumors I heard on almost a daily basis, the only way I could see my news stalling on the gossip launch pad was if the hotter rocket of a story about Marty McCutcheon and the inheritance his bride would be coming into was still soaring.

Based on what I'd heard this afternoon, I couldn't help but wonder about the part Bob Hallahan played in that story.

"You expecting a call?" Steve asked. "You keep looking at your phone."

"No, I was just…. Never mind." I slipped my phone into the back pocket of my jeans. "You haven't heard any rumors about Victoria McCutcheon and Bob Hallahan, have you?"

He shot me a glance. "Haven't exactly had my ear to the rumor mill grindstone."

"She was seen at his house this week."

"Could be for any number of reasons."

"Uh-huh." Considering the woman's husband died a couple of days later, whatever that reason had been, it seemed a little suspect. "She was also referred to as his lady friend."

"By?"

"Estelle. She lives across the street from Bob."

Steve smirked. "The same woman who likes to tease your grandmother about the younger man she's been seeing. Or maybe she referred to me as a young buck. I can't remember."

"I'm sure that's not what she called you. But really, I don't think Bob Hallahan is feeding Marty McCutcheon's wife pot roast a couple times a week."

"She's been seen there more than once?"

"I guess. Enough for Estelle to make the assumption that there's a relationship."

He furrowed his brow. "Don't know what to say about that. If anything were going on that they wanted to keep quiet, I'd expect them to be more discreet."

"Yeah." But Steve and I hadn't exactly been pillars of discretion each time I joined him in his bed the past month. Then again, I didn't have a husband to worry about.

"Don't make too much out of this. You should know by now that witnesses can jump to all sorts of incorrect conclusions about what they think they've seen."

"I know. It's just curious. Possibly not just to me since Darlene McCutcheon was at Bob's house yesterday—the same day she asked me to deliver something to Estelle because she didn't plan on coming into town."

"Hmmm."

"Hmmm, what?" I asked.

"Her plans must have changed for some reason."

"Don't you think that's strange though? Both of Marty's wives visiting the guy who is supposed to be his best friend? And both of them there the week that he died."

Steve gave his shoulder a little shrug. "Like you said, it's curious."

But could it be an indicator of anything significant to this unofficial case?

"Unless you think you need to pursue this with Frankie," he said as if reading my mind, "and I wouldn't unless you've got some fact to go along with this gossip,

I'd recommend that you not share this with anyone else."

I nodded my agreement, but that didn't make Bob Hallahan's sudden popularity with the McCutcheon women seem any less strange.

His lips curled slightly at the corners. "Anything else that we need to talk about?"

I knew I couldn't talk to him about how it had gone with Rox without him rolling his eyes, and there was absolutely nothing I wanted to add to what I'd already told him about Kyle Cardinale. "Nope."

"Then I think we should move on to the next phase of our date," he said, pressing the *start* button on his dishwasher.

My pulse quickened as if he'd pressed my *start* button. "Okay, then!" He'd barely touched me for days, so as long as part two of this date included his hands on me I was all for it.

Reaching into his refrigerator, Steve pulled out two beers. He then cocked his head, and I followed him to the living room where an area rug separated a chocolate brown leather sectional from an overstuffed chair left over from his mother.

I sank into the sectional next to him and set the beer bottle he'd offered me on the cherry wood end table to my left to assume a comfortable make-out position. Unfortunately, I may have assumed too much because instead of reaching for me, he reached for his remote control.

"Hey," he said as his flat screen flickered to life in time for us to watch a baseball fly into the upper deck of Safeco Field. "The Mariners just pulled ahead of the Angels, three-two."

"Good for them."

"It's one of the last games of the year. I thought we could make this a dinner and a movie night, but since it's early…"

I had no choice but to take the bait. "You want to watch the game."

"Do you mind?"

I shook my head. "Remember what we talked about earlier though."

He looked at me with a quizzical expression.

"There could be payback."

"Bring it on," Steve said, his eyes dark as bittersweet chocolate.

I reached for him in invitation and he closed his mouth over mine, playfully kissing me. Leaning into me, the kiss deepened, his hand cupping my breast. But at the crack of the bat, Steve glanced back over his shoulder. "Run!"

"He's going to have to hurry if he wants to get to third base," said the announcer.

I poked Steve's chest. "Don't let that give you any ideas."

He grinned at me. "It's way too late for that, Chow Mein."

✳

It was almost eleven in the morning by the time I brought Gram home from church and had turned down the hill toward my favorite latte stand. Reverend Fleming's sermon on the power of forgiveness had inspired several nods of the head amongst the congregation and an occasional *amen*. Unfortunately, it hadn't given me any bright ideas on how to get Rox to forgive me for holding out on her, so I decided I'd better order an extra double shot mocha latte as a bribe.

Ten minutes later, she opened her front door and eyeballed the paper cups warming my hands. "One of those had better be for me."

"It is if you'll let me in."

Rox took a cup from me and sniffed it as she shut the door behind me. "Mocha?"

"I know," I said, taking a seat on her parents' old pea-green sofa that she'd covered with a crocheted bedspread. "Chocolate in coffee is more my thing, but I figured the occasion called for something mood-altering."

She nodded as she sat in the swivel rocker across from me. "Not a bad call."

Watching her sip her drink, I searched for the right words to remove the awkwardness hanging over us like a storm cloud. "I'm sorry," I said, coming up empty.

Wincing, she stared down at the paper cup in her hands for several silent seconds. "Just help me understand this." She finally looked up, her jaw set as if it had been chiseled from stone. "I never thought there was anything I couldn't talk to you about, but now I find out—"

"No, it wasn't like that." I set my coffee down on the scratched maple table separating us. "It's hard to explain."

Rox squeezed out a fake smile. "Try."

How could I get her to understand something I barely understood myself? "I didn't say anything because I didn't want to make a big deal out of this. You know how people can be."

She puckered.

"I'm not referring to you."

"Then why couldn't you tell me?"

"Maybe I was afraid you'd remind me why I said I'd never cross that line with Steve, and I wasn't ready to hear it."

Her gaze softened. "Are you ready now?"

"Heck, no. Honestly though, there's nothing that you could tell me that I haven't already told myself a hundred times before. But go ahead. Let me have it."

"It's a little late now, but are you sure?"

I hadn't been sure of anything since that moment in the parking lot when Steve first kissed me.

Rox slowly shook her head. "There's no going back from this."

"That's what I told him, that it would change every-thing."

"Has it?"

"Not entirely, but if this doesn't end well—"

"Why are you talking about endings already?" Rox asked, punching out every word as if I'd suddenly become hard of hearing.

"Because in my experience relationships don't always end well, and instead of fighting over the bedroom set that I picked out a year from now, I don't want to be fighting over you and Eddie!"

She blew out a sigh. "Okay, you have a point. I can see how this has the potential to get ugly."

I reached for my coffee. "Thank you."

We sipped our drinks during what felt like an uneasy truce, and then I felt her staring at me.

"What?" I asked.

"You and Steve...together. It may take me a little

while to wrap my brain around this."

I was quite sure Rox wouldn't be the only one in town to feel that way. "But when we're with you and Eddie it shouldn't seem much different from the way it's always been. Steve and I are just *more than friends* now."

"I can't tell you how weird that sounds coming from you after all these years, especially after what I witnessed two nights ago."

"That was a mistake that won't be happening again, and I told Kyle as much when I had…"

Rox had a wary look in her eyes. "Had what?"

I cringed. "Lunch with him yesterday. It was to talk to him about something I'm working on, but—"

"Jeez, Louise! Your life really has become complicated these last few weeks."

"Tell me about it. But I really, *really* want to uncomplicate it, especially between you and me. So, are we okay?"

She smiled begrudgingly. "We're fine. Just tell me, who knows about the two of you? I don't want to say anything to the wrong person."

"Obviously, Donna knows. Other than that, I told Lucille when I was at Duke's yesterday." I pulled my phone from my tote bag. "It's weird though—almost like a *calm before the storm* thing. I served them up a juicy story on a silver platter, and not one of our friends has texted me to confirm it."

"That is weird. Maybe the news hasn't made the rounds yet."

"Maybe," I said, checking my phone. "Or maybe I spoke too soon. Looks like I have a text."

"Who's it from?" Rox asked as I opened the message.

"Seriously?" I could feel the blood draining from my face with each word I read. "You're coming now?!"

"Who? Who's coming?"

"I'll fill you in later." I grabbed my tote. "Right now, I need to get home."

Because a storm was about to blow in, and her name was Marietta.

Chapter Twelve

TWENTY MINUTES LATER, I was changing the sheets of my double bed when Gram came in and set a juice glass on my nightstand.

"What's with the juice?" When I wanted to mainline sugar I preferred it in a chewy, gooey form, not some insidious nectar with the potential of going supernova in my bloodstream and giving me cravings for cookies for the rest of the day.

"It's not juice. It's that expensive chardonnay your mother likes. I opened a bottle to let it *breathe*," Gram said, a smirk firmly planted at the corner of her mouth. "We'll have it with lunch, and as long as it was open...."

"A little early, don't you think?"

"Your mom told me on the phone that she wants our help with the wedding."

Swell. My mother had never solicited my advice or assistance for her first three weddings. Given the fact that she managed to get swept up in a whirlwind romance with my high school biology teacher the second her divorce papers were dry, I saw no reason for her track record to change.

Gram grabbed a corner of my quilted comforter and helped me smooth it over the bed. "She also mentioned that she plans to be in town for two weeks while they don't need her on location."

"Two weeks!" That meant two long weeks of Marietta commandeering my bedroom, and me having to act like the nice, accommodating girl Estelle thought me to be.

The way my last couple of days had gone I didn't know if I had that much *nice* left in me.

"It's after five somewhere," I said, reaching for the glass.

"I thought you might see it that way." She pointed at my closet. "Be sure to make some space for your mother. You know how she tends to over-pack."

"Yeah." She tended to overdo lots of things. I could only hope that the next wedding in her future wouldn't be one of them.

After I pulled a few outfits for the work week from the closet and grabbed my black jeans and favorite slouch sweater, I was downstairs at the door to the study when I caught a whiff of my mother's signature musky jasmine scent.

"There's my girl!" she exclaimed, prancing toward me in a pair of spiky black boots worthy of Catwoman that made her long, shapely legs look even longer and gave her a two-inch height advantage over me.

Marietta crushed me to her double-D's, and then frowned at the clothes in my arms. "Oh, Chah-maine. Ah do hate putting you out."

Not enough to stay at a hotel, especially if a five-star resort wasn't attached to it.

I looked at Barry Ferris, my former biology teacher,

standing behind her.

He gave his head a little shake.

I interpreted it as another failed attempt on his part to convince her to stay over at his house—something my image-conscious mother refused to do prior to tying the knot. As evidenced by the continued use of the fake Southern accent she'd adopted when she was cast in a Georgia-based *Charlie's Angels* clone, maintaining her genteel image had become as fundamental to her as breathing. Plus, I didn't think she wanted Mr. Ferris to see her first thing in the morning without makeup.

"It's not a problem." But the perfume assailing my sinuses was. So was waking up in the middle of the night because of a hide-a-bed spring that had a nasty habit of poking me in the butt.

Yep, I would have two long, sleepless weeks of jasmine-infused wedding planning ahead of me unless I came up with an escape plan, and fast.

I opened the front door to see if my sex buddy with the spare bed was home. Not that I was eager to test Steve at his word about wanting me in his bed, but since I already spent half of my evenings over at his house, maybe it wasn't a stretch to make it one hundred percent.

"I'll be right back," I said, welcoming not only the fresh air but the sight of Steve's truck parked in his driveway.

"Back? Chah-maine, where're you goin'?"

"To ask Steve to join us for lunch after I drop my clothes off."

Marietta sucked in a sharp breath. "You're staying with Steve?"

"In his guest room." If she could play the propriety

game, so could I.

She stepped off the front porch and grasped my arm. "Are you sure that's wise?"

"I don't need to keep our relationship a secret anymore. It's fine."

She frowned with as much disapproval as her Botox-treated brow would allow. "I don't know that I think it's so *fine.*"

Mary Jo Digby had given up the right to give me parental attitude when Marietta Moreau got cast in her first featured movie role and dumped me off at my grandparents' house the next day.

"In fact," she added without a trace of her trademark accent, "maybe I should stay over there instead of you. I can't imagine that Steve would mind."

Oh, he'd mind, and I'd never stop hearing about how much he minded. "No, you'll be more comfortable at Gram's."

"But—"

"Trust me."

"I do, but I feel like I'm chasing you away and into a situation that could be misconstrued."

I was in no mood to debate the consequences of this decision with her. "You're not," I said, turning so I didn't have to lie to her face. "I'll be right back to help Gram with lunch."

Seconds later, Steve stood at his door, surveying the pile of clothing draped over my arm. "Are you running away from home?"

"My mother's in town for the next two weeks. Is it okay if I camp out in your guest room?"

"My *guest* room?" He took my clothes from me. "No,

that's not okay."

I followed him to his bedroom and watched him push aside the slacks and polo shirts I'd seen him wear dozens of times to make room for my things in his closet.

It seemed a little too familiar to see one of my shirts touch his. Was coming over here too much too soon? I'd never spent an entire night with Steve before.

Having no prior experience with this *friends with benefits* thing I felt like I might just have made a big mistake, and the apprehension swelling inside my chest did nothing to convince me otherwise. Not that I'd ever admit that to my mother. "I...I wonder if the guest room wouldn't be a better idea."

He closed the distance between us and placed his hands on my shoulders. "Are you trying to tell me that you'd rather sleep in there?"

"Maybe." If sleep were the only thing we were talking about.

The laugh lines at the corners of his eyes tightened. "I've seen you without makeup. You're not that scary."

"Very reassuring."

He gave me a peck on the lips. "You can always count on me."

I breathed a sigh of relief that he didn't think I was trying to stake any permanent claims on his personal space.

"Good because I could use an ally across the street. Have you had lunch yet?"

"No, I was going to go to the store and—"

"You can go to the store later." I looked down at his bare feet. "Put some shoes on. You're coming to lunch."

His mouth flatlined. "This doesn't sound like it's

optional."

"If you want me in your bed," I said, heading for the door, "choose wisely!"

An hour later, Marietta sat at the dining room table, staring across at Steve over her wine glass.

He shot me a sideways glance.

"So," I said, getting his none-too-subtle hint to offer up a distraction. "Can I get anyone anything? More fruit salad, Barry?"

He smiled politely. "No, thanks. I had plenty."

Gram dabbed her napkin at her lips. "I'm sorry that I can't offer you any dessert. If I'd known you were coming, I would have baked a cake."

Or I would have yesterday.

"I wanted it to be a surprise," Marietta said, patting Barry's hand.

Grinning, he shook his head. "You surprised me, all right."

"So, you didn't know she was coming either?" Gram asked.

He wrapped his hand over my mother's. "She'd told me about coming up after the reunion appearance she and her co-stars were making at the convention down in Portland, but she didn't say a word about the DeLorean."

Marietta giggled like a school girl. "That would have ruined the surprise!"

Gram turned to me like she needed a translator. "I'm confused."

"Me, too. Last I heard you had started filming on location in Baton Rouge."

"Just two scenes this last week," Marietta said. "They won't need me again until mid-October, which worked out beautifully because I had the other commitment in Portland."

My mother was losing me again, and I had a bad feeling that I should have been listening more closely the last time she mentioned her appearance schedule. "A reunion commitment?"

She gave me a chemically minimized frown. "The last stop on the thirtieth anniversary tour of *The Peachtree Girls*. We wrapped up last night, then I arranged to ship the DeLorean to Barry's house and caught the first flight out this morning so that I could be here when it arrived."

Gram reached for her wine glass. "That car you always drove on your show? It still runs?"

"Not as well as it should. My ex...someone I know who was into cars says it needs to be driven more." Marietta cocked her head toward Barry. "And I know just the man who should drive it."

"I still can't believe that car's sitting in my driveway." His eyes beamed as he looked at her. "You are single-handedly upping my cool factor with the kids at school."

A smile of satisfaction tugged at her lips. "It was only going to rust at my house."

"It can't rust," Steve stated. "It's stainless steel."

Marietta narrowed her kohl-lined green eyes at him. "Whatever."

In stilted silence he poured the last of the wine into her glass as if he hoped it would improve her mood and then directed his attention to our former biology teacher. "Have you taken it for a spin yet?"

"Just a short one. It was running pretty rough so we

should probably have a mechanic take a look at it."

I looked at Steve. "Little Dog would slobber all over himself to work on a DeLorean."

He smirked. "Probably."

Marietta's gaze intensified. "I don't know that I want someone named *Little Dog* working on my car."

"You do if you want the best mechanic in town," Steve said flatly.

"Mom, it's George Jr. You've met him. A big redhead? He's the head mechanic for his dad over at Bassett Motor Works." He was also a huge fan. There would definitely be slobber.

Shaking her head, she shrugged a slender shoulder.

Obviously, none of that rang any bells. "He'll probably give you a discount for the bragging rights of working on your car."

Marietta, always on lookout for a bargain now that the movie offers were few and far between, perked up. "Oh, alrighty then. We might give him a try."

Steve pulled out his cell phone and gave her Little Dog's contact information. He then turned to me and thumbed in the direction of the kitchen.

No doubt he'd had enough of my mother for one day. I certainly was approaching my fill limit. "I'll take care of the dishes and get the coffee started."

"No coffee for me. I need to get going." Steve scooted out of his chair and bussed his dishes to the kitchen.

I followed his lead. Unfortunately, so did Marietta.

"I can take care of everything in the kitchen," I said to head her off at the pass.

She gave Steve a sideways glance. "I'm sure you can."

I sighed, inching ever closer to that fill limit.

Steve pressed my hand with his. "I'll go in and say goodbye to your grandmother."

Standing at the kitchen doorway, I smiled at the way Gram brightened up when he kissed her cheek, but I sensed some raised hackles in Catwoman behind me. Clearly, she needed to finish her chardonnay and chill. Maybe even bask in the glow of the emerald-cut diamond ring on her finger.

After Steve said goodbye to Barry, he headed for the front door.

"I'll walk you out," I said, turning to see that Marietta was blocking my path.

Using the advantage her four-inch boot heels gave her, she leveled her gaze at me. "*I'll* walk him out."

Good grief. What was she up to?

Following the two of them to the entry, I watched with dismay as she linked arms with Steve and shut the door in my face.

I added another item to the growing list of things I wished I could undo this weekend: this miserable lunch.

"Please tell me you're kidding," I said, looking at Steve's reflection in his bathroom mirror as I put away my plastic grocery sack of toiletries.

He leaned against the door jamb, his arms folded across his chest. "Your mom wanted to know my intentions."

I inwardly cringed as the band of tension that had been squeezing my temples since her arrival cinched a little tighter. "Sorry. That mother role that she was cast in must be rubbing off on her."

"She is your mother. From her perspective I might be asking the same questions."

From her perspective as a multi-divorced woman jumping into an ill-conceived fourth marriage? Or as the actress who was too consumed with her budding career to raise her own daughter? Either way, she had no business inserting herself into my relationship with Steve.

I turned to face him. "I think you're confusing her with your mother." The cookie-baking Girl Scout leader, who had bandaged my knee after I skinned it playing flag football in Steve's back yard.

A wry smile played at a corner of his lips. "Hardly."

"I'm really sorry that she put you on the spot like that. I'll talk to her."

"Not a big deal."

It was to me.

Steve lowered his gaze. "Want to know what I told her?"

I was dying to know, but at the same time I didn't think my head could contain the explosion if he told me something I wasn't prepared to hear.

I held out my hand. "This is so ridiculous I can't believe we're even talking about it. And that's exactly what I'm going to tell her if she brings the subject up again while she's here."

Pulling open a drawer, I saw a box of condoms and a first aid kit. "Are you sure you don't mind me taking over this bathroom?"

"I rarely use it, so it's all yours."

It didn't feel like it was all mine. It felt like I was intruding, and now, thanks to my mother, in every way possible.

"You're a nice boy," I said, stealing Estelle's line. "No matter what my mama thinks."

His eyes darkened as he stepped into the bathroom. "She and I would probably agree that I'm not that nice."

Oh, my. What did he tell her?

Lowering his head, Steve covered my mouth with his. The kiss deepened, and I wrapped my arms around his neck as he leaned me against the granite countertop, his erection pressing against my midsection. Feeling myself melting from his body heat, I savored his taste, his every touch.

Just as he pulled me to a sitting position on the countertop and reached for my zipper, my phone buzzed with a text message.

"Was that your butt?" he asked, running his fingers over my back pocket.

"Ignore it." That's what I planned on doing.

He unzipped my jeans and it buzzed again.

I reached for my phone to turn it off and saw that I had two messages from my mother. Gritting my teeth, I swore under my breath. Her timing was as bad as Donna's, but at least Donna had enough patience not to call if I didn't answer right away.

"Marietta wants to know when I'll be home. She also wants to make reservations for dinner." I met Steve's gaze. "Want to come—"

"Hell, no." He took my phone and tossed it into the carpeted hallway. "Now, where were we?"

My phone started ringing.

Steve blew out a breath. "Will she get the hint and leave a message or keep calling?"

Marietta Moreau wasn't accustomed to taking hints.

"She'll keep calling."

He zipped up my jeans. "Your mother's a real mood killer."

"Tell me about it."

"When you get back from dinner, we'll pick up where we left off."

Goody.

He retrieved my ringing phone and pressed it into my hand. "And don't even think about sleeping in the guest room tonight."

Chapter Thirteen

WHEN I ARRIVED at work the next morning and greeted Patsy, it felt like some semblance of normality had been restored after what had been a crazy last three days.

Gone was Friday's Patsy, the songbird. Monday's version of the legal eagle assistant perched outside Frankie's office looked like she wanted to shred someone with her talons. I just hoped that someone wasn't me.

She shifted her gaze to the glass-domed anniversary clock on her desk. "You're here early."

Thanks to Steve setting his alarm for six a.m. and making a big pot of coffee for us to share before he left at seven, I'd arrived at work a half hour early and that was after stopping for a mocha latte and a scone. "The early bird gets the worm, right?"

Not that I was after a proverbial worm. I didn't feel right hanging out at Steve's house without him there, and I didn't have anywhere else that I wanted to go, especially considering all the parental disapproval that would be waiting for me at my house.

Staring at me in silence, Patsy opened her mouth and then closed it again. Whatever was going on behind those steely gray eyes, she wasn't sharing.

I peeked into Frankie's office and saw it was dark. "She's not in yet?"

"She's in a meeting."

Dang. I was hoping to ask her about the report I'd sent her. "Do you know if she's made any decision on the Marty McCutcheon cause of death?"

Patsy heaved an impatient sigh and held up a blue folder from the *pending* basket behind her desk. "I just faxed the release form to Tolliver's, so I'd call that a yes."

Tolliver's Funeral Home worked in concert with the coroner's office to provide a temporary morgue, but Curtis Tolliver's real money was in the funeral services he offered. No doubt he'd soon be making a call to Marty's widow.

"Okay." That was that.

Now there was nothing to do but wait for the funeral announcement and the lab results that would free Marty's blue folder from the file purgatory behind Patsy's desk.

Since Patsy was tapping her keyboard with mounting irritation, I figured that was my invitation to leave. "Thanks," I said, making a quick exit down the hall to brew a fresh pot of coffee for my fellow third-floor caffeine addicts.

A minute later, I heard the door to the breakroom click shut behind me.

Patsy's mouth was little more than a grim line as she held her empty coffee cup in front of her and resumed the staring contest I wished she had let me know we were going to have.

I had to do something to break the silence, so I held the coffee pot up to the light to showcase the grounds floating in it. "I don't think you want this. It looks a little chewy."

"I can wait." She took a seat in one of the aluminum chairs at the table between us.

"Okay." It was a little unnerving to have an audience as if coffee-making had suddenly become a spectator sport, but clearly Patsy wanted something beyond fresh caffeine. If she could wait, so could I.

After I started the coffeemaker I turned to her so that she could clue me in on my next move.

"Would you sit down a minute?" she asked without hesitation.

My mind raced as I sat in the chair across from her. What on earth did we have to talk about that warranted a closed door? Certainly nothing work-related, and I knew she'd never come to me seeking diet advice.

I smiled.

She didn't.

Gripping her cup as if she needed something to hold onto, Patsy cleared her throat. "May I ask how well you know Mitch Grundy?"

I blinked. Not in a million years would I dream that Patsy Faraday would want to talk to me about her boyfriend. "Not all that well. I met him years ago when I was working at Duke's."

"Do you know anything about his personal life?"

"No." And I didn't want to. "I only know him as a restaurant supply salesman. Why?"

Patsy stared into the depths of her empty cup. "I think he might be something of a *player*."

"Mitch Grundy?" Sure, he was a salesman through and through and had always impressed me as an opportunist, but did that make him the type to prey on the affections of lonely middle-aged women? I might not especially like the guy, but I had a hard time wrapping my imagination around the notion that Mitch was a *player*.

She nodded. "His profile is still up and—"

"His profile?"

"Online dating. That's how we met. And now that we're supposedly in an exclusive relationship, I'd like to know if he's seeing other women."

I had a bad feeling about where this was heading. "Maybe you should just talk to him about this."

"I have, but his profile is still out there like he's hoping for a better offer."

"Patsy…" I wanted to say more, to give her something to bolster her confidence in this relationship, but I knew the woman well enough to know that my words wouldn't be welcome.

She waved me off. "I'm a realist. But I won't be played for a fool. Not again."

According to my grandmother, everyone in Port Merritt knew Patsy's husband had been cheating on her for most of their twenty-year marriage. Everyone but Patsy.

"That's where you come in," she added.

Hell's bells. This felt like high school all over again. Some of my friends setting up chance encounters so that I could put their boyfriends to the test and find out if they were two-timing them. "This isn't a good—"

"Nonsense. You can join us for lunch next week, when his business brings him back to town. You ask him a few questions like two old friends getting reacquainted. How we met. You're single again. Show some interest in online dating. It should be easy to get him to open up."

She sharpened her gaze. "You're sneaky and he's a talker. It's a perfect way to get to the truth."

I didn't particularly care for the way I was being characterized. "And find out if Mitch is seeing anyone else."

"Exactly."

Sheesh. Just like high school. But with one major difference—we weren't friends, so why was she coming to me?

The coffeemaker started sputtering, venting its steamy proclamation that the brew cycle was at an end. Patsy stood as if this also signaled the end of our conversation. "Of course, I'll expect you to respect my privacy just as I will respect yours."

"Of course, I'll respect your privacy, but what do you mean about respecting mine?"

The curl of her lips told me I wasn't going to like the answer. "If you're living with Detective Sixkiller, you might not want to be seen in Port Townsend with Doctor Cardinale."

Criminy, did somebody have my street staked out? "I don't know who you've been talking to but—"

"I stopped for a quick bite at Duke's this morning," Patsy said on her way to the coffee pot. "Unlike some of those ladies, I'm not judging, and I haven't said anything about seeing the two of you at the Grotto Friday night."

I heard a *yet* loud and clear.

She picked up the carafe and filled her cup. "So, may I count on you to join us for lunch next week?"

Was this my penance for letting Kyle charm me into a dinner date? Or for not telling Steve about it when he came over later that night? No matter how I sliced this I was screwed. "Sure."

"Excellent. I'll set it up."

She left the breakroom, humming a tune that sounded an awful lot like *Your Cheating Heart*.

Yep. Definitely screwed.

*

After three hours of making copies for one of the assistant prosecuting attorneys and catching up on the filing, I took an early lunch so that I could return Victoria McCutcheon's plate—my one loose end from last week.

Forty minutes later, I pulled into her driveway and parked next to a sporty new four by four with chrome wheels.

Very showy. Victoria's visitor had sunk some money into this truck.

I knocked at the front door and once again the lace curtains covering the bay window fluttered seconds before the door swung open.

What a difference a few days had made. Marty McCutcheon's widow couldn't have looked lovelier. Her blood red lipstick matched the tone in the red and black brocade jacket she wore over a pair of black cigarette pants, giving her an alluringly exotic look. Add in the healthy blush of her cheeks and the pleasant smile on her glossy lips, and the beautiful Victoria McCutcheon didn't bear the slightest resemblance to a heartbroken widow.

"Charmaine." She stepped back like a gracious hostess. "Please come in. Do you have news?"

I smelled notes of garlic and onion wafting in the air. "Not much in the way of news but I wanted to return your plate."

Her smile disappeared as she took the ceramic plate from my hands. "You caught me in the middle of making lunch, which is going to burn if I don't—"

"Sorry to interrupt you," I said, following her into the kitchen, where I saw Jeremy sitting at the counter with a steaming cup of tea in front of him.

Victoria splashed some soy sauce on the vegetables she was stir-frying. "Of course you know Jeremy."

The guy who looked like he wanted to break that cup over my head? Yeah, I knew him.

I smiled politely. "How're you doing?"

A corner of his mouth quirked. "I've had better days."

Me too.

"Would you like to join us for lunch?" Victoria asked. "It will be ready in a few minutes."

I glanced at Jeremy to gauge his reaction as to whether three would be a crowd, and got a big nothing as he stared straight ahead and sipped his tea. "Thank you, but I can't stay."

"You know what? I need some onion from my greenhouse." Turning down the heat under her wok, Victoria stepped over to the French doors that led to the back yard. "Walk with me and tell me your news."

I didn't have much news to tell, but this gave me an opportunity to speak to her without Jeremy listening in, so I stepped out onto her patio and waited until I breathed in the earthy scent of the greenhouse near the fence to say what little I could disclose.

"The Coroner released your husband's body this morning. This means that—"

"I know," she said with a sad smile. "That's why

Jeremy is here. We're meeting Curtis Tolliver at one-thirty to make the arrangements."

It seemed to me that Jeremy had gone out of his way for a free lunch since Tolliver's Funeral Home was located a block south of his dad's flooring shop. From what Austin had told me about the way Victoria could wrap the men in her life around her little finger, I wondered if the assistance Jeremy had offered had been his idea.

At least she was getting some help. "Good."

"Is that all the information you have for me?"

I nodded. I knew she would want to hear something about the testing of the items I had taken into evidence, but I didn't want to be the one to tell her that it seemed highly unlikely that was ever going to happen. "That's pretty much all I know."

Sighing, Victoria turned her attention to the green onions growing in a container at her left, and I wandered to the back of the greenhouse, where several varieties of fragrant lavender and lemon verbena commingled into a delightful bouquet. On the shelf next to the verbena sat two flats of assorted herbs at the ready for use in her kitchen. Behind them tall spikes of deep blue-violet flowers on slender stems appeared to be segregated from their edible neighbors by a laminated *do not touch* sign. Tubs of tomato plants heavy with fruit nestled on the shelf to the right of the herbs, and in the far corner a spiky aloe plant rested on the top level of an old wooden ladder.

"I envy you all the fresh herbs," I said, missing the herb garden I'd had in the kitchen window greenhouse of my old apartment.

"It smells good back there, doesn't it?"

I leaned over one of the herb flats to get a better look at the blue-violet, bell-like blooms behind it. "This flower is unusual." It also looked vaguely familiar.

When I tried to breathe in its scent Victoria grasped my arm with a firm grip. "You don't want to get too close to that one."

"Why? What is it?"

"Monkshood. Very pretty, but very dangerous if you don't handle it with the proper precautions."

Monkshood! No wonder it looked familiar. It was one of the toxic plants I'd read about two days ago.

I turned to her, my heart thudding in my chest. "Because it's poisonous."

She locked gazes with me. "It can be."

I struggled to maintain some semblance of calm while alarm bells clanged between my ears. "Why—"

"I'll save you the trouble of asking. I used the monkshood in Marty's tea. It's quite safe when properly diluted as anyone familiar with Chinese herbal medicine would assure you."

Victoria was telling me the truth, but that didn't mean that I was ready to buy everything she had told me hook, line, and sinker.

"Several members of your family, including you, were concerned that your husband ate or drank something that led to his cardiac arrest. I've learned enough about poisonous plants the last few days to know that the symptoms he had…"

Squaring her slender shoulders, her nostrils flared. "It wasn't my tea."

Whether that was the case or not, I knew it was what she believed to be true.

"Does anyone else know that you have this poisonous plant in your greenhouse?" I asked, pointing at it from a safe distance.

"Everyone in the family does. In case anyone wandered back here to help themselves to some fresh herbs, I needed to let them know not to touch the monkshood."

"Is everything okay?" Jeremy called from the doorway.

Victoria smiled at him. "Everything's fine."

Everything was not fine. I now understood exactly why Darlene and Nicole were accusing Victoria of poisoning her husband.

"I was just giving Charmaine a little tour of the green-house," she said.

He stepped aside to let her pass. "The timer went off for the rice."

She smiled up at him. "Then lunch is almost ready." She stood by the door to close it behind me. "You're sure you won't join us?"

"Thanks, but I have to get going." And tell Frankie about the key ingredient in the tea Marty McCutcheon had been drinking.

Jeremy held the French door open for us. "Don't let us keep you then."

Subtle.

"Thank you for your time," I said, heading toward the foyer with Victoria at my heels.

"If there is any other news, please let me know." Her voice was scarcely more than a whisper when we reached the front door. "I really do want to know what killed my husband."

So did I.

✳

"Monkshood," Frankie said, scowling at her computer monitor as she searched a plant toxin database.

I stood by her side, still trying to catch my breath after running up the steps of the courthouse. Yet another reason to lay off the cheeseburgers.

"Aconite. Certainly an infamous poison in ancient times, but an alkaloid not that uncommon in homeopathic medicine." She tapped her pen against a notepad as she read. "That joke about how Marty's wife was trying to kill him certainly makes a lot more sense now that we know what was in his tea."

No kidding.

Frankie tucked a wayward strand of graying auburn hair behind her ear and gazed up at me. "But you believed her when she was telling you all this."

"Mrs. McCutcheon didn't give me any indication that she was lying or holding anything back and was very emphatic that the tea had nothing to do with her husband's cardiac arrest."

"Still, given the witnesses' accounts of what happened at that dinner party, it may have been a contributing factor." She pulled a toxicology lab request form from a file in her desk, put a checkmark next to *Pending Tox*, and wrote *Aconite* in the *Drugs Suspected* column. "Give this to Patsy," she said, handing me the form. "She'll know what to do with it."

"What happens if the results come back positive for aconite? Will there be an official investigation into Marty's death?"

"Let's get the lab results back first. Until that happens

this changes nothing." Frankie sharpened her gaze. "So if Darlene McCutcheon or any family members ask you any questions about this you either refer them to me or say that we'll know more in six to eight weeks."

"Right." I headed for Patsy's desk.

"And Charmaine."

I turned to see Frankie smiling at me.

"You did the right thing to bring this to my attention."

It was my second attagirl in the last two days. If I hadn't stalked Phyllis Bozeman on Saturday to practically accuse her of poisoning her ex-boyfriend, I might have happy-danced my way down the hall.

Instead, I handed the form to Patsy. "We need to send this to the crime lab."

She jutted her pointy chin at me. "We?"

If I ever needed to be cut down to size, I knew who I could rely on. "Frankie asked me to give it to you. It's for Marty McCutcheon."

Patsy scanned the form. "Aconite? That's a new one."

"It's a poisonous alkaloid. Commonly used in ancient times. In fact, it's widely believed that the emperor Claudius died of aconite poisoning."

Her eyes narrowed slightly, reminding me of Myron right before he swatted me in the face with his tail. "Uh-huh."

"Do you think you can get it out today?"

Okay, I admit that I was enjoying my little moment of professional success a tad too much, and I shouldn't have poked the mama bear in front of me. But since Patsy had roped me into playing *Truth or Consequences* with her boyfriend, I thought it only fair that she share in my moment.

She puckered. "I'll get right on it."

I whistled all the way back to my desk. Maybe things were looking up. I had a great guy who wanted to share his bed with me, I had a boss who didn't think I was a total screw-up, and if my hunch was right, a significant level of aconite was going to be found in Marty McCutcheon's urine.

My feet froze to the threadbare carpet as the full weight of that thought made me shiver.

If—and it was still a big if—but if someone had made sure that Marty had consumed enough of the poison to kill him, wouldn't that person have wanted to be there to control the situation? Control who consumed it? When to call for medical assistance?

I rushed back to my desk and pulled out my interview notes, carefully re-reading them.

Both Jeremy and Austin had made it clear that Victoria didn't want to make that call. Even Victoria chided herself for waiting as long as she did. If the salsa had been tainted, Cameron was the only person who mentioned being warned away from it—again, by Victoria.

My pulse pounding in my ears, I did a mental rewind of all the times she seemed to be emotionally off, too helpful, too in control.

No matter how many times Victoria McCutcheon said that she wanted to know what killed her husband without registering a ping on my *liedar*, I couldn't help but think that she already knew.

She certainly wasn't wasting any time burying husband number three.

I'd dismissed it early on as something out of crime fiction, but maybe Darlene had been dead-on when she pointed an accusatory finger at her successor.

Victoria McCutcheon was a black widow.

Chapter Fourteen

A FEW HEADS turned when the silver bell above the Duke's Cafe front door signaled my arrival, but that was nothing out of the ordinary, so the coast seemed clear for me to grab the lunch my growling stomach had been reminding me that I'd missed.

I slid my butt onto the barstool next to ninety-year-old Stanley, who had the sports section of Sunday's newspaper spread out on the counter in front of him. "How's it going, Stanley?"

His eyes, magnified through the thick glasses that were always sliding down his bulbous nose, lit up as he smiled at me. "You disappoint me."

Uh-oh. "Why?"

"I thought you were saving yourself for me."

"A girl can't wait forever, Stan."

"I like to move slowly. Don't want to rush a good thing."

Lucille squeaked up to refill his cup with decaf. "Any slower, old man, and we'd have to call Tolliver's to come pick you up."

He stuck his tongue out at her.

"What'll ya have, hon?" she asked me, her pencil poised over an order ticket.

"A turkey sandwich on wheat to go." I glanced over at Duke, who didn't look pleased to see me. Understandable. He'd been like a second grandfather to me, and while Steve had always been one of his favorites, I was pretty sure Duke wasn't too keen on the notion of Steve and me as a couple.

"Actually, why don't I make it myself, and you can keep me company for a couple of minutes." Because I didn't need any extra ears to overhear the discussion I needed to have with the queen of Gossip Central.

With a nod Lucille followed me into the kitchen.

"What are you two up to now?" Duke grumbled as I washed my hands at the sink behind him.

"Nothing. I'm saving you the trouble of making me a sandwich."

"Uh-huh, and why is Luce back here with you?"

She planted her hands on her hips. "I'm on a break."

He blew out a breath as he flipped a beef patty on the grill. "You've got until this burger is done to finish that break."

Lucille pulled me back to the table where my great-aunt Alice was rolling out pie dough. "Talk first, sandwich later."

Alice looked up at us. "What's going on?"

"That's what I want to know," I said.

Lucille sat on the wooden stool next to Alice. "Like what?"

"Have you heard anything about Victoria McCutcheon being seen around town?"

Lucille and Alice looked at one another and shook

their heads.

"So there's no gossip floating around about her?"

Lucille shrugged a shoulder. "Nothing recent."

I sat down across from her. "What's that supposed to mean?"

"Yeah," Alice chimed in. "What do you know that I don't?"

Lucille looked at my great-aunt like she'd suddenly become senile. "Remember when Pearl came in telling us about Marty breaking it off with her sister after he met someone online?"

I vaguely remembered a music teacher in town named Pearl from when I was a kid. "Who's her sister?" I asked.

Lucille aimed the same look across the table at me. "Phyllis Bozeman, who was none too happy when that pretty young thing came on the scene."

Other than the online part—one of the ways Victoria could have been trolling the region for a rich husband—this sounded like ancient history. "Okay, we're short on time here, so new subject. What do you know about Bob Hallahan's personal life?"

Alice wrinkled her brow. "I know he lost his wife a couple of years back. One of the boys is in the military. The other one's an engineer at Boeing."

"And he sold their big house and recently moved into something smaller over by the school." Lucille hesitated, her eyes searching mine. "But I don't think this is the kind of information you're looking for."

She was right. "Do you know if Bob's been seeing anyone?"

"He's certainly had the opportunity—good-looking man like that. Can't be more than fifty-five, a perfect candidate for some of the younger widows and divorcees around here. Maybe he hasn't been ready to move on."

I wondered if that were still the case.

"Order up!" Duke bellowed.

Heaving a sigh, Lucille pushed herself to her feet. "That man has the worst timing."

Alice chuckled. "He prides himself on it."

The moment that Lucille left to pick up her order, Alice placed her warm palm on my wrist. "What's with all the questions?"

"Don't repeat what I'm about to tell you to anyone, okay?"

Leaning closer, she nodded.

"Estelle Makepeace saw Victoria over at Bob Hallahan's house the Tuesday evening before Marty died."

Alice frowned. "Doesn't necessarily mean anything."

"She referred to Victoria as Bob's *lady friend*, so I think that wasn't the first time she saw them together."

"Oh. Well, that may mean something."

"It may have nothing to do with anything. I just thought that if they had a relationship, that it might have some bearing on..."

Alice sharpened her gaze. "On what?"

"Nothing." I'd already said too much.

"Liar."

"If you hear anything, let me know, okay?"

She patted my hand. "Sure, sweetie. Oh, as long as you're here, when's dinner tonight?"

Huh? "Dinner?"

"Mary Jo said six-thirty or seven. Which is it?"

Since Duke could barely tolerate my mother and her fake accent, I saw no reason for him to arrive early.

"Seven."

Alice picked up her rolling pin and shot me a knowing look. "Be sure to tell Steve to come. From what I'm hearing he's practically family now."

"Don't get too carried away. Like Stanley, I'm trying to take things slowly."

"That's not what I heard this morning."

I cringed. "Well, don't believe everything making the rounds. And he's coaching the peewees tonight, so he can't make it."

She smirked. "Lucky him. He's going to miss out on hearing all about your mother's wedding plans."

Yeah, lucky him. I wondered if it were too late to volunteer for the job of assistant coach.

Almost seven hours later, I split the last of the second bottle of cabernet with Duke while my mother ignored the now cold chicken cacciatore on her plate.

"Of course, we're not looking to make this some grand affair." She beamed at Mr. Ferris as if he actually had some say in the matter. "Simple elegance is what we're going for. I'm thinking classy, serene, understated. With low music and candles."

"Girl, you just described a funeral service at Tolliver's," Duke said, reaching for his wine glass. "I'm sure Curtis would make his chapel available to you for a good price."

Marietta bristled. "I am *not* having my wedding at a funeral home."

"Suit yourself." He pointed at her plate. "You gonna eat that chicken sometime tonight?"

"I'm working on it!" she said without a trace of accent.

"Then make it snappy. Some of us working stiffs have to get up in a few hours."

Alice waved her husband off as if she were shooing a pesky insect. "Mary Jo, we might be able to help you find a hall in town if we knew how large of a wedding you were thinking."

My mother blinked. "A hall? No, no, no. That wouldn't have the ambiance, the *chi* that we're looking for."

"What the hell is chi?" Duke asked.

She smiled across the table at him as if she were a princess addressing one of the less fortunate commoners in her realm. "Energy."

"Energy." He almost spat the word out. "I should have guessed as much." Downing his wine in two big gulps, he pushed his glass toward me.

Figuring that he needed it more than I did, I poured the contents of my glass into his.

Marietta stabbed a bite of chicken with her fork. "The energy of a room is actually quite important. Take this room for example. A little too much negative energy is swirling around if you ask me."

Duke turned to his wife of fifty-two years. "Yeah, so knock it off with the hall suggestions. We need a chi-chi place with ambiance."

Alice glared at him. "What we need is for Mary Jo to tell us more about what she's looking for so that we can help her find it. It's her big day." She looked across the table. "And yours of course, Barry."

"We appreciate that, Alice." Mr. Ferris gazed into Marietta's eyes. "But honestly, I'd be perfectly happy going in front of a judge at the courthouse or hopping on a plane to say our I dos in Vegas."

My mother dropped her fork, awkwardly tittering in a high pitch as if she were auditioning for the role of Glinda in a *Wizard of Oz* remake. Probably because she'd already experienced both those options with marriages that had lasted less than a year. "Don't be silly. We're going to do this right."

"I'm sure you'll find the perfect location. You have two weeks to look around." Two *long* weeks that would require a lot more wine to get through if this evening were any indication.

She looked at me and sighed, "Where do your friends get married?"

Nowhere that would remotely interest her with one exception. "Donna had an outdoor wedding in Port Townsend at Manresa Castle." The first time anyway. "Very pretty grounds. You should check it out."

My mother pointed a lacquered nail at me. "*We* should check it out. After all, you are my maid of honor. You're supposed to help me with these decisions."

She and I both knew that Emily Post wouldn't agree with her. "Let's chat about this later." When I would remind her that this was the type of decision she should be making with her future husband, not me. "Who's ready for dessert?"

Without waiting for an answer, I collected all the dinner plates except for Marietta's and headed into the kitchen, where Alice's famous sour cream apple pie sat on the counter, along with six dessert plates.

Seconds later, my mother set her plate on the stack I'd placed in the sink and turned to face me. "I really could use your help with this." She lowered her voice. "Barry's such a sweetheart, but he's useless when it comes to planning a wedding. He just wants to hurry up and get married. I swear, if I hear that man say *whatever you want to do* one more time, I'm going to lose it."

And if she thought that I was going to spend my every waking hour planning this wedding with her, I was going to lose it!

"Chah-maine, I need someone who will give me an honest opinion."

She didn't want to hear my honest opinion about this wedding. Because I'd be telling her to wait at least a year—well past the typical duration of her infatuations.

"Mom."

"I mean it. You're the only one I trust to tell me what you really think."

"I'm working. I don't have time..."

She inched closer, a hopeful gleam in her emerald eyes. "I'll be happy to work around your schedule."

Marietta wasn't known for working around other people's schedules. Quite the contrary.

While I stared at her, looking for signs she was lying, she took my hand and smiled sweetly, lovingly, and I heard a flushing sound. It was either my resolve going down the crapper, or Duke's prostate was acting up again.

She searched my gaze. "What do you say? Could we take a couple hours tomorrow night and go to Manresa Castle?"

"It will have to be after five."

She clapped her hands. "That'll work out perfectly! There will still be plenty of natural light to see everything when we first get there, but we'll also have an opportunity to see it lit for an evening event."

I forced a smile. "Great."

"And of course we'll need to have dinner there. No point in talking catering before test-driving the menu."

"Fine." No doubt she'd order one of almost everything, take one bite, and leave the rest for me. I made a mental note to wear my fat pants.

"Wonderful! Oh, and I'd like to check out a little chapel up north. Botanical garden, view of the Sound. Barry thought it was a little too far away, but it's supposed to be one of the best wedding venues around. That's worth a look, don't you think?"

I gritted my teeth because the one road trip I'd agreed to had just become two. "Sure."

"When we go, we should probably check out some of the bed and breakfasts up there. The wineries, too. We could even do some wine tasting!"

This *look* she wanted to take was sounding more and more like an all day tour of the north end of the peninsula. "Make a list of all the places you want to see, and we'll try to hit most of them this weekend." *Try* being the operative word. Until Marty's funeral was announced I wasn't going to commit to anything.

"Goody!" She shot me a dazzling smile. "This is going to be fun."

"Yeah, fun."

As I was leaving work the next day I received a text from my mother.

Slight change of plans. Pick me up at Bassett Motors. Driving there now in the D.

Bassett Motor Works was located a few short blocks

away from the courthouse and was on the way to the
north end, so this slight change actually worked to my
advantage. I just hoped that my accident-prone mother
meant that Mr. Ferris was the one driving the DeLorean.

Five minutes later, I pulled in behind Marietta's car
and saw George Junior sitting in the driver's seat with a
big, goofy grin on his face. My mother was in her element
next to him while the Big Dog, George Senior, snapped
several pictures with his camera phone.

"This is so danged cool!" Little Dog said, crawling out
of the car and straightening to his six-foot-six-inch height.

Posing by her DeLorean while George Senior continued his photoshoot, Marietta waved at me. "We'll be
done in a minute."

"No rush." I didn't want to ruin the Bassett boys' fun.

I couldn't say the same for Austin, who was walking
out of the shop with one of the other mechanics.

With his back to Austin, Little Dog grinned at me.
"Hiya, Char! Look at what I'm going to be working on."

"I know she wouldn't trust just anybody with it." And
she was probably reveling in all the attention.

Beaming with pride, he nodded. "Seriously cool."

"Hey!" Austin pulled at Little Dog's arm to spin him
around. "I've been waiting to talk to you."

Looking like a bull threatening to hook Austin with a
horn, Little Dog shook him off. "You want me to work
on your car or not?"

Austin's cheeks reddened and puffed. "That's what I
want to talk to you about."

"Just a minute." Little Dog turned to Marietta. "I'll
give you a call tomorrow to let you know what we find."

She pressed her delicate hand into his grease-stained,

meaty paw. "Thank you, George. Ah appreciate you fittin' me into your busy schedule."

Marietta looked at George Senior. "Ah wonder if you could direct me to your restroom."

"Of course," he said, leading her toward the office and past a pacing Austin.

I didn't know if my mother really did hear the call of nature or if Georgie had just slimed her with a bit of axle grease. Whatever it was I didn't care because Austin looked like he was ready to blow a gasket, and I wanted to hear why.

Sitting in my car with the window cracked open, I pulled out my phone so that I wouldn't appear to be eavesdropping and listened to Austin accuse Little Dog of jacking up a price on him.

"Hey," Little Dog growled in response, "I told you a new transmission would run you around twenty-four hundred."

Austin raked his fingers through his dark hair. "Man, I don't have that kind of money. Not yet anyway."

If he was referring to the money that Nicole would be inheriting, he probably wouldn't see any of it for at least another month.

"I can rebuild it for around seventeen hundred. Will take a little longer, but if you're not in a big hurry—"

"How much longer?"

"I can probably get you in the schedule by the end of the week and have it ready by next Wednesday."

"Another week without her car. My wife is gonna kill me."

I heard a rap on my passenger window and reached over to unlock the door.

"Okay, I'm ready," Marietta announced, fastening her seatbelt. She glanced past me at Austin. "What's his problem? Aside from just being generally disagreeable."

I started the engine and rolled up my window. "I think he has lots of problems. Money being a big one." At least he and Nicole would soon be coming into their portion of Marty's fortune.

"Oh well, I'm sure George and he can work something out. The Bassetts were both very nice about working me into the schedule. Said it was a good day to get me in. Perfect timing in fact."

"Yeah, timing can be everything." For cars and coming into money.

Chapter Fifteen

BY THE TIME Friday rolled around, my mother had prepared a two-page handwritten list of all the wedding venues she wanted to visit this weekend. With Marty McCutcheon's funeral service scheduled for eleven o'clock tomorrow, that would leave little time to spend with Steve, so when he suggested that we meet at Eddie's after work, I jumped at the chance.

It would guarantee great company, delicious food, and a good time, providing a certain doctor didn't show up with a similar idea in mind for his girlfriend.

Walking in while the rhythmic beat of *Addicted to Love* pulsed through the overhead speakers, I scanned the crowd. No Steve, but I spotted Donna sitting at the end of the bar.

"Hey," I said, sliding onto the barstool next to her.

"Hi, hon." She combed her fingers through the bangs that had been hanging in my eyes. "Are you ever going to make an appointment, or do I need to make one for you?"

"I will. Maybe next weekend."

"What's wrong with this weekend? I'm sure I can get you in."

"My mother is planning her wedding to Mr. Ferris, and I've been volunteered to be her wedding venue tour guide for the next couple of days."

Donna wrinkled her nose at the mention of our biology teacher's name. "Why the big rush?"

"He wants to get married as soon as possible."

"Excuse me if I'm speaking out of turn, but this wedding has quickie divorce written all over it."

Probably. "Maybe." I motioned to Eddie who was tending bar, forming a *C* with my thumb and index finger to order my usual chardonnay.

"I'm sure he's nice." She shook her head like she was at a loss for words. "In his own way. But really, never in my wildest dreams would I ever think that your mother would fall for Mr. Ferris."

Me either. "I know."

"It's like a steady diet of vanilla ice cream when you could have something with chunks of chocolate or cookie dough in it, something decadently creamy you want to savor, letting every delicious morsel roll over your tongue."

"I know!" Wait, were we only talking about ice cream? Because my brain was headed somewhere naughty.

"It's gonna spread like a wild fire when the news gets out."

I nodded. Such was life in a small town.

She drained her glass. "It'll be like when Marty McCutcheon ran off and married what's her name."

"Victoria."

"Yeah, her. Everybody was asking one another how did they get together? It wasn't like he was filthy rich. That didn't happen until later." Donna shrugged. "I guess sometimes the attraction is just a mystery. Only it will be a hundred times worse because it's your mother and Mr. Ferris."

I straightened. "Back up. What didn't happen until later?"

"The money Marty inherited from his dad." Donna blinked, her long lashes fluttering. "You didn't know about that?"

I shook my head, leaning closer so that I could hear her over the Van Halen song blasting my eardrums.

"I guess that happened a few months before you came back to town."

"Sorry to keep you waiting," Eddie said, setting my glass of chardonnay in front of me while everyone packed in front of the flat screens erupted into a cheer. "It's a thirsty crowd tonight." He pointed at Donna's glass. "Want another?"

"Can't. Meeting someone in…" She looked at the time on her cell phone. "…ten minutes. Yikes! I need to scoot."

As she reached for her clutch bag, I gripped her wrist. "Finish telling me about this inheritance first, including who you heard this from."

She pursed her full, glossy lips. "Well, it's not like it's a big secret. Remember hearing about how R&E Lumber used to own pretty much everything around here?"

"Sure." R&E was the major player back when Port Merritt was still a mill town. My grandfather had even worked for them.

"The R in R&E was Reginald McCutcheon, Marty's grandpa, and the E was for his wife—Edna or something. The way I understand it from Denise, who volunteers at the museum—nice lady, but she wants to give me a history lesson every time I do her hair. Anyway, according to her, Reggie left everything to his two sons, who ended up selling to a big conglomerate back in the seventies."

"So, when you say filthy rich you mean—"

"They split a fortune worth millions."

Holy crap!

Straightening, Donna got to her feet. "Of course, who knows how much dough was left by the time it made its way to Marty."

I'd bet a chunk of that money that Victoria knew. It probably made Marty quite the catch, and with a father who had to be in his eighties or nineties, she wouldn't have had to wait long to come into some serious money.

Donna hugged me. "Wish me luck."

"Why? Where are you going?"

"I'm meeting a guy. Friend of a friend. If I'm back in an hour, that will make it official."

With everything I'd learned in the last few minutes, I was having trouble parsing Donna's shorthand. "What will be official?"

"That thanks to you, there are no more available men under the age of forty in this town."

I made a face at her.

"That I'd consider doing anyway."

"You could always go out with Kyle."

"You leaving?" Steve asked Donna as he came up behind us.

I hoped he hadn't heard me mention Kyle's name over the music and crowd noise. The last thing I needed to do was to reopen that can of worms.

"Yes, and I'm late, but I took the time to warm the

seat up for you." Donna winked at him. "You'll have to warm her up on your own."

Settling on the barstool she had vacated, Steve looked me up and down. "Do you require warming up?"

"I'm sure I will later."

His lips curled into the disarming smile that first made my heart pitter-pat back in the sixth grade. "Now you're talking."

"Donna was just telling me something interesting," I said as Eddie tossed a coaster in front of Steve.

"Want to try the new microbrew I just got in?" Eddie asked.

Steve didn't answer right away. "Do I ever ask to try something new?"

Eddie arched his eyebrows. "I don't know. Should I ask the lady?"

I could feel my cheeks burning.

"Just give me a draft," Steve said, unamused. "Where's your bride?"

"Kitchen. We're a little backed up because of the playoff game."

While Eddie went to the tap, Steve squinted at the closest TV. "Cool. It's only the third inning." He pressed his warm palm to my knee. "So what was it that Donna was telling you? Some enthralling gossip hot from her salon?"

"Not so hot, but rather topical considering whose funeral you and I are going to tomorrow."

Leaning back, Steve blew out a breath. "Why do I have a feeling that I'm not going to like this?"

"What? Something wrong?" Eddie asked, delivering Steve's beer.

Steve shook his head. "Trust me, you don't want to know."

Eddie smirked. "You're no fun."

"You haven't even heard it yet," I said the second that Eddie turned his back to us.

"I know you."

I made a face at him. "But did you know that Marty was the grandson of the couple who owned R&E Lumber?"

"Yeah, so?"

"And that he came into a lot of money when his father died earlier in the year?"

He gave me the same squint he'd aimed at the TV a minute earlier. "What's your point?"

"If I were a woman looking for a wealthy husband, he'd be quite the prize."

"You keep trying, but I'm not getting on the murder train with you."

"I'm just saying that if what Nicole told me about her father's will is true, Victoria will most likely inherit millions."

"Probably, and not a bit illegal."

I sighed. "It would be if she gave him something that led to his cardiac arrest."

Steve stared at me. "You just can't leave this alone, can you?"

No. "She was making tea for him from a poisonous plant."

His gaze tightened. "I assume that Frankie knows about this plant."

"Yep, she's added it to the tox screen that the lab's going to do."

"Then you'll know soon enough if that had anything to do with his death."

Now it was my turn to stare at him. "Tell me you don't find this suspicious."

He reached for his beer and took a long drink. "Can't do that, Chow Mein."

That wasn't an answer. "So you agree with me that it's suspicious."

"I didn't say that."

"Come on, it's definitely suspicious."

"You obviously think so. Just like you thought Phyllis Bozeman poisoned her grandson."

I scowled at him. "That was a weird coincidence. Anyone could have jumped to the same conclusion."

Steve leaned so close I could smell the beer on his breath. "But no one else did. You did. That should tell you something."

If he was trying to make me feel like a rank amateur investigator he was doing a great job of it.

I reached for my wineglass. "I still think that it's suspicious."

"You're entitled to that opinion."

"Awfully big of you."

His gaze darkened as his lips brushed mine. "You know what else you're entitled to?"

"What?"

"Some warming."

"Mmmm. You'll have to feed me first though."

He grabbed a laminated menu from a holder at the end of the bar. "Pizza?"

"Kitchen's backed up, so it might be a bit of a wait."

"Some things are worth waiting for."

I thought he was talking about the pizza until he winked at me.

Let the warming begin.

*

"It looks like most of downtown Port Merritt is here," I said as we stepped into the packed funeral home chapel.

Gram clucked her tongue. "I told you we should have left earlier. Even Barry and Mary Jo had the good sense to leave by ten-thirty."

That was around the same time that I discovered that I couldn't fasten the waistband of my cheap black funeral suit and had to run across the street to find a safety pin in Gram's sewing room. Dang pizza!

I made the mistake of exchanging glances with Steve, who had a smug look on his face.

"Don't even start about me getting up earlier to go jogging with you." Because I was never going to give him an up close and sweaty view of just how out of shape I was.

Not bothering to hide his amusement, he averted his gaze. "Did I say anything?"

"You didn't have to," I said, following Gram down the aisle to where Duke, Alice, and Lucille sat in the fourth row on the left.

Gram frowned at her sister. "I thought you were going to save us three seats."

"We did." Alice pointed at the empty seat between her and Lucille.

"You two are back here with us," Marietta said, sitting with Mr. Ferris directly behind Alice.

I slipped into the padded folding chair next to my mother and breathed in notes of musky jasmine, mercifully subtle this morning. *Thank you, Mom.*

"You're up early." Unless she was being paid a respectable appearance fee any public sightings before noon were about as rare as pictures of me in a bikini.

Marietta crossed her long legs, barely covered by a short black leather skirt. "Not that you'd know because you haven't been home any morning this week, but I'm still on Louisiana time."

Much more interested in Darlene, Austin, and the McCutcheon children taking their seats in the front row, I ignored the jab. "Hmmm."

While soft piano music pumped through the speakers and tapered candles flickered by the bronze urn draped with a wreath of roses on the table in front of them, I watched the four of them sit in silence. Not that it was any surprise—Austin wasn't touching Nicole.

Seconds later, Curtis Tolliver led Victoria to her front row seat.

Marietta leaned into me. "The widow I take it?"

I nodded.

"Younger than I thought she'd be."

Victoria stopped to hug Cameron, who had been sitting in the second row next to a slim brunette in a navy blue suit.

"Who's that?" my mother whispered.

"He's one of Marty's employees. I don't know her." But by the way Darlene appeared to be staring across the aisle at the woman, it was a safe bet that she had seen her before.

Cameron's mother? He certainly had her coloring.

Bob Hallahan and Phyllis Bozeman sat to her right, both of them with their sights set on Marty's widow.

As Victoria took her seat I noticed Darlene sneaking another glance at the brunette, but this time Victoria, Cameron, and the woman were all staring back at her.

"Oh, mah." Marietta fanned herself with the program for Marty's memorial. "It appears to be heating up in here."

She wasn't kidding. Nor were we the only ones aware of the tension rising on both sides of the aisle. Curtis immediately gave a hand signal to Reverend Fleming to take the podium and then stood to the side for the next hour like a watchful Secret Service agent.

With an instrumental version of *What a Wonderful World* marking the end of the ceremony, we funneled into the foyer following Marty's women and progeny, who Curtis was herding into two separate corners of the reception room.

"Looks like he wants to keep Darlene and the family away from Victoria," I whispered to Steve as we made our way to the punch bowl.

"The woman who was sitting behind Victoria, too."

As usual, Steve had missed nothing.

"Who is she?" he asked, handing me a paper cup of fruity punch.

"I can guess."

"Well?"

I shook my head. "Later." When there weren't so many ears around us.

Lucille stepped out of the receiving line for Victoria

and sidled up beside me. "Okay, who's the dame in the blue suit?"

"Don't know."

She frowned. "Do you think she could be Bob's girl-friend? The one you were asking about?"

"I have no idea and please don't mention that to anyone else," I whispered in her ear.

"Hey, if it was a state secret you should have said so!" she stage-whispered back, turning a couple of heads.

As soon as she rejoined Alice and Duke in Victoria's receiving line, Steve pulled me close. "And why were you asking about Bob Hallahan?"

I painted my most innocent smile on my face. "No reason. I was just chatting with the girls."

"Sure you were."

"And speaking of chatting," I said, hooking my arm through my grandmother's when she stepped up to the punch bowl. "Let's go pay our respects to Darlene." Especially since that was the direction Cameron and the woman in blue were headed.

Gram looked back longingly as I led her toward the other side of the room to where Austin and the rest of the McCutcheon family stood near a white sheet cake on a cloth-draped table. "But I wanted to get some punch."

Falling into step behind Cameron, I handed Gram my cup. "You can have mine."

She looked at me quizzically. "What are you up to?"

"Nothing. The line's shorter, that's all."

Assessing the two people in line in front of us, she narrowed her gaze. "Uh-huh."

While we waited for the mayor and one of the city council members to stop glad-handing Jeremy and his mother, I watched the way Darlene kept staring at Cameron, now standing at the front of the line.

She knows.

She whispered something to Jeremy, then walked away from the crowd to the unoccupied far corner.

The brunette in front of us took Cameron's arm and they set out to join Darlene.

"What's going on?" Gram asked.

"Couldn't say." But since Darlene had moved the conversation away from her children, it clearly had to do with something she didn't want them to hear.

"Well, heck!" Gram grumbled, stepping out of line. "I can't very well pay my respects to Darlene if she isn't here. This might have been the shorter receiving line, but it was a big waste of time."

No, it wasn't. Darlene had obviously recognized the woman Cameron was with, probably because Darlene had seen her while she was still married to Marty. I didn't get a close enough look to tell if she'd been surprised to see Cameron. My gut told me yes, but that the surprise was seeing him here in Port Merritt, not that another son of Marty's existed. And if that were true, Darlene was very good at keeping secrets—from her children and from Marty.

I spotted two of Gram's mahjong buddies, Estelle and Angela, sitting with Alice and Lucille. "Why don't you sit down with the girls and have some cake."

"Sounds good. I'm ready to get off my feet," Gram said.

Me, too, but since the meeting that Darlene had called in the corner appeared to be breaking up, now wasn't the time for cake. As long as I had a safety pin at the waist of my too-tight pants, I didn't need cake anyway. Much like I hadn't needed that fourth slice of pizza last night.

I sighed. For someone who needed to lose thirty pounds I sure made some stupid decisions.

"You okay, honey?" Gram asked me as Cameron and the woman walked past us.

"Sure. I think I'm just a little bit lightheaded." And perplexed because they had just disappeared into the foyer.

Gram handed me the punch she'd been sipping for the last few minutes just as I knew she would. "Drink this."

I quickly downed the cup and deposited her in the chair by Estelle. "I'll get you some more punch."

Right after I got a breath of fresh air so that I could find out where they had gone. I was a little hot in my too-tight suit, so I could definitely use some fresh air. At least that's what I hoped would sound believable to Steve, who had followed me into the foyer.

"The party's back here," he said.

Watching Victoria act like a bereaved widow in front of a hundred people she barely knew wasn't nearly as interesting as what I'd just witnessed. "Yeah, just getting a little air."

He placed his hands on my shoulders. "So, who is she?"

"I think she's his mother," I whispered.

"He has his dad's eyes."

This certainly wasn't the easiest secret to keep. "Yes, he does."

"Probably not a big surprise that they left so quickly given the circumstances."

"Probably." But it made me wonder who besides Darlene and Victoria knew about those circumstances.

Chapter Sixteen

AN HOUR LATER, I was sitting with Gram and Steve and eating the piece of cake I didn't need while I watched my mother and Mr. Ferris bring up the rear of Victoria McCutcheon's receiving line.

"That poor woman," Gram said between sips of punch. "She looks like she's been through the wringer."

Poor would never be an adjective I'd use to describe Victoria. Like Darlene had told me the day after her ex-husband had died, Victoria would be receiving quite a windfall for the twelve months she had been married to Marty.

As for her emotional state, I suspected that the lovely woman in the black pencil dress was the best actress in the room. Like Marietta who was giving her a consoling hug, Victoria knew how to work a crowd. She knew exactly what to say and how to look, especially for the men in that crowd.

Since one of the men by her side was Bob Hallahan, this appeared to be the perfect opportunity to offer my condolences and have a few quiet moments with the two of them.

"You're right, Gram. She looks worn out. I'm going to see if she'd like some tea." And not the kind of tea she had been serving her husband.

Steve arched an eyebrow.

"There's tea?" Gram said, looking around. "I'd love some tea."

"Steve will get it for you." I smiled sweetly at him and headed in Bob's direction before Steve could offer any challenge to my volunteering his services.

The tall man with the graying dark brown hair stood off to Victoria's side like her personal protector.

I extended my hand. "I don't know if you remember me. I'm Charmaine. I used to work at—"

"At Duke's, where you always gave me extra coleslaw with my fish and chips." He shook my hand. "Of course, I remember you."

"Good, because you and Marty were two of my favorite customers."

Okay, that was a stretch because Stanley and Steve had them by a mile, but like my grandmother told me when she once had explained why people sometimes chose to lie, you catch more flies with honey.

Bob's gaze lowered, his lips registering a fleetingly sad smile.

"It got so I never even asked Marty what he wanted for lunch. Duke would see him come through the door and throw a couple of patties on the grill for his cheeseburger."

"The man loved his cheeseburgers." Bob shook his head. "It's amazing that he was able to keep eating them and still lose weight."

"I hadn't realized that he'd lost weight." Especially

with the way everyone had characterized him as a big eater.

"Forty pounds. I only know because he said something about celebrating that on his birthday."

Thank you for opening that door. "Victoria mentioned that you weren't able to attend the dinner party at his house."

The creases at the corners of his eyes tightened. "No, I had a conflict and couldn't make it."

Lie.

"Seems wrong, doesn't it?" I asked, watching him for a reaction.

He stood statue still as silent seconds ticked between us. "What?"

I leaned a little closer. "To pass away on your birthday. It just seems cruel somehow."

"Maybe." He glanced over at Victoria, speaking in hushed tones with Curtis Tolliver. "No matter what, it's hard on the ones left behind."

It came as no surprise to hear him ally himself with his best friend's wife.

"I imagine it's particularly difficult at work. What do you think will happen there?" I already knew that Jeremy had taken over, but I wanted to hear how Bob felt about it.

A humorless grin flashed across his face. "It's going to be challenging."

At first I thought the grin had everything to do with Jeremy, but since Curtis had moved on from Victoria to my mother and was now regaling her with all his favorite moments from *The Peachtree Girls*, I wasn't convinced. "I'm sure Jeremy will do his best to step into his dad's shoes."

Bob's lips flatlined. "I'm sure he'll try to."

I heard the sound of footfalls behind me and turned to see Phyllis Bozeman offer a hug to Victoria.

Whatever words were exchanged with Phyllis caused Victoria's eyes to well up with tears for the first time this afternoon.

I had to hand it to her. The waterworks looked real. Maybe not to Darlene, who was aiming daggers at Victoria from the other side of the room, but they sure did to me. Bob, too, who had gone to her side to offer her the handkerchief from his jacket pocket the instant that Phyllis stepped away.

"I'm okay," Victoria said, head lowered, her eyes squeezed shut.

Marietta flanked her while Curtis rushed up with a folding chair. "Honey, you don't look okay. Maybe you should sit down."

"Would you like some tea?" I asked. A little late but at least I'd made good on the excuse I'd used to come over here.

Victoria trembled, struggling to speak as tears streamed down her cheeks. "I…"

Bob wrapped his arm around her back, turning her away from the watchful eyes of Darlene and her children. "There's nothing more that you need to do here. Let's get your things."

While Curtis and Bob escorted Victoria into the funeral director's office off the foyer, I inhaled a whiff of jasmine as Marietta edged up next to me.

"The poor thing," she said without a trace of accent. "I may have gotten rid of three husbands, but at least they didn't all die on me. It has to take a toll."

"I'm sure." Maybe it did. It was hard to fake the emotion I'd just witnessed in Marty's widow. That didn't mean that she wasn't the one who grew the poison used to kill him, or that it wasn't agony to watch him or any of her husbands die. But I had a feeling that several million dollars would soon help her cope with the pain.

Marietta glanced back at Mr. Ferris, who was sitting with one of the other Port Merritt High teachers. "I think Barry wants to leave soon, which is fine with me." Leaning into me, she hooked her arm around mine. "But I was thinking."

Uh-oh. I could feel several hours of chauffeur service coming on.

"If your grandmother is ready to get out of here, why don't the three of us head up north to see that chapel? The botanical gardens, too. It's a little after two so we should have plenty of time to see everything before it gets dark." She brightened. "It could be like a girls' day out—something fun after all this somber stuff."

It wasn't my idea of fun, but I'd already agreed to help her find a wedding venue, so I couldn't very well say no. "Okay, if Gram's game."

"Not a chance," Gram stated after I floated the idea to her. She reached out a hand and Steve pulled her to her feet. "I have weeding to do."

I lowered my voice so that my mother and Barry, saying their farewells to his teacher friends, wouldn't hear me. "You'd rather weed your garden than help your own daughter plan her wedding?"

I'd resorted to a heavy handed guilt approach. I knew she'd recognize it because my grandmother had used it on me enough times over the years, but I didn't care.

Gram pursed her lips. "And walk all over Timbuktu to find the perfect place for a wedding I think she's rushing into? I'll pass."

I turned to Steve. "Want to—"

"No," he said flatly.

"You're a big help."

He winked at Gram. "I'm needed to make sure your grandmother gets home safely."

Before I could get a good glare off at him, Marietta and Mr. Ferris had joined us. "Are we ready to go?" she asked.

Gram handed me her car keys. "Have a good time. Barry, may we intrude upon you for a ride home?"

"Of course," he said without hesitation.

Marietta wedged herself between her fiancé and her mother. "You're not coming?"

"Don't think these old feet could handle that much walking." Gram smiled at her. "You two go have fun."

Yeah, I thought, heading out the door. *That could happen.*

"You know, I hadn't considered all the walking." Marietta shot me a sideways glance as the chunky heels of her short boots thunked, thunked, thunked down the stairs to the parking lot. "Maybe we should change into jeans and more comfortable shoes."

I didn't relish the idea of spending the next few hours in a too-tight pantsuit, but since Bob Hallahan and Victoria were in the silver SUV easing past me, the only side trip I wanted to make was to get a sense of where they were headed.

And given the fact that Bob was turning left onto Main Street instead of right toward Clatska, I knew I needed to hurry. "Let's get as much done as we can. Do you have your list?"

Marietta patted her tote bag. "Got it!"

I opened the passenger door of my grandmother's Honda, double-parked behind Mr. Ferris's car. "Then let's roll."

Forty minutes later, I was headed northwest on 101, twenty car lengths behind Bob's SUV, when I saw his right turn signal flashing.

I put on my turn signal.

"According to the directions they gave me over the phone, the exit for the botanical gardens is the next one," my mother said, pointing at the map that she had been studying for most of the trip.

"I saw a sign back there for a bed and breakfast. It's on the way so let's check it out."

"This wouldn't have something to do with the car that we've been following, would it?"

"What car?"

Marietta peered at me over her designer sunglasses. "Give me some credit. You've been pacing them ever since we got on the highway."

I sighed as I took the exit. "Fine. Victoria McCutcheon is in that car, and I was curious about where they were going."

"We've been following Victoria and that nice man she was with ever since we left the funeral home?"

"There are some possible extenuating circumstances concerning her husband's death and—"

"She had something to do with his death?"

"No, no, no," I said, taking a right turn at a stop sign

and following the flash of silver in the distance. "This is just… I'm just trying to…" Criminy, I couldn't think of a believable lie.

"You do! You think she had something to do with his death, and you're tailing them to find out where they stashed something that went missing." She slapped her knee. "Oh, my gosh, it's like the episode when I had to follow a suspect to an abandoned warehouse, but he spotted the DeLorean and drew a gun on me."

"There won't be anyone drawing any guns on us. I'm just conducting a little research."

She pulled something out of her bag. "Well, in the event that anyone gives us any trouble, I'm ready."

I didn't like the sound of that and glanced over at the Taser resting on the map. "Are you crazy? Put that away!"

"It's in the case. It's perfectly safe. So, who is he to her exactly?"

"Her husband's best friend."

"He doesn't look at her like a friend."

That's what I thought.

"I take it you think they're lovers?" she asked.

Having lost sight of Bob's car, I turned left at the sign for the bed and breakfast. "I don't know."

"And her husband died suddenly."

"Yeah."

"Sounds like a movie I made a few years back, only I was the rich wife my cheating husband and his girlfriend killed off." Marietta heaved a pensive sigh. "Probably one of my best death scenes ever."

And she'd had plenty in all the horror films she'd been in.

"Pity most of it ended up on the cutting room floor.

You saw it though, right?"

I never missed any of her movies. No matter how bad most of them were, she was still my mother. "You were good in that."

She stared straight ahead, a smug smile on her lips. "You're darned right I was good."

Making a steady climb to a bluff overlooking Protection Island, we followed an arrow up a driveway to the River Rock Inn.

"This is lovely," Marietta said, removing her sunglasses as we drove past a wishing well fashioned out of the same river rock as the quaint cottages on the manicured grounds behind it.

Maple trees aglow in the copper tones of early fall lined the short drive that led to a parking area in front of what had to have been the original house on the property.

A short white picket fence bordered the rose garden that separated the four-car parking area from the gabled two-story house with the rock turret.

With the exception of the two modern-day cars parked in front of it, the house looked like something out of a fairytale. Since one of those cars belonged to Bob Hallahan, I knew I needed to get out of sight and fast.

Seeing that the driveway continued down a gentle slope where it curved around a stand of young fir trees, I pulled in behind them and killed the ignition.

My mother dropped her Taser back into her tote. "Goody," she said, reaching for the door handle.

I gripped her arm. "Where are you going?"

"To look around."

"No, no. Remember when you did stakeouts on your show?"

"Yeah?"

"You didn't get out of the car and look around. You stayed put, where it was safe."

She folded her arms. "Fine."

After a minute of fidgeting, Marietta took off the olive green suede jacket she'd been wearing. She glanced at me. "Aren't you hot?"

Heck, yes. I'd been parboiling in my wool funeral suit for almost five hours and by the smell of my rapidly failing deodorant, I should have been about done. "I'm fine."

"Suit yourself." Marietta chuckled. "No pun intended."

"Yeah, very punny."

Smirking, she started drumming against the center console. "What do you think they're doing in there?"

I could think of one thing. "I have no idea."

"How long do you think we're going to be sitting out here?"

"Again, no idea."

I heard another minute of drumming.

"I'm going to need a bathroom soon," she said.

"It's barely been an hour. I swear you have a bladder the size of a walnut."

"Sorry, I had two cups of tea before we left."

I looked up and saw movement by the SUV. Seconds later, Bob drove away, alone.

"He's leaving." Marietta glanced at the time on her cell phone. "Wow, if that was a quickie—slam, bam, and thank you, ma'am."

She fastened her seatbelt.

"We're not going anywhere just yet," I told her. "Victoria's still here, so let's give him a half hour to get to that little store we passed and back."

Sighing, Marietta unbuckled her belt and crossed her legs.

A half hour later, after no return trip by an SUV, I started the ignition and turned on the air conditioning. "Okay, let's go find a bathroom, then we'll check out that chapel."

She buckled in. "Yay."

"Where is it again?"

"Near Protection Arch Botanical Gardens. If we go back to 101 and take the next exit—"

"An actual address would be helpful."

"River Rock Chapel, 600 Old Bluff Road."

"We took Old Bluff Road to get here."

"Then we must be really close."

Driving past the house I noticed a hand-painted shingle with the number *600* hanging from the picket fence.

I hit the brakes. "Here? Your chapel is on the grounds of this bed and breakfast?"

"How wonderful! Park the car."

"But Victoria is here somewhere."

"Relax. She knows about the wedding, so it's the perfect cover story."

"It's too coincidental. She'd never buy it."

"We probably won't even see her. Plus, I need to pee, so park the flippin' car!"

"Fine!"

I backed up and pulled into the space Bob had vacated. "Let's keep a low profile, so try to be more Mary Jo than Marietta if you know what I mean."

"Just relax and let me handle this."

Relax, right. A serial killer might be inside the house

and my mother wanted me to relax. "Keep your Taser handy."

Marietta patted her tote bag. "I've got this. Now stop acting like a nervous Nellie."

Who was acting? Certainly not me.

A minute later the front door opened and a middle-aged woman with soft brown curls and plump cherub cheeks smiled politely at Marietta.

"Hello! My daughter and I are planning a June wedding and were hoping to take a look at the chapel."

"Certainly. But June is filling up fast so we should check the schedule book to see if your date is available." The woman stepped back from the door. "If you'll follow me."

"This is lovely," Marietta said as we stepped into a hardwood entryway that looked much newer than the World War I-era home. "Very homey."

"Thank you. We do our best to make our guests comfortable." The woman led us past a sitting room to a small office opposite the white banister staircase. "Please, have a seat."

She settled behind a desk with Marietta sitting across from her. While they discussed dates the chapel was available, I looked at some of the pictures on the wall.

"Look at this one," my mother said, pointing at the photo hanging closest to the desk. "The light streaming through the windows is absolutely gorgeous."

"Nice." I took a closer look at the bride—a beautiful Chinese woman in a sleeveless ivory sheath—standing next to a bear of a man.

Holy moly! It was a picture of Victoria and Marty McCutcheon.

"As you can see, the stained glass creates a lovely backdrop for wedding pictures." The cherub pointed at a grainy photo of a man with a bushy gray mustache standing in the chapel with a young woman in black. "The original owner imported it from Italy as an anniversary gift for his wife."

"And are you the current owner?" I asked, wondering why she had hung the picture of Victoria and Marty next to the one of the original owner.

"I'm Rhonda, the manager." She pointed at Victoria's wedding picture. "Mrs. McCutcheon is the owner."

Chapter Seventeen

"IT'S JUST AS well that your grandmother didn't come with us. My feet are killing me," Marietta said, rubbing a bare foot as we cruised past the *Welcome to Port Merritt* sign at the north end of town. "At least we were able to cross the chapel and the botanical gardens off the *must see* list."

And I was able to discover Victoria McCutcheon's home away from home. From what Rhonda had told us, it was where *poor Mrs. McCutcheon* had met her late husband. Maybe Victoria used her charm in tandem with that of the River Rock Inn much like a fisherman made use of a shiny lure, representing herself as a financially independent woman to attract big fish.

A multimillionaire like Marty was a whopper of a fish, especially in these parts. I wouldn't say the same for Bob. As one of the people at the flooring shop who had access to that bottle of salsa, maybe he was more of a scavenger fish, a less attractive functionary to perform the more unpleasant tasks. For a price? If Bob was expecting a share of the wealth, I'd take a clue from his dead friend and remind myself that some people weren't very good about sharing.

I also wouldn't attend any dinner parties at Victoria's house.

"So, it's two down and five potential venues to go, right?" I asked, hoping that we could use tomorrow afternoon to wrap up this episode of *Wedding Impossible*.

"Actually, six."

"What? When did the sixth one get added?"

"Today, when we passed a cute little chapel behind a big totem pole. It looked darling."

"Next to a big brown building with lots of RVs in the parking lot?"

"Yes! That's the one. I didn't care much for the look of that building, but it seems like the parking would be a plus. Especially since some of Barry's family sound like RV people."

"Sheesh, listen to you, Miss Priss."

"I'm just saying that the parking might come in handy."

"Uh-huh. If there are any grifters or riverboat gamblers in the family, they might enjoy that big brown casino. I know Gram and all her penny slot friends would."

"A casino?" My mother crossed the last item off her list. "I am *not* getting married at a casino."

And then we were back down to five.

Driving past Old Town, I put on my right turn signal.

"Why are we turning here?"

"I want to check something out."

"Does it have something to do with Steve?" she asked as we passed the police station.

"Nope." And he wouldn't be overjoyed to know where I was headed.

"Speaking of Steve, don't you think moving in with

him is rushing things?"

"I'm in his guest room." At least that's where I had moved my clothes in case Marietta came over to have another motherly chat with Steve. "And it's temporary."

"Be that as it may, think of how it looks."

I had been the odd duck in this town ever since my mother brought me here to live with her parents. Now that Rox and Eddie knew about Steve and me, I guess I didn't care about how it looked as much as I cared about how Steve felt about me.

I tightened my grip on the steering wheel. "As you told me a few hours ago, relax and maybe think twice about which one of us is rushing things."

Marietta folded her arms while she vented a little steam. "I am waiting nine long months to marry the man I love—a man who would prefer to run off and tie the knot tomorrow. I could have a baby sooner! Okay, not now I couldn't, but I had you in eight and a half, so don't talk to me about rushing things!"

I clenched my teeth. "You started it."

"And I'm finishing it." She straightened, lifting her chin with the air of a queen who would not deign to have RV-driving relations.

While she fumed during a few moments of blessed silence, I turned right on E Street and eased past Bob Hallahan's house, where his silver SUV was parked in the driveway.

"Isn't that the same car that you followed to the River Rock Inn?" Marietta asked.

"Yep." And now I knew where he had gone after he left Victoria.

Maybe this was part of the plan, to avoid drawing

attention to their relationship. Or maybe he was simply a nice widower who had made the mistake of falling in love with the wrong woman. Whatever it was, Bob was involved somehow, and I was dying to know how.

Almost twenty-four hours later, my mother and I were driving back in Gram's Honda after an afternoon of wine tasting at three of the northern peninsula wineries. As it turned out there wasn't a wedding location in the bunch to suit her. At least we discovered a fume blanc that pleased her discriminating palate along with the wine-infused chocolate truffles I plied myself with to get through our five hours of *togetherness*.

As for the wedding venues on my mother's list, her top candidates were still the River Rock Chapel, complicated by the fact that it was owned by a possible serial killer, and the gazebo in the botanical garden. With two more locations to visit, I was leaning toward any venue (with some semblance of the *chi* she had to have) owned by someone who didn't leave dead people in her wake.

Since I'd been away most of the day, I turned up Third Street and looked for Steve's car at the police station. No car. Good. I could only hope that he was enjoying his day off. At least one of us should.

Marietta shot me a sideways glance. "You can't leave it alone, can you?"

Good grief! She was starting to sound like Steve.

I shook off the mental whiplash and turned on E to do a drive-by of Bob Hallahan's house. "I'm just looking."

"What for?"

Answers. Clues. Something to help me understand

what the heck the McCutcheon women had been doing at
his house the week of Marty's death. If Bob had some sort
of symbiotic relationship with Victoria, I could rationalize
taking the risk to meet at his house. But what role did
Darlene play in all this?

I slowed as we approached the dark green house with
the cream trim. "Remember the extenuating circumstances
I mentioned yesterday?"

"Yes, but—"

"Ditto that."

She sighed. "I see a house, cars, and no people. I don't
know what's here to help with those circumstances, but I
need to pee soon so let's hurry up and get home."

Since one of the cars she was referring to was parked
directly in front of Bob's house, I pulled up behind a row
of mailboxes a door down from Estelle's rambler to make
a note of the license plate.

"Do you recognize the car?" Marietta asked.

"Not really." The late model coupe looked a little
familiar, but that was probably because I'd seen it parked
downtown or at Eddie's.

"Maybe Estelle knows who it belongs to."

"I don't want to involve her in this." I'd done more
than enough of that already.

Marietta waved. "Too bad, because she's headed this
way."

Stifling a cringe, I rolled down the window. "Hi,
Estelle. I was just showing my mom…" I pointed at the
first thing I saw. "…this hydrangea in your neighbor's
yard. Amazing color this late in the season."

She waved it off as if the gardener next door couldn't
compete with her green thumb. "If you think that's

something, come with me."

I didn't want to leave the cover of the car, but if Bob happened to look out his window and see us, at least this would have the appearance of a social visit to Estelle.

"If I do say so myself," she said proudly as my mother and I followed her to the side yard, where two tall hydrangeas full of blue and lavender blooms hugged the outer wall of her living room, "these two put that other one to shame."

"What glorious colors and so many different shades." Marietta stepped in front of me, giving me the perfect opportunity to hang back and casually glance across the street.

Fortunately, the sun had set twenty minutes earlier and Bob's lights were on, so I had decent visibility through the sheer curtains covering his picture window. Unfortunately, all I could see was an unoccupied living room.

After a few minutes of seeing nothing more than the occasional shadow across the street while Estelle gave us a tour of her garden, she and my mother headed inside so that Marietta could use the bathroom.

"Want to come in?" Estelle asked me as she reached for her front door. "It's getting chilly out now that the sun's down." She sniffed the air. "Smells good though. Someone must be grilling burgers for supper."

And they were making me hungry. But what I wanted a heckuva lot more than a burger was a better vantage point to get a look at who was inside that house.

Scanning the immediate vicinity, I spotted a *For Rent* sign in the overgrown front yard of the house next door to Bob's.

I pointed at the sign. "Actually, I'm going to check out

the rental across the way."

Marietta looked at me quizzically, like she was trying to figure out why I was suddenly interested in this rental house. "I'll just be a minute."

"Take your time," I said, meandering across the street to see if the house was occupied.

Walking up the driveway I spotted no curtains over the windows. A basket on the wooden porch contained a short stack of informational flyers that the owner must have set out. When I leaned over to pick one up I looked through the front window. No furniture.

Perfect. There was no one here to chase me out of their yard.

The rental didn't have much landscaping to speak of, just a weed-choked lawn that was overdue for mowing and some mounds of heather and scrubby azaleas bordering the lot. Except on Bob's side, where he had a six-foot-tall fence surrounding the greenery in his back yard.

As I quickly found out when I rounded the attached garage, that fence was going to present a problem. There was no raised deck, no vantage point I could use to see inside the house short of climbing the cedar tree in the back corner, and my tree-climbing days were way behind me.

That left me one option: the fence.

I'd look more like a spy than a prospective renter, which was so not the image I was going for over here. All the more reason to be quick about this and skedaddle back across the street before Estelle, the neighborhood watchwoman, saw me.

At least it was getting dark and I was wearing a black

hoodie and jeans, so unless someone shined a light on me, I shouldn't look like anything more than a shadow if I picked a spot behind some foliage. Of course, that bit of logic didn't keep my heart from thudding in my chest as I tiptoed around a clump of heather and peered through a gap in the fence.

I did a quick scan of the back yard to check for movement. Nothing.

So far, so good.

The spotlight mounted above a sliding glass door was on. Because someone was on the deck? I didn't see anyone, just some patio furniture—four chairs and a table—and a gas grill with the burgers that I'd been smelling for the last few minutes.

I saw a figure move by the door, but a bushy rhododendron on the other side of the fence was obscuring my view, so I shifted to my right until I found a knothole in the clear. Closing one eye I focused on the person by the door—Bob Hallahan.

He was talking to someone.

The door slid open. Standing very still I held my breath.

Bob looked back at the person inside the house. "You have to exercise some patience. I know it's tough but it's only been a little over a week."

Since what? Since Marty had died?

"I know," a male on the other side of the door said. "But you weren't there. You didn't see it."

"Just keep your cool." Bob stepped to the grill, turned off the flame, and transferred the burgers to the plate in his hand.

My cell phone in my back pocket started vibrating. I

couldn't risk Bob seeing the illumination of the display if I pulled out my phone to turn it off, so I had to trust that he couldn't hear the buzzing from thirty feet away.

The other guy stepped to the door. "Hey, man, I'm trying."

I was trying, too, to get a better angle so that I could see him. While my phone buzzed with another text message, he turned toward me.

Holy smoke! Cameron!

"Try harder," Bob said as he stepped back into the house.

The second he slid the glass door shut I took it as my cue to scamper to the car as fast as my legs would carry me.

It was also the same moment that my phone started ringing.

Crap!

Sprinting to the far side of the rental, I sounded like I'd run a hundred-yard dash by the time I finally answered.

"Where are you?" my grandmother asked. "And what have you been doing? You sound out of breath."

"I had to run to the phone."

"Oh, that explains why you didn't respond to my texts."

Jiminy Christmas, she was as impatient as her daughter.

"Dinner's going to be ready soon." The implication was clear in her voice, just like it had been when I was a kid. I had better come home. Immediately.

No one needed to convince me that it was time to make like a homing pigeon returning to the nest. "We'll be there in a few minutes."

"Good, because Steve and Barry are here, and while

I'm sure they find my company quite charming, I think they'd enjoy yours more."

I pocketed my phone, collected my mother, and headed for home, where my favorite cop was sure to be very pissed if Marietta breathed a word about what I'd just done.

I could feel her staring at me. "What?"

"You tell me. What'd you find out?"

"I found out who belonged to the car." And then some.

"Well?"

"It was just a guy he works with." I shook my head as if seeing Cameron there had been of no consequence.

"That's it? I was in that house with all those cats for a guy from work?"

I didn't dare tell her what I thought that guy from work might be involved in.

She ran her palms down the legs of her designer jeans. "I am positively coated with cat hair."

"Hey, you're wearing an angora sweater. I'm sure no one will even notice. Just don't mention anything about what just happened. Steve isn't involved in this case, and I'd like to keep it that way."

Marietta groaned, scratching the base of her throat. "I feel like I need to be deloused."

She was still scratching ten minutes later when she sat down next to Mr. Ferris at the dining table.

"So, where did you two go today?" Steve asked, watching her.

Fortunately, my mother was eager to prattle on about

the wineries we had visited while I poured the fume blanc.

Steve reached for his glass. "Did you have a run-in with a cat while you were there?"

Marietta locked gazes with me.

"More than one," I said, covering for her. "Which is exactly why one of those wineries is out of the wedding sweepstakes."

Mr. Ferris turned to her. "What about the others? Any possibilities?"

She gave her head a little shake. "Pretty grounds but other than the wine, not much to offer. I just *loved* the stone chapel we saw yesterday though." She turned to me. "What was the name of it again?"

Dang, I thought she would have finished talking about it during their date last night. "River Rock Chapel." I passed her the mashed potatoes with the hope that she'd start focusing her attention on the meal in front of her.

"Ooooh, that's right. It was so lovely, and it had the most beautiful stained glass. You should see the way light shines through it. Oh." Marietta stared across the table at me. "I should have asked what time of day that picture was taken."

"What picture?" Barry asked.

I jumped in to keep my mother from mentioning any names. "A wedding picture we saw in the office. One of the many weddings that have taken place there over the years."

She spooned a thimbleful of potatoes onto her plate. "Wait until you see it."

Barry grinned. "I don't think I can wait after listening to all this. We should go tomorrow, after school. I could pick you up—"

"No!" My cheeks burning, all eyes at the table turned to me. "I mean, Mom and I have plans to see the rest of the places on her list tomorrow."

"Good heavens, honey," Gram said, passing Steve the platter of biscuits. "You don't have to act like it's a matter of life and death."

As long as Victoria McCutcheon was staying on the property like a black widow in her nest, I wanted my mother to keep a safe distance. "Life and death." I laughed Gram off. "It's just that we have an appointment at one of the places tomorrow."

Mr. Ferris narrowed his eyes at me.

I'd seen the look before, back when I was giggling at the dead-on Barry Ferris impersonation Austin was doing behind me in science lab.

"Is there something you'd like to share with the rest of the class, Charmaine?"

Nope.

"Fine," he said. "We'll go later in the week."

I could only hope that Victoria was back home by then.

"You gonna tell me what that deal at dinner was all about?" Steve asked when we were getting ready for bed four hours later.

Absolutely not. "I have no idea what you mean."

"Is there some reason why you don't want good ol' Barry to see that chapel?"

I shrugged and crawled under the covers of his king-sized bed. "Yeah, my mother and I have other plans tomorrow."

He slid into bed next to me. "You are such a bad liar."

I rolled onto my side to face him. "She has three more venues on her list, and I'm taking her to see them tomorrow after work. Now what about that isn't true?"

"Nothing."

I reached behind me to turn off the lamp on the nightstand. "I rest my case."

"What's up there that you don't want him to see?"

"Nothing." It was more like who was up there that I didn't want to see my mother, especially if Victoria had spotted us there Saturday.

He blew out a breath. "You know I don't believe you."

I kissed him. "Believe me now?"

"Not yet."

I kissed him again. "What about now?"

"It's gonna take more convincing than that."

I wrapped my arms around his neck and pulled him close. "You drive a very hard bargain."

He rolled me on top of him. "You have no idea how right you are."

Chapter Eighteen

I SPENT MOST of my Monday inside a stuffy conference room, helping one of the more junior prosecuting attorneys interview witnesses for an upcoming elder abuse case. After more than six hours of staring at people's faces, weighing their actions against their statements, my eyes burned, my head felt like a lemon that had been squeezed dry, and my lungs ached for fresh air.

And now they still ached, even after watching the sun set behind the Olympic Mountain range from the wedding gazebo of the Rainshadow Ridge Resort. Of course, that could have been because my mother smelled like she'd been flea-dipped in a bath of jasmine.

"Just tell me that we're done now." At least I could breathe a little easier if she had checked every wedding venue candidate off her list.

She sighed as I took the turnoff for Highway 104. "That was the last one. I really think it's between Rainshadow Ridge and that darling rock chapel."

"Rainshadow Ridge has my vote. Just imagine how beautiful a sunset ceremony would be there." If this wedding had to happen, it needed to take place somewhere that had no connection with a murder.

"I don't know. I do so love that stained glass."

"Give yourself some time and think about it." For another six or seven weeks until the lab results came back.

"You heard what they both said. Their calendars are filling up fast. I need to make a decision before I leave Sunday."

That's what I was afraid she was going to say, making me glad that I had taken this route back to Port Merritt.

She stared pensively out the window for the next few miles until we reached Gibson Lake. "Have we missed a turn?"

"Nope. We're just going home another way," I said, slowing to take the Clatska exit.

"Kind of a roundabout way of getting there, isn't it?"

"If you and Barry plan to see that chapel this week, we need to make sure that Victoria McCutcheon is nowhere in the vicinity. So, we'll do a quick drive-by to see if she's back at her house."

She patted my thigh. "Good thinking."

I took the right turn onto Gibson Lake Road. "Not to say that she's guilty of anything, and I sure wouldn't want you to suggest that to Barry." Or anyone else. "It's just that her husband died under some mysterious circumstances."

"And she and his best friend seem to have become chummy. Yeah, yeah, yeah. Honey, that's been the bread and butter of crime dramas for years. Why on my show, every season one of us girls would have to match wits with a beautiful black widow."

"I don't remember you doing that."

"I was usually dressed in some skimpy outfit to act as

bait for the boyfriend." She finger-fluffed her cropped hair. "The things I had to do for ratings."

Like she had ever minded flashing her goods for the right price.

Turning onto the narrow tree-lined lane that led to the McCutcheon home, I shut off my headlights after about a quarter mile. Between the moon low in the sky and the outdoor lights marking a neighbor's driveway I could barely see where I was going as I crept toward a clearing.

"I don't like this," my mother said, leaning toward me as if she were afraid that an ax-wielding psychopath would jump out of the bushes. "It's creepy skulking around in the dark."

"There's light up ahead." Lots of light. Maybe Victoria didn't like being alone.

No, not alone as I quickly discovered. A very familiar-looking car was parked out front.

Cameron's car.

I shivered, the hair on my arms standing on end. My flight instinct screamed at me to speed away like Marietta's psychopath was chasing us, but I couldn't risk turning on my headlights and being seen.

Marietta pointed at the metallic blue coupe, shining under the spotlight illuminating the driveway. "Isn't that…?"

Spitless, I nodded.

Was Victoria also telling Cameron to be patient, to keep his cool? The only reason such a conversation would take place was if he had been an accomplice and thought someone was onto him.

It wasn't me. I hadn't talked to him for over a week.

It had to have been a person close to Marty with some

suspicions of their own. Someone who had confronted Cameron before I saw him last night at Bob Hallahan's house.

I sucked in a breath. "Darlene!"

My mother stared at me. "What?"

"Nothing, I was just thinking out loud."

"About Darlene? You think she's mixed up in this?"

I flipped on my headlights and accelerated toward the main road. "I don't know." But I needed to find out.

My grandmother greeted Marietta and me with a scowl as we stepped through the back door. "About time you two got back. Dinner's been ready for a half hour."

My mother slung her tote bag over the back of a chair at the kitchen table. "Oh, Mama, I thought I'd told you. Barry and I have plans and he'll be here any minute, so I need to get ready."

Glaring at me while Marietta ran up the stairs, Gram stirred something that smelled like spaghetti sauce. "I suppose you and Steve have plans."

"Steve has football practice tonight, so no. I'm all yours."

She looked at me like I wasn't much of a bargain.

"Something wrong? Aside from the fact that we're late and we didn't call?"

Gram averted her gaze. "No, it's nothing. Really."

It didn't sound like nothing.

"Okay." I washed my hands and grabbed a knife to slice the loaf of French bread she had set out on the counter.

Since she kept worrying her lips I put down the knife.

"Just tell me. Something is obviously bothering you."

"Sweetheart, there are things that are best left unsaid."

"Did I do something?"

Gram squeezed out a smile. "Of course not. Some people are just.... Well, they should just mind their own business, that's all."

"Mind their own business about me and Steve."

She didn't answer me. Instead, she crossed to the sink to strain the steaming pasta.

"One of your friends said something." Given how gossip was a staple of every local gathering place, someone flapping their gums to my grandmother was inevitable.

"It's unimportant. Slice that bread and let's eat."

One woman seemed to have her finger on the pulse of everything going on in town, so I could guess who had been doing the flapping. "It was Estelle, right?"

Gram stared down at the strings of pasta like she wanted to strangle Estelle with them. "I had lunch with her and Angela today." She set the strainer on the counter. "Who's having sex with who was all they wanted to talk about. Of course, my two girls were at the top of their list."

Obviously, this hadn't been a proud day for her. But after almost a year of celibacy I didn't feel like I needed to apologize for my relationship with Steve.

"And then they started speculating about Victoria McCutcheon and Bob Hallahan." She dumped the pasta into a crockery bowl. "You should have heard what those old biddies were saying. Like there's nothing else to talk about around here."

There was nothing else that I wanted to talk about. "What'd they say?"

"Charmaine! It's bad enough that I had to hear it. I will not stoop to their level and repeat it."

Typically, I had nothing but respect for her always wanting to stick to the moral high road, but tonight I needed her to unstick herself and dish some dirt. "What they said could have some bearing on something one of the prosecutors is working on, so think of this as your civic duty to—"

"Do I look like I was born yesterday?"

"Uh, no."

"Then what's this pile of horse manure that you're trying to hand me?"

I buckled under the intensity of her parental glare. "Okay, it's something that I'm working on."

"You mean, having to do with Marty's death?"

I held her gaze. If she could read me half as well as I thought she could she'd have her answer.

Her jaw dropped. "But he died of a heart attack."

Cardiac arrest, but close enough. "Yes, but I really do need to know what they told you."

"Oh, my." She reached for the dishtowel as if the gossip she was carrying had sullied her hands. "It was just Estelle being a little graphic about some visits Bob had from Marty's wife."

I already knew about the visits. "Did she actually see them doing something?"

"I'm not sure, but I wouldn't be surprised if she did. The way she keeps tabs on everything going on outside her window."

Bless Estelle's voyeuristic heart.

"What exactly did she say?" I asked.

"That Victoria must not have been getting enough at

home." Gram winced. "Crude comments like that while the two of them cackled like a pair of old hens about being *serviced* by the likes of Bob."

I patted her hand. "Okay, enough said."

"He certainly was very attentive to Victoria at the service Saturday. Do you think it's true? Were they having an affair?"

I didn't dare share my suspicions about the nature of their relationship. "I don't know."

I also didn't know how Cameron fit into the equation. Some revenge angle having to do with his mother? Or had he come to the conclusion that he'd never be accepted into the McCutcheon family, and Victoria had lured him into her scheme with the promise of easy money? By Darlene's reaction to his presence at her ex's funeral service I wouldn't be surprised to learn that she had wielded some influence in that regard. Maybe even paid a tidy sum to Cameron's mother to stay away from her family.

"Even if they were, it's none of our business." Gram waved her hand as if she held a magic wand to make all the unpleasantness of the day go poof.

If only it were that easy.

She poured the spaghetti sauce on the pasta and headed for the kitchen table, where we usually ate when it was just the two of us. "Grab the salad in the fridge and let's eat."

The doorbell rang. "I'll get it," my mother chirped.

"We're off," she said seconds later, when she and Barry waved goodbye from the doorway.

After the front door closed behind them, Gram turned to me. "I worry about that girl, rushing into this wedding."

"Me, too, but she refuses to budge on the date. For whatever reason, it just has to be June."

"When school's out, so that makes some sense. Still, she's practically galloping to the altar and with someone she barely knows. Barry's a very nice man, but unless she's willing to put him before her career, how is this going to work?"

"Yeah, well…" I was living proof of how famous she was for putting family first. I knew I'd sound petty if I said any more, so I clamped my mouth shut and helped myself to the salad.

When Gram fell silent I noticed her doing the worry thing with her lips again. "What?"

She stared at the bowl of salad as if the bits of red cabbage mixed with the leafy greens had suddenly become fascinating. "It's not that I'm an old fuddy-duddy, and I only want your happiness, but I wonder if your mother isn't the only one rushing into something."

"I'm not the one sporting an engagement ring." Nor did I think that would ever happen. Not if I were being completely honest with myself.

"No, but you're practically advertising your relationship with Stevie by living with him."

"It's only while Mom's here. Everything will be back the way it was by Monday." I knew that was a lie before the words left my lips. As soon as I'd crossed the street with my clothes, I should have recognized the impact of my decision. There was no going back from this.

Maybe I was more like my impetuous mother than I wanted to admit. Leaping across the street when I should have been looking.

At least I hadn't proclaimed myself to be in mad,

passionate love with the man a week after he had first kissed me. That was a good thing, right?

Looking as unconvinced as I felt, Gram nodded and we ate in silence for a couple of minutes until the doorbell rang again.

"Hey, did you eat?" Steve asked when I opened the door.

"Doing that now and there's plenty." I waved him in. "Did practice end early?"

"It started to rain so we called it a night." Grinning, he focused on my lips and I had the sinking feeling that I should have made better use of my napkin.

He kissed the corner of my mouth and then licked his lips. "Spaghetti?"

"Overcooked pasta but the sauce is good."

He winked. "Yes, it is."

"Hope you're joining us, Stevie," Gram said when he followed me into the kitchen. "I made enough for a small army."

"Don't have to ask me twice." He sat down across from her. "So what did my two favorite girls do today?"

"Lunch with a couple of friends." Gram did another little wave of her hand. "I won't bore you with the details."

I put a plate, salad bowl, and silverware in front of him. "More wedding location research with my mother after work, and I won't bore you with those details." Or mention the side trip we took.

"I thought I saw your car go by as we were wrapping things up," he said, heaping his plate with a mound of spaghetti. "Is there some place she has her eye on west of town?"

Dang it! When I got back to town I had driven right by the middle school where the peewees practiced. "More like northwest. Rainshadow Ridge."

"That resort?" Gram wrinkled her nose. "Kind of hoity toity, isn't it?"

"It has very pretty grounds. If Mom wants a sunset ceremony, that's the place to have one."

Steve twirled pasta on his fork. "Did you drive back on Highway 104?"

Avoiding his gaze, I stuffed my face with spaghetti and nodded.

"Kind of the long way home, don't you think?" he said.

I shrugged and chewed.

"Honey, that's at least ten miles out of the way." My grandmother stabbed a leafy bite of salad. "You should know better than that, and that two lane road between here and Clatska is awful at night. No wonder you were so late getting back."

Not helping, Gram.

Steve put down his fork. "Something in Clatska you wanted to see?"

"Gosh, you act like it's a crime to show my mother another way to get home."

"It is if you decided to do some trespassing like your last caper with her."

I glared at him. "I thought we had left that very minor incident behind us." Fortunately, the neighbor who had called the cops on us a few weeks back had a crush on Marietta, so she was able to charm her way out of trouble. I knew better than to think that any amount of charm could rescue me from the volcano rumbling in the chair next to me.

"And I thought you had stopped with the Nancy Drew act and were going to wait for the lab results like everyone else in your office."

I wanted to tell him that waiting wouldn't make it safe for my mother and Mr. Ferris to visit that wedding chapel, but I knew I'd be wasting my breath. "I resent that."

Steve pushed away from the table. "And I resent the fact that you think that little badge of yours gives you the right to poke your nose where it doesn't belong!"

"Children," Gram said. "Let's calm down and finish our meal."

"Sorry, Eleanor. Don't think I can do that." Without a backward glance he headed for the door.

I leapt to my feet. "Seriously, you're just going to leave?"

Steve didn't answer, so I followed him outside. "I don't know what you're so mad about. I'm the one with the *little badge* who got insulted."

He wheeled around. "Listen, it doesn't take much to provoke someone into action."

"Obviously."

"I'm not talking about me. I see people do crazy things all the time and after very little provocation."

"I didn't do anything to—"

"I don't want to hear it."

"Fine!" Obstinate man!

Crossing the street with me on his heels, Steve glanced back over his shoulder. "I'm done talking about this."

"Me, too. I'm just going to get some of my things."

"Char." He stopped, all the sharp edges erased from his tone. "You don't have to do that."

My eyes stinging, I pushed past him so he wouldn't see me cry. "Yeah, I do."

Chapter Nineteen

AFTER THREE HOURS of tossing and turning on the lumpy hide-a-bed in my grandfather's study, I called an end to my grudge match with the *Crippler*.

"I give up," I said to the fat tabby peering down at me from the window sill.

Trying to work the kinks out of my back, I peeked through the curtains, looking for signs of life across the street, while Myron hopped down to claim my pillow.

Of course, no lights were on. Steve was probably sleeping like a baby with his bed all to himself.

Goody for him.

In no mood to continue my late night relationship counseling session with Gram, I threw myself together and headed downtown for some edible therapy and free bad coffee.

"Look what the cat dragged in," Duke announced as the cafe's kitchen door banged shut behind me.

Sitting at her butcher block table, Aunt Alice frowned at the wall clock mounted above a vintage Coca Cola sign. "Land's sake, girl, it's bad enough we have to be here at four in the morning. What gives?"

"Couldn't sleep." I headed for the coffee station and the industrial strength java jolt that my sluggish synapses desperately needed. "So you might as well put me to work."

She had a stainless steel bowl and her chocolate chip cookie recipe waiting for me on the table when I got back. "How about three dozen?"

"Fine." The foul mood I was in, I could buzz through the first dozen myself.

Duke stood by the fryer keeping watch on his first batch of doughnuts for the morning, but his gaze kept shifting my way.

"What?" I demanded as I pulled a pound of butter from the refrigerator behind me.

"You don't look so good. Are you sure you feel okay?"

"I'm fine." I reached for the bag of flour in the center of the table. "I just didn't put much makeup on." I had also pulled my hair up into a top knot. Not my best look, but the hair dryer would have made noise and that wasn't an option since Gram was a light sleeper.

Alice leaned closer, inspecting me through her wire-rimmed trifocals. "And everything's okay at home?"

"Everything's peachy."

"Uh-huh," she muttered. "Looks it."

"I'm okay. I just don't feel like being chatty."

With a knowing smile, she nodded. "Your mother's here. Say no more."

Having a mother renowned for creating family drama had its upside. Mainly because everyone related to me was sick of hearing about it.

Three hours, two cookies, and five cups of coffee

later, I was stocking the bakery shelves with all the cookies, scones, and muffins I'd baked when the silver bell over the door jingled for the fifth time in the last ten minutes.

Port Merritt was awake and hungry, and so it appeared was the detective of its police force.

"Good morning," Steve said, his gaze zeroed in on mine as he approached.

"Morning." I shifted my attention to the pumpkin walnut muffins on my tray.

"How're you doing?"

"Great."

"She's in a bad mood," Duke announced with enough volume for everyone in the cafe to hear.

And he wasn't helping to improve it.

As Steve took a seat at the counter and Lucille went to take his order, a jingle signaled the arrival of another customer.

I looked up to see Jeremy McCutcheon striding toward the bakery counter.

A sardonic smirk flashed across his lips. "Things didn't work out at the courthouse for you?"

Nice. "I like to help my family out when I can." The fact that I was the one who had needed the help this morning was beside the point.

"We have that in common then."

Yeah, we were just two sweet peas in a pod. "And what may I help you with?"

"A dozen doughnuts, two of each of those," he said, pointing at the top shelf in the glass case between us.

I filled a bakery box with his selection and then reached for an apple fritter because his dad always wanted at least one with his orders. "One? Two?"

"What?" He looked up from the cell phone in his hand.

"Fritter?"

His gaze hardened. "If I'd wanted one I would have told you."

Excuse me.

After ringing up his order, he handed me a ten-dollar bill. With four cents coming to him as change, I reached into the register.

"Keep it." His eyes danced with amusement as he pocketed his thick wallet. "A little tip for you."

Was I wearing a sign or something? *Insults gladly accepted here.*

I dropped the pennies into the tip jar by the register. "Have a nice day." *Jackass.*

"What was his deal?" Lucille asked, squeaking over in her orthopedic shoes.

"He was just being a jerk."

"Really? He's usually pretty nice."

Then Jeremy had wanted to put me in my place for flashing my *little badge* at him and disrupting his father's sale. "Not with me."

I glanced at Steve. Then again, I was the one wearing the *kick me* sign.

He crooked a finger at me.

This was not a good time to motion to me with any finger.

Avoiding his gaze, I grabbed a coffee carafe to refill his cup.

"You didn't have to do that," he said. "But thanks."

I thought of Phyllis and what she had said about still

wanting to do nice things for Marty long after it was over between them.

I didn't want that to become us, so I dispensed with the niceties. "What?"

"Are you going to be home later?"

"I'm not planning on any capers if that's what you're asking."

He blew out a breath. "It's not."

"Hey," Duke said, passing me a bowl of oatmeal. "Hand this to your boyfriend."

He had said it in a teasing tone, but I was in no mood to hear it.

I set the bowl in front of Steve. "Enjoy."

With nothing more I wanted to say to him in front of an audience, I headed for the kitchen.

"Wait. Char!" he called after me.

I shook my head. "Not now."

Duke's gaze followed me as I tossed my dirty apron into a hamper. "Had enough fun, huh?"

"Yep." Given how my day had started, I had a bad feeling that the fun was just beginning.

✳

"You're early again?" Patsy remarked when I walked by her desk. "Going for a record?"

"You betcha." Apparently, the most butt kicks in a twenty-four hour period.

I headed for the breakroom and had just started to brew a fresh pot of coffee when I heard the door click shut. Glancing over my shoulder I saw Patsy approach.

Now what? "The coffee won't be ready for a few

minutes."

"That's not why I'm here."

Turning to face her, I gritted my teeth.

Scowling, she scanned me from head to foot. "You don't...are you feeling okay?"

I know. I looked like crap and didn't feel much better. "I'm fine."

"Then we're still on for lunch today?"

Today of all days I was supposed to find out if her boyfriend was two-timing her? "We're on," I said with all the false cheer I could muster.

She heaved a shaky breath. "Good. I told Mitch to meet me at Duke's at twelve-thirty, so plan on walking by our table a couple minutes later and I'll ask you to join us."

"Duke's?" We had to do this at Duke's?

"I thought familiar surroundings could be helpful."

I stared at her in disbelief. "We're going to want privacy, so try to get a table in the back."

"Okay. Now, do you understand the plan?"

"Get him to talk about online dating and find out if he's seeing someone else."

She nodded solemnly. "Exactly. Just be subtle about it, and not too many questions about the two of us."

Good grief. "Maybe you should just give me a list of the dos and don'ts."

"Excellent idea. I'll have that to you in a few minutes." She spun on her heel and headed for the door.

Me and my big mouth.

"I need the corner table in the back," I said, pointing

it out to Lucille and Courtney, the waitresses working the lunch shift at Duke's.

"Gonna do some necking back there?" Lucille elbowed Courtney, a sandy-haired single mom who had started yesterday. "You should have seen her and Steve going at it in the kitchen last Saturday."

A misfire of an idea if there ever was one. "It's not for me. Patsy is having a meeting in twenty minutes and needs some privacy." And if I didn't grab that table to tuck Mitch away where Duke couldn't see the two of us together, he would have a different kind of go at me in the kitchen.

"No problem," Courtney said. "As soon as those ladies are done I'll put the *Reserved* sign on it."

Lucille snickered. "This is a diner, honey. We don't have *Reserved* signs."

Courtney pulled out a folded sheet of paper from her pocket and smiled contentedly. "We do now."

"Where the heck did that come from?" Lucille asked.

"Me." I had printed it at work. "One more thing, Mitch Grundy is going to be joining Patsy."

Lucille frowned. "What for?"

"It's a lunch date meeting that I have to be at. So, if Duke sees him come in, just tell him that he's not here to try to sell him anything." At least I hoped Mitch had the good sense not to be a salesman today.

After the girls assured me that they had the situation covered, I ducked out the door and crossed the street to Clark's Pharmacy to make myself scarce for the next twenty-five minutes.

As long as I was there I figured I could buy some shampoo to replace the bottle I'd left in Steve's shower, and maybe pick up a protein bar in case lunch went badly and Patsy wanted me to leave. Preferably a protein bar covered with chocolate. It would be healthy without being sanctimonious about it. Of course, Mr. Clark had to shelve them in the candy aisle, where lusciously gooey chocolate bars were calling my name. And as it happened, where Cameron Windom was buying a pack of sugar-free gum.

"Not tempted, huh?" I said, feeling much braver in the daylight about this sighting than I had last night.

He blinked. "What?"

"By all this chocolate."

A hint of a smile tugged at the corners of his lips. "Oh, I'm not much of a chocolate fiend."

No, he was the non-chocolate variety. "How're you doing?"

"I've had better days."

You and me both. "Are things improving for you at work?"

"I think we're all just trying to get through everything that's going on as well as we can."

He was a little twitchy, his feet in constant motion, just like when I had interviewed him over a week ago.

"And how's Mrs. McCutcheon? Have you had an opportunity to speak with her since the funeral?"

"No, not really."

Is that so, because you saw her last night.

"Sorry, I should get going," he said, inching toward the register. "Got a customer coming…any minute."

Sheesh, this guy was such a bad liar. Victoria needed to give him some pointers.

I nodded politely. "Have a nice afternoon."

I watched him scurry away like the rat I suspected he was. Frightened that someone might be onto him? Good. He should be. Maybe that would lead to him making a big enough mistake that someone with a scarier badge than mine might notice.

I'd certainly made enough mistakes of my own lately.

I tossed a chocolate bar into my basket. "What does one more matter?"

As soon as I spotted Mitch Grundy enter the cafe with Patsy on his arm, I settled up at the pharmacy register and then jaywalked across the street.

Opening the door to the familiar tinkle of the silver bell above my head, I waved at Duke, who was scowling at me from behind the grill.

"What? I haven't even done anything yet," I said, popping my head into the kitchen.

"Didn't you see that turkey, Grundy, come in right before you?"

"He's not here to sell you anything. That turkey happens to be a friend of Patsy's, so you stay on your side of this door and he'll stay on his." At least he'd better. And I knew I'd have to do my best to make sure that the turkey didn't venture back here to have some face time with the salty dog holding the carving knife.

Much like everything having to do with this lunch meeting—whether I wanted to or not.

Stepping in front of the bakery case, I expected to see Patsy waving at me from the far corner. Instead, I saw the same two gray hairs who had occupied the booth twenty minutes earlier. Not good!

Courtney shot me an apologetic smile. "They wanted pie, so I had to move you to a table up front."

The table that Patsy was waving from was in Duke's sight line.

Swell. "Don't worry about it."

Fortunately, Mitch was sitting with his back to Duke.

But that meant that I'd have to sit with the distraction of a pissed off great-uncle in my line of sight, and worse, the police detective taking a seat at the counter.

Envisioning a future as Patsy's personal piñata if I didn't get my butt over to her table in the next two seconds, I ignored Steve's cold stare and painted a smile on my face. "Well, hi, you two. It looks like we meet again."

Mitch pumped my hand. "Always a pleasure."

"Yes!" Patsy said with fake enthusiasm. "It was so fun to bump into you at the Grotto, but you and Mitch hardly had an opportunity to catch up. I have an idea. You should join us."

And people thought my mother was a bad actress. She was an Oscar contender compared to Patsy.

"Thanks! I'd love to." I could feel my smile start to crack as Steve swiveled around and glared at me.

"Gosh, you don't even have menus yet?" Probably because Courtney had been waiting for my arrival. "I'll go grab some."

I crossed the diner and reached for three laminated menus from behind the napkin holder in front of Steve. "Do you mind?" I whispered in his ear. "I'm having lunch with a coworker."

He narrowed his eyes. "Yeah, that didn't sound like a set-up at all."

"Never mind that. Just turn around and eat."

"I want to see you later," he stated, sounding more like a cop than a friend.

"Maybe ask a little nicer next time and I'll consider it."

Lucille squeaked up to refill his coffee cup. "You two fighting?"

"No," Steve and I said in unison as I headed back with the menus.

"Here we are." As soon as I sat down on the bench seat next to Patsy it struck me that the menus presented a problem. The food that Mitch would be ordering did, too. The use of utensils, napkins—anything that might obstruct my view.

I folded my hands over the menus on the table in front of me. "I just hate trying to have a conversation when I'm eating, don't you?"

Mitch gave me a blank look.

"So, let's take this opportunity to catch up, like you suggested, Patsy."

"Sounds good. You two catch up. I need to... uh...wash my hands anyway."

I stood to let her slide out and then scooted over to the warm spot she had vacated. "So," I said with what I hoped was a disarming smile. "Tell me how the two of you met."

"Online actually."

"Like in a chat room?"

"Online dating. With my schedule it's the only way to go."

Courtney brought us three waters. "Do you need a few minutes?"

I nodded, and she got the hint and disappeared to the

table behind me. "So, how does the online dating thing work? You saw Patsy's picture or something?"

"You never tried it? Oh, well of course you're dating that doctor."

No, no, no. We were not going to talk about Kyle, not with Steve sitting twenty feet away. "Nope, never tried it. So, tell me about it."

Since Mitch Grundy was the kind of guy who wanted to explain how the watch was made when you asked for the time, I had to listen to a two-minute, blow-by-blow account of how he'd set up his profile.

I had to move the conversation along or Patsy was going to be back before I had the chance to ask any of the questions on the list she'd emailed me.

"The way I understand it is that interested parties will contact one another," I said.

"Exactly. You get to know one another a little online and—"

"Then you set up dates."

"Right. Like coffee or drinks."

"So, let's say you contacted someone in the last couple of weeks." I waited for him to jump in and deny doing that, but he didn't. "You'd meet the lady somewhere and have a casual mini-date."

"You usually know within a few minutes if it's gonna work or not. If not, at least you can enjoy a nice cup of coffee." He winked. "Unlike the swill good ol' Duke serves."

I lowered my voice. "I imagine it could get complicated. I mean what if you and Patsy had run into one of the other ladies when you were out that Saturday night?"

"Not gonna happen."

"Oh, I hadn't realized you two were exclusive."

He smiled like he had a secret. "She's a special girl."

Patsy was special all right, but she was wasting her time with this guy.

"Were your ears burning, honey?" he asked, gazing lovingly at her as she returned to the table.

Taking a seat she turned to me. "Should they have been?"

"We were just chatting about how the two of you met." I handed her a menu.

"She asked me so many questions, if I didn't know better I'd think that doctor fella might be in trouble."

Oh, please stop talking about that stupid dinner!

"What was his name again?" Mitch asked. "It reminded me of a vegetable. Cabbage, I think."

I shoved a menu in front of his face. "Speaking of cabbage, Duke makes a mighty fine Reuben with his extra tangy sauerkraut, so I know what I'm going to have."

"Not cabbage—kale. Kyle! That's it!" He tapped his temple. "Got a mind like a steel trap."

I wished he'd shut his trap.

Seeing movement out of the corner of my eye, I expected to see Courtney coming over to take our order. Instead, it was Steve stalking toward the door.

Nothing about his demeanor suggested that he was anything other than a busy man—too busy to spare me a glance.

He had to have heard almost every word Mitch had said. Heck, half-deaf Gladys sitting across the room probably had heard him loud and clear.

Courtney stepped to our table, her order pad in hand. "Are you ready now?"

Not me. I'd lost my appetite.

Chapter Twenty

"OKAY, WHAT WAS up with that lunch meeting?" Lucille asked the second after the door jingled shut behind Patsy and Mitch.

"Nothing. Just a lunch." I handed her a twenty for the Reuben sandwich I had barely touched.

"It didn't look like nothing." Leaning an elbow on the cash register as she gave me my change, she lowered her voice to a stage whisper. "It looked to me like you were putting him to the lie detector test."

"Don't be ridiculous." Patsy didn't need that rumor to spread, especially since she'd think it had come from me.

"You gonna tell me that you're suddenly interested in online dating?"

I pocketed my change. "Maybe I was asking for a friend."

Lucille's eyes gleamed with predatory intent. "Which one?"

"Order up!" Duke barked at us.

Message received. *Get back to work.* "Like she'd want you to know."

Squeaking away with a coffee carafe, she shook her

head. "You're no fun."

One small crisis averted, one big one to go—Steve and how much he had heard.

I turned to leave and almost ran into Courtney on her way to pick up the lunch order waiting at the pass-through window.

"I feel horrible about not being able to get that table in the back for you," she said.

"Not your fault."

"Still, that was the type of conversation that needed more privacy." The color of the strawberry milkshake a little kid was sucking down at the counter crawled into her cheeks. "I couldn't help but overhear."

I forced a smile. "Forget what you heard."

"Okay, but I just wanted to say that if you had more questions about online dating that I might be able to help you."

"I don't. Thanks anyway."

I started for the door but Lucille blocked my path. "I might," she said.

Sure. She just wanted to sink her teeth into whatever tasty morsels Courtney had to offer. "Since when?"

"Hey, look at the prospects around here." Lucille pointed at Stanley, slurping his decaf while he read the paper. "The pickings are slim, so I've been thinking about expanding my horizons."

Courtney nodded. "I was in the same boat. My sister kept nagging me to try the dating website she used, so finally I tried it a couple years back."

Duke cleared his throat. "Order up!"

"Coming," Courtney said, backing away from me.

Lucille grabbed her arm. "Not so fast. You were

trolling local waters?"

Courtney blinked. "Huh?"

"She's just looking for dirt," I said. "Ignore her."

Lucille frowned at me. "I beg your pardon, but how can I know if this would be money well-spent if I don't ask about the pool of local talent?"

"If by local you mean within a thirty-mile radius, I'd agree that the pickings can be slim. There was only one man who I thought might work out, but he was involved with someone else." The forty-something blonde squared her shoulders. "But at least I've already seen him here, so I'm over that initial awkwardness."

"Who are we talking about, honey?" Lucille asked, following her to the pass-through window where Courtney loaded her arms with three orders of burgers and fries.

The younger woman whispered an answer, and then whisked away to deliver her order, leaving Lucille to turn to me with a smug look on her face.

"Well? Are you going to tell me or make me guess?"

She returned the carafe to the coffee station, and then pushed the kitchen door open. "Why don't you step into my office for a moment."

"Lucille, I don't have a lot of time," I said, feeling the heat of Duke's stare as I entered his domain.

She dismissively waved me off. "You'll want to make time for this."

I followed her back to the butcher block table, where Lucille took a seat next to Aunt Alice.

"What's this about?" Alice asked, rolling out dough for pie happy hour. She looked at me. "And why are you still here? Don't you have a job to get back to?"

Her clock-watching husband was rubbing off on her. "Yes, and I'll get going as soon as we're done here." I met Lucille's gaze. "So, who's the mystery man?"

Lucille folded her arms under her ample breasts. "Someone you were inquiring about at this very spot a week ago."

My breath caught in my throat. "Bob Hallahan?"

She nodded. "Small world, huh?"

"Very." Especially since I knew that Victoria had met Marty McCutcheon through an online dating service.

"Who are you two talking about?" Alice demanded.

"Courtney dated him for a while. No big deal." At least it shouldn't have been to anyone but me.

I kissed my aunt on the cheek. "I'm off." To work, right after I had a few words with Courtney.

"See you tomorrow probably," I said to Duke as I went by.

He pointed his spatula at me. "Try to make it a little later in the morning, like a normal person."

I thought about the hide-a-bed I'd be trying to sleep on tonight. "I'll do my best." But *normal* felt like something out of my reach this week.

Stepping out of the kitchen, I found Courtney at the counter chatting with Stanley. I motioned toward the door and she followed me outside.

I looked around to make sure no one was within earshot. "Hope you don't mind, but since I help out here Lucille thought I should know about Bob."

A boldfaced lie, but I didn't want to make it difficult on Lucille if Courtney thought she had told her something in confidence.

"That's okay. I'm pretty much over it."

Since her eyes were misting I seriously doubted that. "You dated two years ago?"

"More like a year and a half ago."

Which was close to the time that Marty and Victoria would have started dating. Coincidence? I had a hard time believing in any coincidences where anyone with the last name of McCutcheon was concerned.

Courtney smiled, sweet and sad. "Actually, today was the first time I've seen him since I moved to town."

"Where were you living before?"

"Near Gibson Lake. And now you know another reason why I joined that dating website. There are no eligible bachelors living out there."

Maybe, but I knew of one recently widowed woman.

Could she have been the woman Bob had fallen in love with?

"If you don't mind me asking—you know, for my friend—what was the site you used?"

"Secondchances dot com. Its clientele is typically a little older and all the men I met were either widowed or divorced."

Just like Marty, and Bob, and Victoria.

※

"So, he *is* a player," Patsy said after I sat down with her in the breakroom and told her that I didn't think Mitch was ready to date anyone exclusively.

"No, he's a salesman. I didn't have time to ask, but did he sign up with this site fairly recently?"

"Last month some time."

Since long-time bachelor Mitch Grundy prided himself

in prompt delivery after the sale, I suspected that he was getting too much action to want to cut off his supply chain anytime soon.

I had absolutely no desire to broach the subject of sex with Patsy, so I decided to give it a wide berth. "It may just be too soon for him to commit."

"His loss." She pushed out of her chair, holding her head high. "I am sorry though that he kept going on about Dr. Cardinale."

Not nearly as sorry as I was.

"If that causes you any difficulty with Detective Sixkiller, I regret putting you in that position."

An apology from Patsy—something I had never expected to hear. It barely made a dent in the suckiness of today, but I was grateful for it nonetheless.

She jutted her pointy chin at me. "Now, let's get back to work, shall we? And never speak of this again."

The two of us never talking about the events of today wouldn't make them go away. In my case, it would only make it worse.

I sent Steve a text. *Can we talk?*

Sitting on Steve's front porch with my head in my hands, I looked up to see Gram standing on her sidewalk.

"Honey, you should come home and have some dinner."

Since Steve hadn't responded to any of my texts, I knew I needed to be here when he came home. "I will. Later."

She pulled her sweater tight across her chest. "Brrr. It looks like a storm is moving in. Don't you want a coat?"

Yes. My pullover had been perfectly adequate when I had gotten off work an hour ago, but now that the wind had picked up, I was freezing. And had no intention of moving from this porch. "I'm fine."

"Whatever is going on between the two of you needs to stop. For both your sakes."

I didn't think my grandmother meant that the way it sounded, but somewhere deep within my gut I knew she couldn't have been more right.

"I know, Gram. Go inside and get warm."

An hour and a half later, Steve pulled up in his Crown Victoria. With rigor mortis setting in, I labored to push to my feet.

He looked at me long and hard through the sprinkles dotting his windshield.

I shivered as if I were standing in the middle of an ice storm. "Yes, I know. You're pissed."

"What are you doing?" he asked when he finally got out of the car.

What does it look like I'm doing? "Waiting for you."

A shadow from his porch light cut a cruel slash across the planes of his cheekbones, feeding my trepidation about how well the speech I'd been practicing would be received.

He didn't make eye contact as he climbed the steps of his front porch. "I'm too tired to do this tonight."

"I'd really like to talk to you."

"Yeah? Well, I wanted to talk to you, too," he said, unlocking the door. "Earlier."

"I know and I'm sorry. Can I come in?"

His back to me, he stiffened. "Not now. Go home, Char."

"But—"

He stepped inside and gently closed the door in my face.

When I got to Eddie's Place fifteen minutes later, I was relieved to see that half the chairs were empty. No games on the flat screens, no guys in matching bowling shirts toasting one another in celebration. Even the classic rock typically pulsing throughout the bar had been turned down a couple of decibels, enabling me to hear the rumble of bowling balls from the other side of the brick wall.

I could also hear Rox curse the instant she saw me.

"That bad, huh?" I said when I plopped down at the far end of the bar.

She spun a coaster in front of me like a blackjack dealer. "Honey, you look like death warmed over."

I pushed back the bangs that the blustery evening drizzle had plastered to my forehead. "Probably because that's how I feel."

"Chardonnay?"

"Do you have any hot cocoa? I'm freezing."

"Is it that cold out?"

While she prepared my drink, I told her about spending the last couple of hours camped out on Steve's front porch.

Rox's eyes widened. "He slammed the door in your face?"

I sipped my cocoa with the peppermint schnapps my favorite mixologist had stirred in. "No, no, it wasn't a slam." But the message he'd sent had been loud and clear.

"He just didn't want to see me tonight." And possibly tomorrow and the day after that.

Rox leaned her elbows on the polished oak bar separating us. "I'm sure he needs a little time. You two have had a rough couple of days. Let him cool off and it will be fine."

"No, I really screwed this up." I stared into the murky darkness of my drink. "I let things get out of hand that night with Kyle—"

"Only because I pushed you into it."

"You didn't know. Just check that off as another screw-up on my part."

Criminy, I'd been on a roll lately.

I heard my phone buzz and pulled it from my tote.

"Text from Steve?" Rox asked.

"Donna. She wants to get together this weekend. I'll answer her later." I shook my phone at Rox. "See how I am? I put off my friends so much I'm surprised that any of you even want to be with me."

"You've been busy with Steve and your mom, and we get that." She leveled her gaze at me. "So stop being so hard on yourself."

No, I'd been busy pushing and pulling everyone around me, using them to fit whatever my need was at the moment—Steve, Rox, Kyle, Donna, family members, coworkers, even suspects. How magnanimous of me. I was an equal opportunity manipulative bitch.

I pushed my phone away and grabbed the glass mug in front of me. "Well, I won't be busy with Steve tonight." Not in any sense of the word.

Rox patted my hand. "It's going to be okay."

No, like my grandmother had suggested, I needed to

stop this thing between Steve and me, but it would take a very long time to feel okay about it. "Sure."

"Want something to eat? The kitchen's going to close in less than an hour."

"I had a candy bar." The protein bar, too.

"And now you're having more chocolate."

I sighed. "I know. I'm wallowing."

"I have a customer at the other end of the bar. Back in a few."

I waved her away. "I'm not fit company anyway. You should just shun me."

"Since when did you become a bigger drama queen than your mother?" a familiar male voice asked.

Cringing, I looked up at Steve. "Is that a multiple choice question?"

Without answering he picked up my drink and carried it to the table in the far corner.

"Do you want a beer, Steve?" Rox called after him.

"No." He pointed at a chair. "Sit."

"Okay." I didn't care for the attitude, but at least he was talking to me.

Taking the seat opposite me, he folded his arms. "Your grandmother is worried about you."

He couldn't have made me feel more deflated if he'd reached out and popped me like a balloon. "You're here because of my grandmother?"

"I'm here because you wanted to talk, and you weren't home. So talk."

Blinking back tears of relief that he had come looking for me, I filled my lungs with a shaky breath. "First of all, I apologize for not telling you about that dinner with Kyle Cardinale. I was dressed up for a date that Friday and there he was. Not the man I wanted to be with, but he was nice enough to ask and we had a pleasant time. Then we ran into Mitch Grundy and he jumped to some conclusions. That's it. I should have told you when you came over that night and I chose not to. That was a mistake, and honestly, not very brave of me."

I could have mentioned the kiss, but the tic above Steve's jawline looked like it was counting down the seconds until he exploded, and I had no desire to push him to zero any faster than necessary.

"It was just one of many mistakes I've made lately where we're concerned." I smiled at him while I struggled to find the words I needed to say. "I wanted to take it slow at first, but I wanted things too much to take it slow, so it got *complicated*."

His gaze tightened. "What are you talking about?"

Us! And I was clearly doing a miserable job of it. How could I make him understand what I was trying to say without laying myself emotionally bare in front of him? Because if he decided to walk, if he'd had enough....

"I rushed things. The way I tried to get everything out in the open. I made a mess of everything, especially with Rox, and then I pushed myself into your house." I couldn't take the cop squint he was giving me, so I stared down at my drink. "Into your bed. That was a mistake. Things had been going along okay, and I pushed them into a different stratosphere."

I glanced up in time to see the corners of his mouth flicker into a smile.

He wiped his mouth like he didn't want me to see it. "Stratosphere? You are a drama queen."

"Will you stop saying that? I'm trying to make a point

here!"

"So what's your point?"

"I think we should slow things way down and then see where this takes us."

I breathed a little easier, like a suffocating weight had been lifted now that I had said everything that I'd rehearsed earlier and then some.

I made no demands, set no expectations, while being carefully vague. Depending on his response to what I'd had to say, maybe we could put this genie back in the bottle.

Steve leaned forward, his eyes wary. "Slow things way down? I thought we were fine. Except for the fact that you keep lying to me."

"Excuse me, I have not been lying to you. I just omitted a couple of things."

He smirked. "Yeah. Such a careful distinction."

"I've already apologized for that."

"And I sort of sicced Dr. Cardinale on her," Rox said, clearing the table in the opposite corner. "Sorry, not trying to eavesdrop, but had to fess up for my part in this little drama."

I rolled my eyes. "Will you two stop with the drama stuff? I made a big mistake and I'm sorry!"

"Are you done?" Steve asked.

"I guess." But other than airing myself out in a more public way than I had intended, it didn't feel like anything had been settled.

He pushed away from the table. "Then let's go."

"I haven't finished my drink."

He drained it in two gulps and then grimaced. "What was in that?"

"Peppermint schnapps."

"The girly stuff you drink."

I stood, getting in his face. "Hey, it was *my* drink."

"Yeah, *was*. Let's go."

"I need to pay for it."

He threw a couple of bills on the table, took my hand, and pulled me to the door.

"So, have you two kissed and made up?" Rox asked, calling after us.

I waved at her over my shoulder. "Not yet."

"Well, do it soon. You don't want to go to bed angry."

"You heard the woman," Steve said, pebbles skittering at our heels as we crossed the parking lot. "We need to kiss and make up so we can go to bed."

"Did you not hear a word I said about slowing things down?"

"I heard you, but I think that's something we should sleep on."

I groaned. "You are making my head hurt."

Using his legs, he pinned me against the driver's door of my car. "Perhaps there's something I could do to make you feel better."

"Give me two aspirin perhaps?"

Steve smiled as he lowered his mouth to mine. "Maybe later."

Chapter Twenty-One

I WOKE UP feeling crampy and bloated. At least my body had been spared a rematch with the Crippler. Not to say that I had enjoyed a delightful night's slumber in Steve's bed since I spent more hours staring at him than sleeping. Still, our make-up session before he started softly snoring had been fun.

After pulling on a pair of stretchy black yoga pants and a long cashmere sweater to hide my bloat, I headed to the third floor of the courthouse, where I was handed a white envelope marked with the county seal.

"It's a subpoena for a former caseworker involved in that abuse case and needs to be delivered today," Patsy said, her gaze shifting to her glass-domed clock.

No sunny morning greeting. No blissful chirping. No humming.

All bad signs for Mitch Grundy but good for me. I didn't know how much more of *songbird Patsy* I could withstand.

"No problem." A field trip would provide a welcome break from copying the files that one of the criminal prosecutors had dropped onto my desk late yesterday.

Heading past the breakroom, I read the address on the envelope. Sequim, a destination spot for visitors to the Olympic National Forest, was located just a few miles northwest of Victoria McCutcheon's bed and breakfast.

With each step I took, I mentally replayed my observations leading to that trip to her bed and breakfast. Bob Hallahan's proximity during the funeral, the protective way he looked at her, the care he demonstrated afterward.

If Victoria had been the other woman when he was dating Courtney, it seemed likely that he would have driven her home during that time. And wouldn't that be interesting to know.

I could think of one person who might be able to tell me: Rhonda, the River Rock Inn manager.

Even if she were able to fill in a few blanks about their relationship, would it prove anything? No. But the fact that Marty, Bob, and Victoria had used an online dating service around the same time felt a lot like a puzzle piece. Now all I had to do was take a little side trip and figure out where the piece fit.

I glared at the tall stack of files that appeared to have multiplied overnight on my desk.

Fine. Copying first. Hours and hours of copying. On the plus side, that would give the layer of fog hanging around after last night's rainstorm a chance to burn off.

And that was the only plus as I found out three hours into my marathon when the copy machine overheated.

Seeing that we both needed to cool off, I carried the box of files and all the copies to my desk, grabbed the envelope I needed to deliver, and told Karla that I'd be back in a couple of hours.

By the time I made it to the freeway exit I'd taken with

my mother, it was approaching noon. If the office where I was headed closed for lunch, this was a bad time to try to serve a subpoena, so I took the turnoff to have a little chat with Rhonda.

Parking in front of the two-story house like I had on Saturday, I stepped out into the crisp October air, walked to the door and knocked.

Rhonda opened the door with a pleasant smile. "You're back."

"My mother was quite taken with this place when we were here last weekend."

"I know. She brought her fiancé here to see it yesterday afternoon."

She couldn't have waited a day? It would have helped my cover story.

I nodded to make it look like Marietta's visit hadn't come as news to me. "I'm helping her with the invitations, and I was hoping to take some pictures of the chapel as well as the grounds. Would that be okay?"

"Of course. Take as many pictures as you like. We just ask that you respect the privacy of our guests."

"Thanks. Also, could I take another look at that picture in your office? The one of the owner with the light streaming in through the stained glass?"

"Certainly."

I followed her to the office and sat at her desk so that I could get a good look at Victoria's wedding photo and strike up a conversation in the process.

"It's a lovely picture, isn't it?" Rhonda asked, standing behind me.

"Yes, indeed. I was thinking that I might have seen her when we were here the other day, but this doesn't look like the man she was with."

"Oh, no, that wasn't her husband. Unfortunately, Mr. McCutcheon passed away recently."

I turned so that I could read her face. "When I saw her holding hands with that other man, I guess I assumed they were in a relationship." I hadn't seen them publicly display any affection, so I hoped she didn't call me on my bluff.

"From what I understand he's a good *friend* of the family," she said with a pucker of disapproval at my suggestion to the contrary.

So much for Rhonda being able to help me with the history between Bob and Victoria.

I thanked her and wandered over to the chapel to snap a few pictures with my cell phone. Not that Marietta needed them. I was sure she would have taken several of her own so that she could take images of this place back with her to Louisiana and daydream about her upcoming wedding between takes.

Ambling through the floral garden surrounded by vine-covered stone cottages, I could see why my mother loved the charm of this bed and breakfast. Heck, it looked like it had been plucked out of a story book by a little girl's fairy godmother.

But a pall hung over it much like this morning's fog, something dark and sad that made me want to run back to my car and return to the safety of the courthouse. Maybe because I knew too much about the owner.

Rhonda waved to me from one of the windows as I passed.

"Bye," I said, although she couldn't hear me from the other side of the glass. "Thanks for nothing."

No, not nothing. She might not know much about Bob Hallahan, but that didn't exclude him from fitting into this deadly puzzle somehow. I just needed to keep my eyes and ears open because somebody was going to slip up, and when they did....

I didn't know what I was going to do. Based on how fast I was walking to my car, running would probably be involved.

✳

After a crampy Thursday spent doing scut work to prepare for that abuse case, I wanted nothing more than to crawl into my grandmother's claw-footed bathtub and spend the next hour steaming away the ugliness of the day.

The only thing standing in the way of that steam? The actress at the kitchen table, who had been reading a fashion magazine when I stepped through the back door.

"Oh, goody, you're finally home," Marietta said with a sigh of relief. "I was beginning to worry."

Worry about what? "It's not even five-thirty."

She rose to her feet. "But Bassett Motors closes at six, so we need to go. The DeLorean's ready."

"We can't get it sometime tomorrow?"

"Barry and I have something special planned with his son tomorrow."

Swell. At least I hadn't heard my name mentioned in that sentence.

"Where's Gram?" Not that I wanted her to volunteer as Marietta's chauffeur, but I hadn't seen her Honda in the carport.

"Shopping."

No doubt to get away from my mother for a couple of hours.

She waved toward the door, a half dozen gold bangles clanging at her wrist. "So, let's go!"

I did an about face with Marietta nipping at my heels in her red stilettos.

"You should have George fix this," she said after I reached across the passenger seat to open the car door.

I waited for her to fasten her seatbelt. "That costs money."

"I have money. Let me pay for it."

She had money because of the movie role that had fallen into her lap last month. A year from now would be a different story. It always was with her.

I started the engine. "Thanks, but no. You have a wedding to spend your money on."

She gave me a pained look, so I knew I needed to up the wedding distraction ante. "Speaking of which, have you made a decision on the venue?"

"As much as I love that chapel, an outdoor wedding at sunset would be so romantic."

Whew! It sounded like the River Rock Chapel was out of the running.

"Being in a rain shadow the weather shouldn't be a factor, but I was assured that white tents could be made available if needed." Marietta touched my arm as I drove down the hill toward Main Street. "You don't think we'd really need them, do you?"

"I'm sure it will be fine."

"What if it's windy and damp like it was last night?"

"It's October. We're supposed to get wind and fog

and rain. Your wedding's in late June. It'll be fine."
Maybe.

"I don't know. An outdoor wedding could be iffy."

"I think you should go back to Rainshadow Ridge and take another look. Really, I can't imagine a more beautiful site than that."

"Maybe," she said, fingering the gold necklace at her throat as I turned into the Bassett Motor Works parking lot.

"And you said that their calendar is filling up fast, so when you go you'd better reserve the date."

"I suppose."

Her answer lacked the conviction I wanted to hear, but my mother's wedding was the least of my concerns when I pulled in next to the DeLorean, one of two cars parked in front of the office. Because the other car was Darlene's tan Ford Bronco.

It didn't take long to spot Darlene inside the office, alongside her daughter, who was snarling at Little Dog like she wanted to take a bite out of him.

"Oh, mah." Marietta's Georgia accent was back at full strength as she stepped out of the Jag. "Someone's in a snit."

And from what little I could hear from the other side of the door, it sounded like Nicole had a good reason for that snit. She didn't have the money to pay her bill.

"I don't frickin' believe this!" she exclaimed, storming out of the office, followed by her mother and Little Dog.

Marietta stopped in her tracks. "Are you okay, honey?"

"No, I'm not okay! If someone quotes you a price, they should honor that price."

Little Dog stood in front of the door, his beefy arms

folded across his chest, straining the seams of his blue coveralls. "I told Austin it would be close to seventeen hundred and it is."

"Well, that's not what he told me!" she said, wheeling around.

"Take it up with your husband. You want your car? One thousand seven hundred and eighty-nine dollars."

Little Dog offered an apologetic smile to Marietta. "Be with you in a moment. Want to come in and take a load off?"

She took a step and then hesitated. "I'm fine waiting out here, Georgie."

Probably because she didn't want to miss any of the drama.

He turned his attention back to Nicole. "What's it gonna be?"

She looked longingly at her Volkswagen. "I need my car. I'm sorry, Mom. It's either borrow your car another week or—"

"I'll take care of it," Darlene said, pulling her wallet out of her leather purse.

Little Dog held the door open for her and then looked at my mother. "It will be a few minutes and then I'll be right with you."

She waved him off, bangles clanging, as they stepped inside. "No problem."

Like me, she knew the more interesting story was out here with the daughter, cursing under her breath.

Nicole stabbed a finger in the direction of the DeLorean. "That yours?"

Nodding, Marietta beamed. "From mah show."

"What show?"

The effervescence behind my mother's eyes fizzled as if Nicole had flipped an off switch. "Never mind."

"So, how quickly did George say it would be ready?"

Marietta inspected a nail. "A few days."

"Do you know how long my car has been here?" Nicole didn't wait for an answer. "Over two weeks! Most of the time just sitting because my idiot husband wanted to be the big man. These things are all about negotiation, he told me. What a joke."

None of us were laughing. She'd had a miserable two weeks. A dead car. A murdered father. And some obvious money problems that appeared to be straining her marriage.

I thought about what she had said about borrowing her mother's Bronco—the only car parked outside the house when I spoke to Nicole the Friday after her father's death. "At least your mom had a car you could borrow."

She rolled her eyes. "Which left her stuck at home all day."

But I thought… "So you were driving it that Friday when I came out and took your statement."

Nicole slanted me an irritated glance. "And almost every other day that week thanks to Austin trying to fix my car. At least it was drivable before he screwed around with it."

That meant that Estelle might have been right about the car she had seen, but she'd made the wrong assumption about the driver.

Knowing I would have only another minute while her mother settled the bill, I couldn't waste a second. "By chance, were you driving your mom's car when you visited Bob Hallahan the night after your father's death?"

Nicole stared at me as if she'd seen a ghost. "I'm not sure what you're talking about."

She knew exactly what I was talking about. "One of the neighbors saw the Bronco there."

"I-I just needed to talk to him about something."

"Would it have something to do with his relationship with Victoria?" I asked to gauge her reaction.

She opened her mouth and immediately clamped it shut again.

That would be a *yes*.

"How…did Jeremy say something about that to you?"

Jeremy? "He may have."

"I had my own suspicions. Especially when he wasn't there at Dad's birthday dinner. But after Jeremy said that he saw Victoria and Bob together, I just had to know."

At last, another witness. "So, they were having an affair."

"No! They were shopping for my dad's birthday present." Nicole said it like she was disappointed. "My stupid brother…. No, I take that back. At least he was smart enough to not go over to Bob's house and yell at him like I did."

"Don't be so hard on yourself, honey," Marietta said, shifting her gaze to me. "A lot of people jump to the wrong conclusion when they see a man spending time with a woman."

Like you weren't thinking the same thing.

"Especially that woman." Nicole lowered her voice when Darlene swung open the door. "Because she killed my father."

Darlene handed a set of car keys to her daughter. "We're all set." Frowning, she looked at me. "What are you talking about? Is there some news?"

Pointing toward the office so that my mother would get the hint that she had heard more than enough, I waited until the door swung shut behind her to answer Darlene's question. "No news. We're still waiting for the lab results to come back."

"She's going to get away with it, isn't she?" Darlene asked, the same murderous look in her eyes as Nicole's.

Not if I could help it. "We're doing everything we can."

She grimaced. "Which isn't much."

"I'll let you know if I hear anything."

"Sure."

I wanted to ask about her private conversation with Cameron and his mother after the funeral service, but I didn't dare broach the subject with Nicole standing there. "And I would appreciate you letting me know if there's any additional information that we need."

The little tug at Darlene's crow's feet told me that she understood my meaning. "Of course."

Turning, she kissed her daughter's cheek and then climbed into the Bronco.

I got the sense that Nicole was waiting for her to leave, so I stood next to her while her mother drove away.

Nicole met my gaze. "I realize that you haven't seen me at my best, but I'm not just some pissed off bitch that wants to find someone to blame for my father's death."

I was sure there was some truth in that statement, but since it followed another "she killed my father" line, Nicole couldn't have laid more blame at Victoria's feet if she tried. "I know. There just isn't much that anyone can do until we get the test results back."

She sighed and turned toward her car.

"If you don't mind me asking, what was the birthday present?" Because most men I knew would balk at the idea of going shopping, unless this had been a way for Bob to spend some time with his best friend's wife.

"A stupid fishing reel. I guess it was something Dad had wanted for a while." She wiped away a tear. "All that money and he hardly spent any of it on himself. But you can bet who's gonna be spending it pretty soon."

Yep. Probably a safe bet.

Chapter Twenty-Two

"DID YOU SIGN up for that online dating website?" I asked Lucille when I stopped at Duke's to pick up Frankie's Friday morning doughnut order on my way to work.

Looking over the cash register at me, she pursed her coral painted lips. "Did you?"

"I wasn't the one who said she wanted to expand her horizons."

"Well, don't believe everything you hear."

I didn't, especially at Gossip Central where half-truths were served up as often as the pancakes my great-uncle was flipping on his grill.

I handed her a twenty.

"Speaking of dating," she said, a mischievous glimmer in her eyes as she counted out my change. "How's it going between you and Steve? He hasn't come in for breakfast once since Tuesday."

Probably because I'd been serving him healthier breakfasts at his house each morning. "Everything's fine." I'd been PMSing and hadn't been the most fun the last couple of days, but things now felt like we were back to normal—whatever *normal* meant when it came to me and Steve.

She scoffed. "Everything's fine, eh? That seems to be the catch phrase of the day."

"What do you mean?"

"It's the same thing that new kid working at McCutcheon's Flooring said after he had a little scuffle with Jeremy outside."

A scuffle? "When did this happen?"

"Ten minutes before you got here. Duke had to go out and break it up."

Duke looked over and frowned at the mention of his name. Either that or he was spying on me to make sure I didn't help myself to one of his apple fritters.

Lucille leaned closer. "I think someone's getting fired today."

If Cameron got fired, that would eliminate the one thing that appeared to be keeping him in town. "Well, that's not good."

"Hey, mess with the bull and you're gonna get the horn."

"Yeah." Walking to my car with the pink bakery box I wished Jeremy McCutcheon were the kind of man to keep his horn to himself, but I knew better.

With any luck, Cameron would stick around to get his reward for his part in his father's death. Maybe even reveal himself as Jeremy's half-brother as a parting shot.

I sucked in a breath. What if that revelation was what had precipitated the fight? What if Jeremy had provoked him into throwing the one punch that Cameron knew would send his big brother reeling?

I rushed to my car, all the while playing the *what if*

game. Because if Cameron had told Jeremy the truth about his identity he may have just made that mistake I'd been waiting for.

During an hour spent catching up with the filing I'd neglected yesterday, I'd had plenty of time to think of excuses to ask for a follow-up interview with Cameron. The trouble was all of them were lame. Since I really didn't expect to see him at the shop, maybe that didn't matter. I should be able to get the answer I needed from Jeremy.

I glanced at the clock hanging on the wall next to the bank of black filing cabinets. Ten-thirty-five—a good time to go have a chat before Jeremy left for lunch.

Waving a registered letter at Patsy that Karla had asked me to take to the post office, I slipped my tote over my shoulder and skipped down the marble steps of the courthouse as quickly as my feet would carry me.

When I stepped onto the sidewalk on Main Street five minutes later, I turned to see Steve's unmarked cruiser pacing me.

He rolled down the passenger side window. "A little early for lunch, isn't it?"

"My goodness, you are so suspicious," I said, maintaining a steady stride. "You'd make a good cop."

Steve gave me a lopsided smile. "So, where're you going?"

"Errands." Not a complete lie.

"Would you be interested in a date later?"

If he had wanted to grab my complete attention, he'd just said the magic words. We both hit our brakes, and I leaned against his open window. "What did you have in mind?"

"Dinner, a little black dress I heard you mention, maybe some conversation."

"You'd talk to me, too?"

"Yeah, don't let it go to your head."

"Golly, when you put it that way, I can hardly wait."

"Six?"

"You've got yourself a date!"

He turned on Third to head back to the police station, and I walked another five blocks to McCutcheon Floors & More.

A buzzer announced my arrival as I stepped into the shop. Seconds later, Bob Hallahan emerged from a back room with a guarded look in his eyes. "May I help you with something?"

"I was hoping to have a word with Cameron."

"He's out doing an installation," he said as a phone started ringing.

So much for him being fired. "Is—"

"We're short-handed. You'll have to excuse me a minute."

While Bob ran to answer the phone, I browsed the laminate floor display.

"Are you being helped?" a female voice asked.

I turned to see Phyllis, who looked even more alarmed to see me than Bob had. "I was just waiting for Bob." To try to get some information out of the keep cool guy who wouldn't want to tell me a thing. "But maybe you can help me. Could we talk in your office?"

Averting her gaze, she clamped her lips shut.

Yes, I know. You don't want to talk to me.

I followed her down the hall to a smaller, less cluttered version of Marty's old office, where the colorful home page of the Second Chances dating website was displayed on her computer monitor.

She turned off the monitor, a crimson flush crawling up her cheeks as she took a seat.

"Popular site." Much more popular than I ever would have guessed two weeks ago.

"I suppose." She pressed her palms together as if in prayer. Probably for a do-over of the last few minutes. "Now, what can—"

"Been using it long?" If she had, or if Bob or Marty had shared any of their experiences with her, I wanted her to start talking.

"Not long. One of the guys told me about it, and…well, it probably seems foolish at my age, but I thought I'd give it a try."

"Marty was close to your age when—"

Her eyebrows arched, and I realized that I'd made a mistake. I shouldn't have let on that I knew how he met Victoria. "Sorry, in my interviews someone mentioned that he met his wife online."

That someone had been Phyllis's sister, but she didn't need to hear that from me.

"No, he didn't. They met through Jeremy. He was the one who met her online."

"Oh."

"Shortly after that, Victoria became a customer when she needed some work done at her B & B. Marty took over when the job became a little too big for Jeremy. Hardwood, I think."

The way Phyllis said *hardwood* I sensed that she wasn't

just talking flooring.

"This isn't what you came here to talk about," she said dismissively. "What did you want to ask me?"

I didn't want to ask her anything. Not now. "I actually should speak with Jeremy about the matter. Is he around?"

She shook her head. "He's gone for the day. Some business he had to tend to."

I thanked her and headed out through the showroom.

Bob looked up from the deskwork he was doing. "Did you get what you needed?"

And more than I had bargained for. "I think so, thanks."

Outside on the sidewalk I reconsidered what I'd just learned. So what if Jeremy was the one who had introduced his father to Victoria? "Does that really change anything?" I asked myself as I headed to Duke's for lunch.

She still married the richest guy around—a guy who just happened to have a bad ticker.

She and Bob might not have been having an affair, but he still looked like a man in love. And people in love had been known to do some stupid things, beyond buying the "stupid fishing reel" Nicole told me about yesterday.

Nothing about Cameron appeared to have changed. He had still lied to me. He was still a guy who appeared to have a problem keeping his cool, and yet Jeremy hadn't fired him. I didn't get that last part at all. Unless he had something on Jeremy.

Had anything really changed?

Knowing that Jeremy and Victoria had once dated made me wonder about his feelings toward her now. How far did Victoria's ability to wrap Jeremy around her little finger extend? And what would he be willing to do for a bigger piece of the pie?

Heck. I now had four murder suspects and no proof of anything.

Steve had said that we'd have some conversation with dinner. Would he be willing to listen to what I'd learned today?

I thought about the last date we'd tried to have and what a mess it had turned into.

"Date first, talk later."

"I am wearing a pair of killer stilettos so don't you dare tell me that you're cancelling on me again," I said when Steve called at six o'clock sharp.

"Killer stilettos. Sounds dangerous."

"They are, but mainly to my balance, so are you going to be here soon, or do I take these things off and make myself comfortable for an evening in?"

"I should be done here in twenty minutes. Since our reservation is in Port Townsend, to save some time why don't you go to Eddie's and I'll pick you up there."

The last time I went to Eddie's wearing my black dress it hadn't worked out so well. "Okay. Twenty minutes but—" I heard a click and looked down at my phone. *Disconnected.*

I grabbed Gram's beaded clutch bag. "I hope the second time's the charm."

Ten minutes later, while Rox poured me a glass of chardonnay, I saw Bob Hallahan and Cameron come in. It was a typically busy Friday night with no tables available, but an empty barstool was next to me, so feeling brave with my cop buddy on his way, I waved them over.

"I didn't realize this place was so formal," Bob said over the din of the crowd. "Or perhaps this seat was being saved for someone."

"Who won't be here for a little while, so please," I scooted over to make room for Cameron, "make yourself comfortable."

"Some people around here have dates on Friday night, and some of us poor souls have to work," Rox said, delivering my chardonnay.

"I remember date night with my wife." A wistful smile played at the corners of Bob's lips. "The best night of the week."

He pointed at the stool vacated by a big guy in a Hawaiian shirt, and Cameron pulled it over while a Joan Jett song filled the awkward silence.

Rox tossed coasters in front of them. "What'll you boys have?"

Bob ordered a couple of beers and handed Cameron a laminated menu. "Figure out what kind of pizza you want," he said, sounding more like a father than a coworker. Then he turned to me. "I almost forgot. You wanted to talk to Cam earlier."

Heck. My lame excuse for talking to him seemed even more lame now.

Cameron looked past Bob, sitting between us. "What about?"

"I'd heard there was some trouble outside my family's cafe this morning." Like it was really any of my business.

"Sorry." He averted his gaze. "I let something get out of hand."

I leaned closer. "It's just that my uncle Duke is getting

along in years and shouldn't over-exert himself." Never mind that the old coot competed in the regional Ironman competition every year.

Rox stifled a chuckle as she delivered two frosty mugs of beer.

Bob turned to Cameron. "I'm sure it won't happen again, will it?"

Cameron heaved a weary sigh like a teenager. "No." He glanced at the flat screen to his right. "Hey, the playoff game's on."

The second Cameron parked himself in front of the TV, Bob glanced at me. "The kid's having a hard time with Jeremy. Cam told me that you know about his *situation*."

He had told Bob? These two were even tighter than I'd thought.

"Now that his dad's gone, he's trying to honor Darlene's wishes and give her the opportunity to tell Jeremy and his sister, but," Bob reached for his beer, "I keep telling him he needs to take a step back and calm down."

Criminy, was that why he had told Cameron to keep his cool?

Bob took a long drink. "Sometimes, you can only wait so long before you have to take matters into your own hands."

I turned to get a better angle on his face. "Do you think he's going to say something to Jeremy?"

"Wouldn't you want to if you'd found out you had a brother?"

According to Marietta, I had an older half-brother and sister somewhere in France. Since I had absolutely no desire to meet them, he was asking the wrong girl. "Maybe. Speaking of Jeremy, since you know the family as well as you do, help me understand his relationship with Victoria."

I figured if I could get him talking, I could get a bead on his feelings for the woman.

His brows furrowed. "Are you suggesting that there's something inappropriate going on?"

"You know people around here. They talk."

"Then they've got their heads up their asses if they think Victoria has been anything other than a good friend to Marty's son. Actually, both his sons."

While I could plainly see that Bob believed what he said to be true, I couldn't make everything I'd witnessed with my own eyes fit into the family portrait he was painting for me.

"I hadn't realized that she'd become that close to Cameron," I said.

"Victoria's determined to carry out Marty's wishes." He shot me a sideways glance. "I know Darlene is accusing her of being some sort of murderous gold digger, but she doesn't know her. She never saw how good they were together."

This didn't sound like a man who was anything more than a faithful friend. "But Bob, Victoria stands to inherit millions."

He turned to me. "Don't tell me that you're buying into this load of crap."

"Hey," Steve said behind me, saving me from having to tap dance around the truth.

"Sorry, that took a little longer than planned." He extended his hand to the man on the next barstool.

"How're you doing, Bob?"

"Can't complain."

"How's the house coming along?"

"Faster now that I've got some help." He pointed at Cameron, whose eyes were focused on the Yankee at bat. "Although I may have a hard time pulling him away from the game tonight."

Steve took a step toward the TV. "What's the score?"

I downed half my wine. "I'll tell you what the score is going to be if we don't make that reservation."

"Guess it's time to go," Steve said with a wink.

I paid for my drink, said my goodbyes, and took his arm as we headed for the door. "That was interesting."

"What?"

"My conversation with Bob."

"Seeing that he was a friend of Marty McCutcheon's, do I dare ask what was so interesting about it?"

"I don't think he had anything to do with killing his friend."

Steve laughed all the way to the car.

Back at his house after our candlelit dinner, I handed Steve a bottle of beer, sat down on the couch next to him, and shared everything that I'd uncovered in the last two weeks.

"After tonight's conversation with Bob, I'm beginning to think that he's right. Darlene is bitter and jealous and spiteful where her ex-husband is concerned. She believed every word she said, so of course I found it easy to buy into her black widow accusation when the other people I talked to made it look bad for Victoria."

"Of course," Steve said between swigs of beer.

"Hey, you would have, too, if you had talked to some of these people like I had."

"Uh-huh." He handed me the beer bottle. "I also would have waited for some evidence to suggest there had actually been a crime committed."

I took a sip. "Details."

"Your buddies in the prosecutor's office can't do anything with the case without those details."

"Well, they'll have them in another six or seven weeks."

He stole back the bottle I'd been resting on my lap. "So, there's nothing to do but wait, is there?"

Steve's tone suggested that I should agree with him. "I still have questions."

"I'm sure you do, but it's not your job to ask them."

I sighed. "Somebody needs to. A man was poisoned."

He drained the bottle. "That won't be confirmed for another six weeks minimum. Correct?"

"Yes."

"And if ... *if* the lab result comes back positive, a criminal case will go to the Sheriff. Correct?"

Sinking deeper into the couch, I folded my arms, not crazy about his line of questioning. "Yes."

"And in this six-week period, everyone on your suspect list has some money to inherit, so they aren't going anywhere. Wouldn't you agree?"

"I suppose."

Steve pulled me close. "So, if some questions need to be asked at some point in the future, they won't need to be asked by you."

I leaned my head on his shoulder. "I hate it when you

get all logical on me."

"Somebody needs to," he said, serving my answer back to me.

"You done?"

"Are you?"

I was for tonight. "Yep."

He gently pushed me away and unfolded himself from the couch.

"Where you going?" I asked.

"It's time for dessert."

The last time he said that we were in bed, finger-painting one another with chocolate ice cream. "I'm sorry, but I'm really not in the mood for anything beyond a couple of aspirin."

He came back from the kitchen cradling one of Aunt Alice's apple pies in his hands. "I meant this kind of dessert."

"Oh."

Chapter Twenty-Three

AFTER STEVE LEFT to coach a football game, I headed home and joined Gram in the kitchen around nine the next morning.

Wearing her pink robe and fuzzy slippers, she filled my favorite mug with coffee and handed it to me. "Want some breakfast? I was thinking pancakes, maybe with some blueberries to make it healthy."

"Healthy, huh? So, no butter and no syrup on these pancakes."

Gram grinned. "Let's not take this healthy stuff too far."

She was my kind of girl.

"Do you want to ask Steve if he'd like to join us? Your mother won't be up for at least another hour."

It was no secret that Marietta possessed a unique ability to drain Steve's patience dry faster than I could suck down a mocha latte. As much as Gram enjoyed the pleasure of his company, she knew better than to expect to see Steve with any frequency during my mother's visits.

Leaning against the counter, I stirred some milk into my coffee. "The peewees have a game this morning, so he won't be back until later this afternoon."

"What about you? Any plans?" she asked, a hopeful glint in her eyes as she reached for a mixing bowl.

"No plans other than the ones I think you're making for me."

Chuckling, her rosy cheeks plumped. "Moi?"

"Yeah, you."

"Now that you mention it, I was thinking about going for a drive and seeing some fall color. Maybe visit that herb farm near Gibson Lake and pick up a few things."

She had me at herb farm. "I'm in."

"Good. We can stop by Darlene's on the way and pick up an order she said was ready. I never really got the opportunity to extend my condolences at the service, so I'd like to do that before too much time goes by." She shot me a glance on her way to the refrigerator. "You don't mind, do you?"

Heck, no. Maybe I could glean a little information about that conversation that took place in the corner with Cameron and his mother. "Nope."

"Okay! Breakfast and then we're outta here," she said, a carton of eggs in her hand.

I assumed that also meant get out of here before my mother woke up. "You realize that Mom will probably smell the pancakes. Then she's going to want to come with us."

Gram returned the eggs to the refrigerator. "Actually, I think I'm fresh out of blueberries. Maybe we should go out for breakfast."

"Uh-huh." Yep, my kind of girl.

✳

An hour and a half later, I drove down Darlene McCutcheon's rutted dirt driveway and parked Gram's Honda near the yurt so she wouldn't have far to walk.

With the dogs sounding the intruder alert at the fence along the other side of the red farm house, we didn't need to ring the doorbell. Darlene appeared in front of her home just as I was helping Gram out of the car.

"Jake! Elwood! Knock it off!" Darlene rolled her eyes. "Those darned dogs. They won't shut up today."

Gram gave her a friendly smile. "Well, they're excellent watch dogs. Just what I'd want if I were out here on my own."

"They're good boys. Most of the time," Darlene said over her shoulder as if that would encourage them to settle down.

It didn't. But with the steady drone of a lawnmower blaring nearby I couldn't fault the dogs for their verbal protests. I only hoped that the posts in that dilapidated fence were sturdier than they looked.

"Darlene, dear." Gram took the younger woman's hand. "I'm so sorry I didn't have an opportunity to spend much time with you at Marty's service."

Darlene nodded. "It was a good turnout. The kids and I were really touched to see so many of his old friends. Even…"

Even who? Cameron's mother?

"…people we hadn't seen for years." Withdrawing her hand, she dried her eyes. "Funerals are for the living, but I think he would have been pleased."

I took a step closer to my grandmother as if she might need my arm for support. "Gram and I were waiting in line when you stepped out to talk to a couple of people.

The line grew so long after that." I winked at Darlene to clue her in that I was trying to preserve my grandmother's dignity. This also gave me an opportunity to observe the fire torching Darlene's cheeks. "When a chair opened up, I grabbed it for her."

Gram scowled at me. "I guess I couldn't have found that chair by myself."

"Sorry that I made you wait," Darlene said. "That was an old friend."

Lie. That was no friend.

"You know how it is." Darlene was nodding like a bobblehead, as if that would increase the plausibility factor. "Sometimes you just have to have a few moments alone to catch up."

Catch up? More like unceremoniously dispatch based on how quickly Cameron and his mother left the funeral home.

Gram patted her friend on the shoulder. "It's not a big deal. I just wanted to let you know that I would be around if you need anything. And that still goes."

That brought on more nodding from Darlene. "Thanks. I appreciate that."

"Now, on to more pleasant things." Gram brightened. "The yarn you said was ready."

Chatting up her new batch of yarn, Darlene led the way to the yurt.

While I admired the scarves and hats my grandmother knitted for almost everyone she knew, I was far more interested in Darlene's relationship with Cameron's mother than the blend of fibers in yarn, so I hung back, debating with myself about how confrontational I should get with Darlene.

Should I tell her that I already knew that Cameron was Marty's son? That would be as good as calling her out on her *old friend* story. Was I ready to force Darlene's hand, or should I just tell her that I knew she had lied to me and give her an opportunity to come up with something closer to the truth?

I wandered behind the yurt to weigh my options and breathed in the sweet scent of the clematis while I paced. Noticing a few rocks scattered in front of the purple flowering vine where there hadn't been any before, I stopped and inspected the lumpy patch of dirt between the clematis and the white tent reflecting the bright sunshine. Something looked different. Was something missing?

Thinking back to the last time I stood at this spot, I remembered that there had been three flowering plants of various shades of violet back here. One of them had sported a couple of blueish-purple blooms hanging from a spike like hooded bells.

Oh, my gosh! The same kind of blooms that had been hanging from the plant that Victoria used for Marty's tea!

Adrenaline surged through me, making my legs feel heavy and wooden when I knew they should have been pumping like pistons. Instead, I stood inert as the dirt I was staring at while my brain tried to rationalize everything I'd seen.

Rationalize later. "Move!"

Placing one foot in front of the other as if I were trudging through mud, I rounded the yurt and almost knocked Darlene down, inciting a fresh round of barking from her dogs.

"Is everything okay out here?" she asked, frowning at

me.

I glanced over at Gram, sitting on a bench next to a rack displaying skeins of yarn. *Good. Stay there for a minute.* "Sorry, I was being chased by a bee."

"Oh, is that all. I thought that Jeremy might have frightened you back there. He can't hear a thing with those headphones he wears when he mows the lawn. I swear that boy has tunnel vision, too. Been more than once that he almost mowed me down."

"Jeremy's here now?" I hadn't seen his pickup when we arrived.

Tilting her head, she nodded. "Yep, sounds like he's still at it in the back forty."

I forced a couple of shaky breaths into my lungs. "Nice of him to help out."

"Charmaine, he does more than just help out. When my fiber business took off last year, he volunteered to take over all the gardening." She gave me an impish grin. "Personally, I think he missed getting his fingers in the dirt living at that apartment in town."

"I bet he did." I'd also bet that more than just his fingers were dirty. "Before that bee came after me I noticed that it looked like something had been dug up back there."

Darlene shrugged. "Jeremy had a plant that he was experimenting with. Told me not to touch it. It was kind of scrawny so maybe he decided to give up on it."

Not touch it? It had to be the same poisonous plant.

"Must have been this morning though," she added. "It was back there earlier in the week when I was watering."

Holy crap! He was getting rid of the evidence that could connect him to his father's death.

"Where's Jeremy's truck?" I asked, trying to sound nonchalant while my quavering voice betrayed me.

"Why?" Darlene narrowed her eyes. "What's going on?"

Stretching my trembling lips into a smile, I pointed to the south side of the farm house. "Over here?" The two Great Pyrenees barked at me with a dozen alpacas bearing silent witness as I took cover behind a tall rhododendron and peeked into the side yard.

Partially obscured behind a livestock trailer, a black four by four with shiny chrome wheels sat in the shade of a towering Douglas fir. I listened for the lawnmower. The drone barely audible over the protests of my furry audience, I inched my way to the truck, the barking dogs clawing to get at me from the other side of the fence.

"Nice doggies," I said. "Be quiet for just a minute so that we don't attract the attention of your big brother." A much more dangerous animal who was wearing head-phones and wouldn't hear me or the dogs.

"Never mind." The noise level was clearly the least of my concerns.

I dashed over to the truck and looked into the bed. Grass clippings. Lots and lots of grass clippings and no blue flowers to be seen.

Swell.

I needed a stick and saw one by the paw of the bigger of the two dogs. "Don't suppose you want to push that over here, do you?"

Frothing at the mouth, he growled at me.

"Fine." I dug around in my tote bag and found a pen. Dropping the tote, I leaned over the side of the truck and started combing through the grass. After several passes, I uncovered a bell-shaped bloom. "Yes!" I said, lifting the branch with my pen at the same time that I heard the lawnmower getting louder.

I looked up, saw Jeremy's sandy blonde hair, and ducked.

"Crap!" I muttered, scampering behind the base of the fir tree. I fumbled for my camera phone to get a picture in case he took off before I could get the Sheriff out here.

As long as you hear the lawnmower you're okay.

Squatting and quivering like a scared rabbit behind that tree, I listened for the lawnmower while the dogs yapped at me from ten feet away.

Still droning. *Whew!*

I saw movement in the front yard. So did the dogs, who took off the other direction to bark at Gram as she peeked around that rhododendron.

"Charmaine?" she called. "I don't know what's going on, but if you're back here somewhere, I think it's time to go."

"Get in the car, Gram," I yelled, waving her away. "Now! And call nine-one-one!"

She disappeared and a heartbeat later I heard nothing but barking. *Uh-oh.*

"She's over there somewhere," Darlene said, heading in my direction.

I had a quick decision to make. Continue quivering like a rabbit and be ripped apart by a muscle-bound predator, who would be on me in a matter of seconds, or run for the relative safety of the car.

Some decisions are no-brainers.

I bolted out from behind the tree as if I'd heard a starter's pistol. Unfortunately, I could hear the former athlete turned killer gardener gaining on me.

"Not so fast," Jeremy called out, a deadly calm in his voice as if he were all too aware that I couldn't offer him any real competition in this race.

Breathless, I waited until he was almost on me to swing my tote at him like a bag lady defending her turf. Unfortunately, I didn't have a good angle on him, and I was the one who tumbled hard to the ground.

"I'll take that," he said, standing over me and pointing at the phone in my hand.

"I'm not giving you my phone. What's wrong with you?"

"What's wrong?" He smirked, drips of sweat watering the patch of grass between us. "Nothing and it's going to stay that way." Reaching down he grabbed my phone, pocketed it, and then yanked me up by the arm.

"Ow! Darlene! Your son is hurting me!" I shouted, staring into his eyes.

He appeared more amused than worried about me telling on him to his mother.

Not good.

He pushed me to the driver's side door, his mother's dogs barking and clawing at the fence. Opening the door, he sank his fingers into the soft flesh of my upper arm and shoved me toward the seat. "Get in."

"No." If I got into his truck I was as good as dead.

"Get in!" he growled, twisting my arm behind my back.

"In the driver's seat?" If he wanted me to drive I'd do an *Estelle* and ram his rig right into the fence. I'd probably be mauled by those dogs, but at least I'd deny Jeremy the pleasure of putting me into a head lock and squeezing all the air out of me.

"No, idiot, the passenger seat."

Struggling to clear my thighs past the stick shift, I hesitated so I could get a better angle.

He pushed me. "Just get your ass over!"

"This would have been a whole lot easier if you'd let me get in the other side."

"Shut up."

I looked up at Darlene, staring at me with her mouth gaping open in stunned silence. "Aren't you going to do anything to help me?" I shouted.

Jeremy glanced over at his mother. "Everything's okay, Mom. I'm just going to take Charmaine someplace where we can have a little talk."

Grimacing, she took a tentative step toward us. "Are you sure?"

"What?" *Are you completely blind to what your son is capable of?*

"Yeah. I'll come back later to finish up," he said reassuringly.

I locked on her gaze. "You can't possibly believe that. He—"

Dripping beads of sweat on me, Jeremy wrenched my arm back, the pain in my shoulder white-hot as I fell into the passenger seat. "If you say one more word I'll break it," he whispered, his fetid breath warm against my cheek.

He slid behind the wheel and waved to his mother. "I'll be back in about an hour."

The implication in Jeremy's words couldn't have been more obvious. He'd return *alone*.

Turning the key, he shifted into reverse and backed to the driveway, swinging toward where I'd parked Gram's car. Thankfully, he didn't appear aware that an eighty-year-old lady with peach spun sugar hair was watching us through the cloud of dust he had stirred up as we barreled toward the road.

Since that old lady was known for siccing Steve on me at the slightest sign of trouble, I sure hoped that he was near his phone.

"So, what do you want to talk about?" I asked, searching the cab for something I could use as a weapon while he drove through farm country like a bat out of hell.

Nothing, not even a stick of gum I could throw at him.

Since Jeremy didn't answer, I figured that I'd better start talking and hope for an opportunity to distract him on the road ahead.

"Okay, I'll talk and you can listen. I was thinking about how you must have been planning to kill your father for a long time."

No response.

"How long were you experimenting with that plant in your mother's yard? I bet it would take at least a year for it to get to that size."

He stared straight ahead, his face impassive.

"It's going to show up on the toxicology report, you know."

The corner of his mouth curled.

My little threat about the toxicology results gave him pleasure? What sick bastard gets off on someone telling him that he won't get away with murder?

I looked back at the blades of grass taking flight from the bed of his truck. Only a thin layer of green covered the plant he had used to kill his father—a plant that would soon be thrown over a bank somewhere off of State Route 17, along with my body.

"And when it does and the Sheriff comes calling, Nicole will be happy to show him the greenhouse where Victoria grows the kind of plant used to kill your father. Maybe you can manage to shed a tear when you blame yourself for introducing her to him."

He grinned. "You're not so stupid after all."

"Gee, thanks." Since I was sitting in the truck of a killer I doubted Steve would agree. Why, why, why hadn't I trusted my instincts when I first talked to Jeremy? I knew something was off. There were too many mixed signals and for good reason. He had taken pride in the planning and the execution of his father's murder. That explained the smile I had spotted that day, the business as usual attitude. I had seen no sense of loss because none existed. Worse, he hadn't been conflicted by regret.

"I didn't sense any remorse," I muttered, my thoughts escaping my filter.

"Remorse?" He chuckled. "Not really my style."

I shivered. This guy was as sick as he was deadly.

Somehow I needed to get out of this truck. If I jumped out I'd probably kill myself, but if I did nothing I was as good as dead.

Staring at the road ahead I looked for tall grass, a landing place that could cushion the blow my body would take at this speed. If I were lucky enough to survive the fall, what was to keep Jeremy from backing up to finish the job?

No, I might be scared spitless, but I hadn't been scared stupid—at least not yet.

I needed to make a move when there were people

around. Maybe if he slowed to take a turn and there were a car behind us—someone to act as a witness. Maybe that would be my best chance to escape.

But if that chance never came, if this were it, I didn't want to be driven to my grave without some answers. "Why kill your father on his birthday?"

Jeremy turned to me with a gleam of delight in his eyes. "Nice touch, don't you think?"

"No." I mentally replayed the descriptions all the witnesses provided of Marty's final hours, bile rising in my throat. "It's awful."

"Maybe physically, but the old man forced my hand."

I knew of only one thing that had changed recently—an addition to the family. "Because of Cameron."

Jeremy slanted me an amused glance. "Look at you. Uncovering the skeletons in my dad's closet."

"How long have you known?"

"I figured out who he was a couple of weeks ago, after I saw Pop crying in his office. My dad didn't cry, not even when he left my mother."

"Your mother knew about Cameron."

Nothing registered on his face.

"And with him working at the shop she must have figured that it would be just a matter of time before your father acknowledged him."

Again, no reaction.

"Maybe even included Cameron in his will," I added, fishing.

Jeremy smirked.

Bingo!

Now it made sense why Darlene had been in no hurry for Cameron and his mother to meet the rest of the family. She didn't want anyone hanging around to challenge Marty's will prior to Jeremy and Nicole receiving their inheritance.

"It was about the money." I stared at him. "That's what you meant about your father forcing your hand."

"I didn't want to share with my baby brother or my new mommy. Does that make me a bad guy?"

No, it made him a sick and twisted guy. "Does your sister know?"

"No, and she never will if I have anything to do with it." He squinted at his rearview mirror. "She has enough problems with her deadbeat husband."

Probably true, but since I was sitting in a vehicle with her murderous brother, my problems trumped hers at the moment.

I noticed his knuckles blanch as he angled to look in his side mirror. Something had gotten under his skin and clearly it wasn't me.

"What?" I turned to see what he was looking at and noticed a car in the distance. Were those flashing lights?

Jeremy hit the brake as we passed a sign for Haughton Lake, an old fishing destination of my grandfather's.

"Do you plan on doing some fishing out here?" I asked, holding on as he took the sharp right turn.

"Wrong season, but it should be nice and quiet. You know. For the rest of our talk."

Jiminy Christmas! I was going to be in big trouble if I didn't come up with an escape plan in the next five minutes.

I noticed him glaring at his rearview mirror again as his truck bounced from pothole to pothole in the narrow road, and an obscenity escaped his lips.

I looked in my side mirror and realized that he hadn't sworn because of what this bumpy road was doing to his wheel alignment. The car with the flashing lights had taken the right turn and was gaining on us.

Good.

"You should slow down. That cop back there might arrest you for speeding."

He frowned.

"Plus, this road's really bad," I said as we rumbled across a cattle guard marking the entrance to the dairy farm we were blasting by. "And there could be some cows in the road up ahead."

"Shut up."

There were certainly plenty of black and white faces near the farm's wooden fence to support my prediction, but none of them looked like they wanted to make a break for it.

I sure did.

I just needed Jeremy to shift his attention to his rear-view mirror for a moment.

Watching, I sat breathlessly waiting, a tight coil of tension gripping my gut.

Come on, come on, come on.

Just one look back, one split second of distraction was all I needed.

My fingers twitched in anticipation. My pulse pounded in my ears.

I heard a siren. Jeremy must have, too, because he directed his attention to his rearview mirror. And as soon as he did, I lunged for the wheel and put all my weight into turning it to the left, toward a big Holstein grazing on the other side of the ditch we were careening into. With a sharp thud we banged to a stop.

Fighting my way out from under the airbag pressing against my chest, I scrambled out of the truck and ran toward the white and green Sheriff's vehicle that had pulled up behind us.

"Are you okay?" a deputy asked, aiming his weapon at the guy crawling out of the truck's passenger side.

That was the same question Steve asked me an hour later, after I ran into his arms at the Sheriff's office.

"I'm fine," I said, while he frowned at a bump I had on my forehead. "Other than the fact that I'm going to be a little sore the next couple of days, the paramedics gave me a clean bill of health. I take it Gram called you?"

"Fortunately, our game had just ended. Otherwise, I don't think I would have heard the phone." He wrapped his arm around my shoulder. "Everybody around here knows Jeremy's rig, so I didn't have to give much of a description. Most of the credit goes to your granny for watching which way he went. After that it was a matter of guessing where he was headed."

I shuddered to think of what he would have done when we got there. "I told Deputy Barnhart about the poisonous plant in the back of Jeremy's truck."

"I heard. Looks like those lab results will become a formality."

"He poisoned his father. Killed him for the money. Can you believe that?"

Steve shook his head.

"And he was setting Victoria up to take the blame." Even after what Jeremy had divulged in the truck, I was having difficulty wrapping my brain around the words coming out of my mouth.

"Makes sense in a warped way," Steve said. "Convict Victoria and it's a few more million for Jeremy and his sister."

I stared at him in disbelief. "How could someone do something like that?"

Steve cupped my face with his palms. "I used to ask the same question when I worked Seattle Homicide. Never thought I'd have to ask it here."

I shivered.

He pulled me close. "Are you sure you're okay?"

I nodded.

"You did good getting him to talk."

"I also managed to get myself into harm's way," I admitted with the hope that if I cleared the air, I wouldn't have to hear a lecture about it later.

"Yeah. We're going to have to work on avoiding that in the future."

I liked the way he said *we*.

"We're ready for you," the Sheriff's Detective said, holding a door open for me.

I turned to Steve. "I have to give a statement."

He smiled. "I'm familiar with the drill."

"I don't know how long I'll be."

"I'll be right here waiting for you."

Almost an hour later, Steve passed the *Welcome to Port Merritt* sign at the south end of town—a sign that I never thought I'd be so happy to see.

"I think you have a decision to make," he said.

"It had better be an easy decision. I don't have enough energy for anything else."

"Understood. Just know that I promised your grandmother I'd bring you home as soon as I can. But after that, what would you like to do?"

"Well, I never got to go to the herb farm. That's where Gram and I were headed, so that might be nice."

His mouth was a grim line when he turned to me. "Herb farm? Not happening."

"I feel fine, so I'm sure—"

"I'm sure you should take it easy and relax."

"At home? Is my mother going to be there?"

He nodded. "She's there, waiting for you."

All worried and motherly. "Great." In no way, shape, or form was that my idea of a relaxing afternoon.

"Seeing how she's leaving tomorrow, she might even have more wedding stuff that she needs help with," he said, his voice as solemn as if he were testifying in court.

"Seriously?"

He grinned.

I folded my arms. "You're an ass."

"I beg your pardon, and here I was about to suggest that we get a pizza later and make out in front of the TV."

"Is a baseball game going to be on that TV?"

"Possibly."

"But we'd at least make out during commercial breaks?"

"Absolutely. In fact, I think the paramedics mentioned that it would help you relax."

"It wouldn't hurt."

THE END

About the Author

Wendy Delaney writes fun-filled cozy mysteries and is the award-winning author of the Working Stiffs Mystery series. A long-time member of Mystery Writers of America, she's a Food Network addict and pastry chef wannabe. When she's not killing off story people she can be found on her treadmill, working off the calories from her latest culinary adventure. Wendy lives in the Seattle area with the love of her life and has two grown sons.

For book news and to sign up for Wendy's newsletter please visit her website at www.wendydelaney.com.
Email address: wendy@wendydelaney.com
Connect with Wendy on Facebook at:
www.facebook.com/wendy.delaney.908

Made in the USA
Las Vegas, NV
21 July 2021

26824186R00173